THREE STEPS
TO OBLIVION

BOOK FIFTEEN OF
THE GUILD WARS

Ian J. Malone & Chris Kennedy

Seventh Seal Press
Coinjock, NC

Chris Kennedy/Seventh Seal Press
1097 Waterlily Rd.
Coinjock, NC 27923
https://chriskennedypublishing.com/

Publisher's Note: This is a work of fiction. Names, characters, places, and incidents are a product of the author's imagination. Locales and public names are sometimes used for atmospheric purposes. Any resemblance to actual people, living or dead, or to businesses, companies, events, institutions, or locales is completely coincidental.

Cover Design by Brenda Mihalko.
Original Art by Ricky Ryan.

Ordering Information:
Quantity sales. Special discounts are available on quantity purchases by corporations, associations, and others. For details, contact the "Special Sales Department" at the address above.

Three Steps to Oblivion/Ian J. Malone & Chris Kennedy -- 1st ed.
ISBN: 978-1648552472

For our families.

Prologue

FTS *Long Reach*, Camdone System

"Captain, we have hull breach in three places!" the damage control officer reported.

The free trader's captain took a deep breath and let it out slowly. *I never should have taken the cargo. I knew this was coming.* But he'd been unable to pass it up; he needed the money, and the rate he'd been able to charge would have made him solvent again. *But only if I survive.* "How many at each breach?"

"At least 10," the Zuul security officer replied. "There may be more. I saw 10 before they shot out the camera. They're moving too fast for us to get a good count."

"Meet me with all your forces at hold number one. They'll be going there." The captain switched to the ship's intercom system. "All hands, this is the captain. The ship has been breached in three places. Arm yourselves and kill as many as you can. We may yet get out of this alive."

Although the captain had said it to encourage his crew, he didn't believe it. For the last year, rumors had abounded in the sector about ships that mysteriously vanished. Their goods often showed up again on the black market, but the ships and their crew were usually never seen again.

They all had one thing in common—they were carrying an ancient treasure. And, unlike the normal goods the cargo ships had been carrying, the artifacts were never seen again.

The captain's thoughts flashed to the ceremonial blade resting comfortably in its protective case down in cargo hold one. He knew nothing of the saber's origins, just that it had belonged to the ruler of some ancient reptilian race that'd been drummed out of the Union several thousand years ago for crossing the Cartography Guild. That, and its value, of course—which was substantial.

Everything inside the captain had screamed *walk away* when the Talgud merchant he'd been dealing with had approached him about carrying the item to a Sidar buyer on Ulvaud Station.

"No one knows of this, save for us," the Talgud had said. "I'm only telling you because I know you can be trusted to be discreet with the saber's delivery."

Someone else knew. The captain drew his laser pistol and faced his XO. "Lock the bridge after I leave. Don't let anyone but me back in. Coordinate the defense as best you can."

The XO nodded toward the hatch. "Do you think it's wise to go?"

"No, it most assuredly is not, but I'd rather go down fighting and try to save my crew." *Especially if the other outcome is that I'm never going to be seen again.*

The captain raced down the passageway, hoping to reach the hold before the pirates.

* * *

M strode onto the merchant ship, still adjusting to his new form, as two of his pirate units cleared the nearest junction leading onto B deck. As expected, the merchant crew consisted mostly of Lotar, with a few Jeha along as engineers. M had known prior to attacking that no one aboard posed a threat to his cogs. That was what he called them, those beings he'd recruited to his cause. Even the merchants' Zuul security officer was scarcely worth watching. Sure, one mercenary could do some damage to his forces, but it would never come close to harming him. The primitive beast couldn't.

M chuckled as he marched toward the staccato sound of weapons fire ahead. Most of the Lotar fled from his cogs; those who didn't were shot down. *It's good to be back*, he thought. It'd been some time since M had led a raid personally, and he'd forgotten how stimulating the danger of the experience could be under the right conditions. *Danger.* He chuckled again. At the very least, the raids were a nice respite from his normal routine, hence why he'd left himself the flexibility to run one on occasion when he'd begun executing his plan.

The plan. M's smile faltered. For all he knew, the others still mocked him for his ambitions. They couldn't understand why he believed as he did about the old ways, and why things had to change. To them, life was merely a game of amassing power and resources. However, to him, it was more—so very, very much more. True, amassing resources was important, but there were other things that made the game worth playing. And, in the end, there could be only one winner.

Me.

The cogs wasted little time carving a path through the merchants' defenses en route to the cargo hold two sections over. To their credit, the crew who stayed behind put up more of a fight than M would've expected, as evidenced by the growing number of corpses lining the corridor at his feet. *No matter.* He would get more.

Spotting his objective ahead, M pressed his forces forward though the torrent of laser fire as, one after another, cogs and merchants fell like dominoes until he reached the hold entrance.

"Fall back for reinforcements!" one of the Lotar said before fleeing from sight. The others went with him.

Typical. M heaved a sigh, then sidestepped a pair of dead Jeha and went inside.

"Give it up, Pirate!" someone shouted.

M turned to find the merchant ship's captain glaring across the room at him from behind a drawn laser pistol. The Lotar was joined by his Zuul security officer, but no one else remained. *Hold positions.*

"I'll make you a deal," the Lotar captain said. "Turn around now and leave my ship, and you've got my word that I'll let you go."

"You'll let *me* go?" M asked.

"That's right," the captain said. "While you're at it, you can take the rest of your pirate thugs with you. But go now."

M met the other's glare with a wry smile. "With respect, why would I ever comply with that order?"

"Because you want to live?" the Zuul growled.

"Agreed, but I also want what I came for," M said.

"Not happening," the captain said. "You should've checked your intel, friend. My crew and I delivered the item you seek to our client on Ulvaud two days ago. It's no longer aboard this ship."

M chewed his lip. "It's not aboard, you say. I find that...disappointing."

"Find it whatever you want," the captain said. "The fact is you and your crew of bandits came all this way and sacrificed all those lives for little more than three tanks of waste sanitizer and 50 crates of Dutya dahva beans. That's it; that's all we have left aboard. The good news is, your losses can end here if you so choose, which brings us back to my offer." He cocked his head. "So, what'll be it? Are you gonna leave my ship conscious and upright, or dead through an airlock? The choice is yours, but decide now."

* * *

The captain watched nervously as the pirate leader seemed to consider the offer. The alien intruder was humanoid, all right. In fact, it looked a lot like the Human males the captain had encountered during his travels to Earth, although this one sported a shorter frame than most, with pale, ghoulish features and a shaved head.

The intruder's eyes flicked to the security officer then back to the captain.

Don't even think about it. The captain stepped forward, gun up, in unison with his security officer. In contrast, the intruder's weapon remained in its holster.

"I must commend you, Captain," the intruder said. "This ship of yours is deceptively fast, given her rather pedestrian model and class. Your engineers have done a masterful job with her systems."

"My deal, yes or no?" the captain asked.

The pirate leader exhaled through his nostrils. "Your proposal is intriguing, to be sure. Alas, in light of the fact that I believe you're bluffing about the artifact, I'm afraid I must respectfully decline."

The captain's gaze narrowed. "You're kidding."

"Not at all," the pirate leader said calmly. "You see, there's a third option you clearly haven't considered. It's the one where I kill you where you stand, take what I want, and retire to my own ship, while my cogs ransack yours and slaughter everyone else on board."

He paused, considering. "Come to think of it, I rather prefer that option. Let's go with that, shall we?"

The security officer twitched.

"Have it your way." The captain sighted on the pirate's chest and squeezed.

Pop, pop.

A plume of crimson misted the wall at the intruder's back as the humanoid crumpled to the deck in a bloody heap.

Greedy fool. The captain holstered his sidearm. "Bridge, we're clear. Have security round up the last of—"

A sun went nova on the captain's chest, and he was falling. *How did…*He glanced up to find his security officer looming over him, a wisp of smoke trailing from the other's pistol barrel.

"Why did…" A gush of blood poured into the captain's lungs, ending his ability to speak, while the world around him went gray.

The Zuul shrugged and marched over to the fallen pirate leader. The latter started to move, and the humanoid hunched onto an elbow with the tortured scowl of a man who felt completely and utterly violated. "Burn in hell, Mercurius!"

The Zuul grinned and pressed his pistol's barrel to the other's temple. "You first."

Pop.

* * * * *

Chapter One

Golden Horde Headquarters, South of Chorvoq, Uzbekistan

"Your...visitor is here, ma'am," Sansar Enkh's XO, Lieutenant Colonel Beth "Bambi" Lobdell, said from the doorway. The way she stressed "visitor" told Sansar she wasn't pleased at being kept in the dark about who it was.

There are some things even the XO of the Golden Horde is better off not knowing. Sansar looked up from her slate with a small smile of condolence. "Send him in, please."

"Go right in," Bambi said to someone behind her. She gave the visitor another glance, then stalked off back toward her office.

A Caucasian male, slightly on the tall side, but otherwise nondescript, flowed into her office. He winked and nodded in Bambi's direction. "I don't think she likes me."

"She doesn't like *secrets*, but I can't let everyone know that senior members of the Gray Wolves visit me here."

The man raised an eyebrow. "'Senior members?'"

Sansar smiled. "Yes, senior members. I heard about your promotion."

"You did?" He cocked his head. "I thought—"

"Oh, come on, Beowulf, you—if anyone—should be aware of the special relationship between the Wolves and the Horde."

"I am," Beowulf said with a nod, "I just didn't realize how much you kept track of the inner workings of the organization."

11

"I'm sure there are things I'm not privy to," Sansar said, "especially things I don't have any need to know. However, Timur and I meet periodically to discuss matters of mutual benefit to our respective organizations."

Beowulf nodded once. "That makes sense."

"In a recent conversation, I may have mentioned something about your doings in the Spine Nebula, and that I thought a promotion or two might be in order."

"So I have you to blame."

While his smile took away some of the sting, he didn't appear as happy about the promotion as she'd expected. "Blame? I don't understand."

"I was given a task to complete prior to being formally recognized."

Sansar cocked her head. "And that involves the Horde?"

"It involves the Wolves, the Horde, the Merchant Guild, the—"

"Wait." Sansar sat forward. "The Merchant Guild? How so?"

"Well, I didn't mean the Merchant Guild, so much as a number of ships under *contract* to the Merchant Guild."

"Some of the Human mercenary units have recently had…problems with the Merchant Guild. Perhaps you should start at the beginning, and I can see if our problems are the same as yours."

"May I sit?" Sansar waved him to a chair, and he carefully sat on the edge, obviously contemplating what and how to tell. He finally shrugged and said, "It all started with a couple acts of piracy."

Sansar nodded. "Piracy is an occupational hazard in your line of work."

"Well, yes, and I'm not saying that we haven't relieved some ships of goods we thought could be better distributed by our organization." He smiled. "We have." He shrugged. "There's always some low levels of piracy going on. Certain systems—and some races, like the Pushtal—are known for it. This is something different, though. Recently, ships have been disappearing throughout the Gresht region at a greatly increased rate."

Sansar shrugged. "As long as we were without contracts, it wouldn't surprise me if some enterprising merc commander decided piracy was a profitable way of life. Maybe more than one. They'd have the arms and ability to do it well, too. Do you suppose that's what's happening?"

Beowulf shook his head. "We thought about that, too, when it started, but things just don't add up. There's no single system or cluster of systems where this is happening. It's throughout the whole region, and it's spilling into the core and Tolo regions, as well. Also, if it were mercs, word would get around. The Wolves are connected to the underworld; we believe we'd have heard something by now if that's what was going on. A rumor here...a strange occurrence there. In this case, though, there's *nothing*. Not a word. It's strange, almost creepy even."

"So what do the Wolves think is going on?"

"We're not sure, yet, but we're pretty sure we're going to need your help to find out."

"Why's that?"

"Because of the scale, if nothing else. These attacks are occurring throughout a vast region; they have to have a large, coordinated force to be able to pull them all off."

Sansar nodded. "We are...between jobs at the moment."

Beowulf's eyebrows rose.

"We had a fight with the SI that runs the Science Guild," Sansar explained. "We almost killed it, but it got away. Finding it and killing it is our number one priority, but it's vanished. Until we find it again, the Golden Horde—and most of the Four Horsemen—are available to deal with this."

"I heard about that. An SI is like a super AI?"

"Artificial intelligences are simple programs written to simulate intelligence. They appear to be smart, but that's just good programming. They don't actually learn and grow beyond their programming. Synthetic intelligences, though, are functioning intellects, capable of creating unique solutions based on stimuli. They adapt and grow, just like organic intelligences."

"So they're worse."

"Much worse. And we suspect there are SIs running most, if not all, of the guilds in the galaxy."

"So what do we do about them?"

Sansar shrugged. "I don't know yet what we *can* do about them, or even if there's something we *should* do. They've obviously been around for 20,000 years, and the galaxy has done all right with them running things."

"Until now."

Sansar smiled. "Until now. I don't think the Science Guild SI—Minerva is its name—is going to let us go back to the way things were. Not that we would let it. Minerva was keeping technology stagnant, rather than letting it grow, and killing people who tried to advance it."

"So Minerva has to go?"

"We think so. I don't see how we'll be able to come to a satisfactory agreement with it."

"And the other SIs?"

"That's yet to be determined. Nigel's on the Merc Guild Council, and he's never heard of an SI in charge of the guild."

"Maybe the Veetanho are the SI's pets."

"Maybe. If so, the SI has to be *pissed* that they let the Goltar take over." She shrugged. "We have people working on that, but, like I said—for the minute, anyway—we're available to help with your pirates. Got anything else to go on?"

"Well, yes, actually, and this is what I was getting to," Beowulf said. "Best as the Wolves can tell, there seems to be no common thread among the pirates themselves. They've been Humans, Zuul, Sumatozou; you name it. We do, however, believe we've identified the staging point where these attacks are being coordinated. It's the planet Kullawee in the Coro region."

"Kullawee?" Sansar arched an eyebrow.

"That surprised us, too," Beowulf said. "Kullawee's star is fairly remote, and its inhabitants have never been viewed as technologically advanced. Nevertheless, our operatives have confirmed that the planet is suddenly home to a noticeably larger merchant shipping fleet. But here's the thing." He hunched forward. "All the ships were supposedly added to the Kullawee fleet decades ago, only no one recalls ever having seen them before."

Sansar drummed her fingers. "Let me guess. The ships in this fleet bear a striking resemblance to the vessels that've gone missing."

"Many do, but not all," Beowulf said. "Additionally, a lot of their cargos are eerily similar to cargos that have been seized in the pirate attacks."

"And that cargo is?"

"Everything under the sun, from weapons and ordnance to textiles and building materials."

Sansar cocked her head. "Weapons and ordnance, you say."

"Yeah, but strangely enough, those are in the minority," Beowulf said. "According to Merchant Guild records, most of what's being reported stolen are everyday necessities like food and medical supplies. We find that odd, given the low rate of return for those on the black market, which is where a lot of this stuff is resurfacing." He shook his head. "I mean, seriously—what self-respecting pirate ever made his fortune off looting ships for fruits and vegetables?"

"People have to eat," Sansar said.

"I guess." Beowulf shrugged.

Sansar clasped her hands on the table. "Maybe the pirates are going after low-value cargos because they're not guarded as well. Like you said, who's going to steal fruits and bandage tape? Maybe the margin is low, but so's the risk. Rather than go for a big, risky score, the pirates are going for lots of minor, low-risk scores and are hoping no one will notice."

"That's what we thought, at first."

"And?"

Beowulf exhaled through his nostrils. "And then a heavily-guarded merchant ship got bagged a few weeks ago."

Sansar's eyebrows pulled together.

"Initially, we thought it might be an expansion of the pirates' operations," Beowulf said, "but then we did some more digging into what sort of cargo the ship was carrying. As it turns out, one of the stolen items was an artifact that supposedly dated back to the Great Galactic War."

"What sort of artifact?" Sansar asked.

"A piece of jewelry from the queen of a race that no longer exists," Beowulf said. "During the course of our investigation, somebody mentioned that one of the earlier ships had been transporting a similar type of relic. We went back and checked. Sure enough, it was true."

Sansar shifted in her chair. "I take it these ships aren't the only vessels to be deprived by pirates of their ancient valuables?"

"Not even close," Beowulf said. "So far, we count at least two dozen ships carrying relics that've been hit in the last 18 months, and that's just what was reported to the authorities."

"I take it the Wolves believe there are more."

"We do." Beowulf nodded. "Working off a lead I got from one of our contacts, I tracked down the owner of one of the ships that didn't list an artifact as registered cargo and asked him about his brush with the pirates. He was reluctant to talk, of course, but he did admit to taking on a high-value item prior to launch that was intentionally left off the manifest."

"I presume the item never resurfaced on the black market," Sansar said.

"Nope," Beowulf said. "None of the artifacts have."

Sansar chewed her lip. "So, what does that mean? That there's a rogue Galactic War collector out there trying to corner the market on Galactic War treasures?"

"No," Beowulf said. "It means there's a rogue collector out there who has immense wealth and the ability to fund a pirate operation at the opposite end of this arm of the galaxy. Not only that, this person has access to the Merchant Guild's shipping database and can somehow backdate vessels into its archives." He grimaced. "Oh, yeah, and they also have a secret intelligence group that can ferret out where these objects are and how they're going to be transported."

Sansar stared down at her desktop. "Immense wealth, an enormous intelligence network, and access to the Merchant Guild's databases…" She frowned. "I don't like where this is going."

"Welcome to my world." Beowulf grunted. "The Gray Wolves came into possession of an ancient Krulig artifact some time ago that we've kept in our custody—a ceremonial saber, actually. I planted it on a freighter using a Talgud trader I've dealt with in the past. The ship went missing, but there was a tracker on the vessel's skin that was supposed to activate two months later. It just went off."

Sansar glanced up. "Kullawee?"

"Kullawee," Beowulf repeated. "I don't mind admitting that I'm out of my league here, Sansar. Deep space pirates, Merchant Guild archives, ancient artifacts." He looked away. "The Gray Wolves are in our element running down intel on these sorts of things, but when it comes to doing something about them, that's not our area of expertise."

"So you decided to call us again," Sansar said.

"It worked the first time, didn't it?" Beowulf smiled. "That and, there's this matter of the Horde having a standing debt that's owed to our organization…"

Sansar waited as his words trailed off. "I'm aware of the debt. Even still, I'd be remiss if I didn't mention that the last time I helped you, I ended up sitting beside a rather large nuke that was about to go off."

"I remember," Beowulf said. "I was there, too, you know."

"And you'll be here for this one as well?"

"Do you think I have a choice?"

Sansar sighed. "No. I doubt you do."

"So, what do you think?" Beowulf asked.

Sansar turned her gaze to the painting beside her desk and considered all that had been said. "I have a really bad feeling that we've found the Merchant Guild's SI, and it's getting as uppity as Minerva." She smiled. "Lucky for us, I recently made the acquaintance of someone with a vested interest in helping us get rid of it."

* * * * *

Chapter Two

Golden Horde Listening Post, Mars, Solar System

Taylor Van Zant descended his shuttle's boarding ramp behind his XO and stepped out onto the open docking bay floor of the Golden Horde's Mars outpost.

"Dear sweet Moses, I'm sick of these things." Billy Dawson ripped off the cloth mask that'd been hiding his face and sucked in a breath. "I kid you not, T. I long for the day when I get to shove this stuffy piece of trash in a drawer somewhere, never to be worn again."

"I hear ya, brother," Taylor agreed, pocketing his mask in his nondescript attire. "You have my word as your CO that on the day we finally track down the Merchant Guild asshole who put this price on our heads, you can cram that thing down his throat sans ketchup. Hell, I'll even supply the napkins."

"Does his head need to be attached to his shoulders when I do it?" Billy asked.

"Chef's choice." Taylor lowered his hood, allowing his long blond ponytail to spill out behind his shoulders.

"Impressive place," Billy noted with a whistle.

"I figure that's kinda to be expected when you're dealin' with one of the wealthiest and most prestigious merc outfits in Earth history," Taylor said.

"You think Swamp Eagle Security will ever own digs like this?" Billy asked.

"Nah; wouldn't want to," Taylor said. "Look around at all this space, man. Do you have any idea how much it costs to maintain a spread of this size? Gimme our campus in Jax any day."

Billy shook his head. "Always the pragmatist."

"Function over form, baby. That's how I roll." In truth, Taylor was just as impressed with the facility as his XO, whom he'd known since childhood. Taylor had expected as much three weeks earlier when the Golden Horde's commander, Colonel Sansar Enkh, had invited them there for a visit. He'd inquired then about the meeting's nature, of course. However, in classic Sansar fashion, she'd merely responded, "See you on Mars in three weeks. Oh, and come alone."

Taylor shook his head. *Gotta love the Horde. Cagey as always.*

Silence filled the bay while the pair waited for their host.

"So," Taylor said, "are we gonna talk about the elephant in the room while we've got a minute, or what?"

"Can't say as I know what elephant you're referring to, Chief," Billy said.

"Oh, cut the crap, Billy." Taylor frowned. "We've known each other way too long to have to dance around awkward subjects like this. I'm talkin' about the call you got from—"

The sound of a mechanized door in motion reverberated through the docking bay, causing both men to turn.

"We really have to stop running into each other like this," a baritone voice said.

"Speaking of elephants in the room," Billy murmured.

Taylor grinned and stepped forward. "Mornin', Japhara. Fancy runnin' into you out here."

The large Sumatozou marched across the bay floor toward the Humans. "Thank you for coming."

"Thanks for inviting us," Taylor said. "Rumor has it I have you to thank for my initial introduction to Colonel Enkh outside the Hell House in Jax starport three months ago."

"I may have mentioned that the Eagles could be useful to her cause, yes," Japhara replied.

Taylor titled his head. "She said you called me 'honorable and trustworthy.'"

The Sumatozou crossed his arms. "Well, then. I suppose it'll just have to be her word against mine, won't it?"

"Fargin Sumatozou." Taylor laughed. "You people are smug to the last, huh?"

Japhara flashed a rare but visible grin. "What do you mean, *you people?*"

"All right, all right. Reunion time's over," Billy said. "Colonel Enkh said she wanted to meet with us personally, right? Let's get on with it."

Japhara escorted the two Humans out of the docking bay, and a Golden Horde corporal took them down through a labyrinth of steel-walled corridors to a lift, which took them two levels up to the facility's state wing. There, they were shown through a pair of hand-carved double doors etched with gold inlay into a large circular briefing room with transparent walls that showcased the vast red Mars skyline on all sides.

"Now *that's* what I call impressive," Taylor murmured.

"Welcome to Mars," a female voice said from out of sight.

The trio turned to see the door beside the Tri-V on the far side swing open, and Sansar Enkh appeared. A small woman of Asian descent with short black hair and prim, bronze features, the colonel was dressed in the Horde's camouflage uniform, and was trailed into the room by two other beings. The first was a Sumatozou like Japhara, but with a darker skin and a visible scar down the right side of his face. He was also a merc, judging by his battle dress uniform and weapons. By contrast, the second newcomer was a Pendal male of significantly smaller stature, most of which was carefully obscured by his cloak and hood. He was also vaguely familiar.

"Do we know him?" Taylor murmured to his XO.

"I doubt it," Billy murmured back. "All the Pendals literally look identical, so it's more likely you've crossed paths with one of his kind someplace else. Around Jax starport, maybe."

Taylor shrugged off his sense of déjà vu as best he could while the others approached the conference table.

"Everyone, please be seated," Colonel Enkh said before following her own instruction. "Allow me to introduce Chief Taylor Van Zant and Major William Dawson of Swamp Eagle Security."

Both men nodded.

"Gentlemen, these are my colleagues." The colonel gestured to the Sumatozou. "This is Fragontic. He's a longtime associate of the Golden Horde and the commanding officer of Fragontic's Fearless. He has a lot of personal experience on the matters we'll be discussing here today."

Taylor greeted the alien with a wave. "Good ta meetcha."

The Sumatozou didn't respond.

"Maybe he didn't hear you," Billy whispered.

"I heard him just fine, Major Dawson," Fragontic grumbled. "I shall do you both the courtesy of being frank."

Frank's my nav officer. You'll just have to stick with Farts n' fights or whatever.

"I, unlike some of my associates—" Fragontic pelted Japhara with a dirty look, "—am not convinced that the two of you are ready to be at this table. You are neither Horsemen, nor even mid-level mercs, even by Earth standards. You are, as you Humans like to say, 'small potatoes.' It's not that I don't think you're capable; I'm just not sure you're capable *enough*. I've seen what we're up against. Nevertheless—" he sighed, "—I've learned to trust the colonel's judgement during matters like these, and I see no reason to stray from that approach now." He leaned in, eyes narrowing. "I hope you prove her judgment correct. For your sakes, as well as ours."

Taylor traded matching smirks with his XO.

"Moving on." The colonel cleared her throat. "Next, I'd like you to meet—"

The Pendal rose to his feet and dropped his hood, thereby revealing his three widespread eyes and central mouth, before extending one of his four hands to Taylor. "Yosiff. My name is Yosiff. It is a genuine pleasure to finally make your proper acquaintance, Chief Van Zant. The last time we met, you were quite busy."

"I was?" Taylor shook the alien's hand.

"You were," Yosiff said. "You, the Sumatozou named Haju, and the other Humans were in the process of clearing my cell block on Droxis when I brushed past you en route to the Tortantulas' drop ship. We were evacuated shortly thereafter, so you and I never formally met."

"You were on Droxis?" Billy asked.

"That's right," Yosiff said, his voice the harsh whisper of his race. "The KzSha attacked my transport ship in the Jainoy system and took our crew captive at the behest of the renegade gate master, Akoya Vehlo. From there, we were returned with the others to

Droxis and forced to work as slave laborers in the red diamond mine your forces destroyed." He hung his head. "I must confess. For a time, I feared we were done for, my shipmates and me. But then the Eagles arrived and gave those wasps the justice they deserved." He glanced up. "On behalf of every poor soul who was ever forced to lift a shovel in that godsforsaken hellhole, I sincerely thank you for your heroism."

Taylor had commanded his own merc company for more than three years, and in that time, he'd experienced a lot of things. None of it had prepared him for a compliment like the one he'd just received. "I appreciate the kind words, Yosiff. I really do. The fact is, though, my people ain't any different than most every other culture on Earth—or the Galactic Union, for that matter—in that we once had our hands in the slave trade, too. Thankfully, our ancestors squared with that history a long time ago, and, by the grace of God, we haven't looked back. Nowadays, when we see someone takin' advantage of others, we Southerners are often inclined to step in. It ain't anything heroic. It's just what's right."

The Pendal offered up a final smile, seeming to understand, then returned to his seat.

"Excellent." The colonel clasped her hands. "Now that the formalities have been settled, why don't we—"

"I have a question before we start," Fragontic said.

Of course he does.

The Sumatozou jabbed a sausage-sized finger at Taylor. "Why is the Eagles' CO called 'Chief?' Is that not an inferior rank to colonel or even major?"

"It is in most merc outfits, but not ours," Taylor said. "It's the title I took when I reopened my brother's company three years ago."

"But why not assume the rank of colonel instead?" Fragontic asked. "It would make things much simpler for others of our craft to determine you are the Eagles' leader."

Taylor raised a shoulder. "Seems to me you figured it out just fine once I explained things. Why mess with something that clearly ain't broke?"

The merc commander's expression turned sideways.

"As I was saying," the colonel continued. "Now that formalities have been satisfied, let us call to order today's meeting of the Gathering."

"The what?" Taylor wondered aloud.

"The Gathering is a collective of beings who've taken up arms against the synthetic intelligence entities I told you about in Jacksonville," the colonel said. "We exchange information and resources about the SIs. In some instances, we even share our forces when the need arises."

Billy sat forward. "Chief told me about these SI creatures after your chat outside the Hell House. With respect, and not to question the quality of your intel, but are you sure these things are as powerful as you suggest? I mean, come on. A group of 20,000-year-old beings roaming Creation and pulling the levers behind the curtain of the massive apparatus we call the Galactic Union? That's kind of a tall tale, don't ya think?"

Fragontic snorted across the table. "I can assure you, Major Dawson," he said, rubbing the scar on his face, "the SIs are every bit the real threat Colonel Enkh says they are. My company has faced one in battle. It did *not* end well for our side."

"I'm sorry to hear that," Billy said.

"Do we know how many SIs actually exist?" Taylor asked.

"Not precisely, though we believe, based on current intel, that every Guild is being controlled by at least one," Sansar said. "As it stands, we've countered Minerva, the SI controlling the Science Guild, at least for the time being. However, I believe we can safely assume we've entered the crosshairs of a second after the Eagles' actions on Droxis."

Taylor steepled his palms. "So it's true, then. The Merchant Guild is being controlled by the same SI who put a hit out on my people."

"I'm afraid so," the colonel admitted.

Billy palmed his forehead and muttered, "One of these days, we're really gonna have to stop pissing in other people's corn flakes and start minding our own business."

Taylor was inclined to agree. "What does the Gathering know about the Merchant Guild SI?"

"Not much, aside from the fact that we now know for certain it was bankrolling Akoya's mining operation," the colonel said. "Since then, it would seem, the SI has shifted its means of procuring wealth to other methods."

"Such as?" Billy asked.

"Pirating, to be exact," the colonel said. "Over the last 18 months, numerous merchant ships have reported being attacked by marauders who seemingly appear out of nowhere to hijack their cargo."

"That actually makes a lot of sense." Billy snapped his fingers. "Think about it, Chief. Who better to know what ships are transporting what goods to what systems, with or without an armed escort, than the Merchant Guild? If this SI really is in control of the guild, it'd be like handing 17-year-old me the keys to my parents' liquor cabinet. There's no way I'm not gonna crack her open for all she's worth."

Sansar offered a round of applause. "Well done, Major. It is also very much worth noting that the frequency and ferocity of these attacks has escalated significantly since Droxis."

That, too, makes a lot of sense, Taylor thought. "What do we know about them? The pirates, that is. What species are they? What sort of ships are they using to execute their attacks?"

"All of them," the colonel said.

"Come again?" Billy asked.

Sansar sighed. "The pirates aren't one species or another using a particular type of ship. These raids have been perpetrated by dozens of species, spread across multiple regions, in multiple systems. The pirates could literally be anyone, anywhere, at any time."

Taylor caught a nervous look from his XO.

"Are you suggesting that this thing..." Billy began, "this SI is capable of manipulating others into carrying out its orders?"

"In some instances, yes," the colonel said. "In some instances, the SI's control runs far deeper."

"Explain," Taylor said.

"The Gathering has observed a handful of instances where someone—or some*thing*—seemed to command large clusters of beings in unison," the colonel said. "During such occasions, the aliens in question responded more like drones than sentient beings."

"So they couldn't think for themselves, then," Billy surmised.

"It appeared they could think for themselves, but only within the confines of the SI's programming," Japhara said. "They were given an order. They performed that order. End of story. When something went wrong or circumstances changed, the drones withdrew, probably to receive new instructions."

"And in other instances?" Taylor asked.

"In other instances, the SI seemed to control the host directly by physically inhabiting the other's body," the colonel said. "In such situations, the host spoke differently, acted differently. They were also far more adaptable and, according to the intel, always in total command of their drone followers."

Billy winced. "You make the whole thing sound like some kind of demonic possession."

"Depending on one's belief system, yes," Sansar said. "Possession isn't an entirely inaccurate metaphor for the joining process."

"I'm afraid it's more complicated than that," Fragontic added. "The SI also has the ability to jump, for lack of a better term, into any being it wishes *at any time.*"

"Jump?" Taylor asked.

"Correct," Fragontic said. "During my company's encounters with Minerva, we experienced several instances when we believed we had it cornered. Every time, it escaped."

Sansar nodded. "I have also received information that shows that, in fighting back, several of the crews who were being pirated actually killed several of the SI's hosts, and every time, the SI resurfaced occupying a new body."

"How is that possible?" Taylor asked. "Don't get me wrong, Colonel. I believe in God and the Bible. Even still, last time I checked, it's been 2,000 years, give or take, since anybody on Earth has witnessed a demon possession."

"The SI doesn't occupy its hosts through spiritual suppression," the colonel said. "Its methods are surprisingly far more practical."

"How so?" Billy asked.

The Golden Horde commander lifted a small hand from the conference table and pointed to one of the pinplant nodes behind her ear. "When I say these pirates can be anyone, anywhere, at any time, I mean that in every sense of the phrase. So long as they have pinplants, anyone is vulnerable to an SI's manipulation."

Billy buried his face in his hands and grumbled a curse. "That's it. I'm officially *done* with those things for the rest of my fargin life."

"If the pirates can be anyone, anywhere, then how do we track them? Taylor asked. "Or the SI, for that matter?"

"That's where we've caught a break." The colonel raised a finger. "Another of my associates recently planted a tracker on a merchant ship, using an ancient sword as bait."

"A sword," Taylor repeated.

"That's right," the colonel said. "It appears that 20,000-year-old beings have a flair for nostalgia. The pirates took the bait, which allowed my contact to track them to a remote world in the Coro region called Kullawee. We suspect that it is from here that the Merchant Guild SI is coordinating its attacks."

"For what purpose?" Taylor asked.

"I beg your pardon?" the colonel asked.

"What's this thing's endgame?" Taylor asked. "Think about it, y'all. This thing is the head of a fargin guild. That means, as things stand, it's already got more money and power than any one of us could ever fathom. Why go through all the hassle of staging these attacks? I mean, is it just bored or what?"

Sansar heaved a sigh. "We definitely know the SI is not after thrills."

"And how's that?" Taylor asked.

"Because it's already amassed a fairly sizable fleet in the Kullawee system," the colonel said.

This time it was Taylor's turn to bury his face in his palms. "Great. So world domination it is, then."

"We can't know that, either," Japhara said. "The only thing we know for certain about the SIs is that they're not like an artificial intelligence. They're not programs built for a specific purpose. They grow and evolve, even going so far as to form their own personalities."

"Japhara is right," Sansar said. "Different personalities crave different things, make different plans. Thus, there's no way to know what this SI has in store until we find it ourselves...which brings us to you."

Taylor glanced up.

"The Gathering needs Swamp Eagle Security to deploy to Kullawee and investigate what's happening there," the colonel said. "Under no circumstances are you to engage the SI or any of its followers. You are merely there to collect information and observe."

"Why can't your associates do that?" Billy asked. "The ones who planted the tracker. I didn't catch their name, by the way."

"That's because I did not give it." Sansar smiled. "The associates you're referring to are presently occupied with other tasks."

Taylor thumbed his whiskers. "Operating in the open like that is gonna be tricky for us on account of the bounty. I'd think that'd make us persona non grata for covert field work."

"Or it could make you the perfect choice," the colonel said. "The SI will never be looking for you on its own soil. Add to that your exceptional adaptability and resilience as observed by our common friend here, and I'm confident you'll figure things out along the way."

Japhara swiveled his chair to face the Eagles. "With permission, I'd like to accompany your crew on this mission."

"Pretty sure we don't need a babysitter, Hoss," Taylor said.

"On that we agree," Japhara said. "Lest we forget, however, I am a member of the Cartography Guild's Grand Latura Corps. I have many contacts throughout Union space who could be useful in a pinch. That and..." The Sumatozou hung his head. "I've already put you in harm's way once, for my own purposes. At the very least, I would prefer to be there with you personally this time if things were to go sideways."

Taylor averted his gaze, his thoughts swiftly returning to Droxis and the sight of one of his best leaders and dearest friends being ripped to shreds right in front of him by the KzSha. *I'm so sorry, Stan.* Taylor swallowed hard, fighting to drag his thoughts back to the present. "Major, are you good with this?"

"You mean having a Grand Latura along for the ride on a crazy-ass mission to hunt down a 20,000-year-old super intelligence with a vendetta against us?" Billy shrugged. "Sure, why not?"

"I, too, wish to join your team," Yosiff added. "With your permission, of course."

Taylor wrinkled his nose. "Why do you wanna go?"

"Suffice it to say, I share Japhara's sense of obligation as it pertains to Droxis," the Pendal said. "Your people liberated me from that gulag, and as far as I'm concerned, that leaves me with a debt to pay."

"Pay how?" Billy asked.

"I have certain…" The Pendal shrugged. "Abilities that may be of use to you on this mission."

Taylor opened his mouth to ask a question but was cut off when Colonel Enkh rose from her seat.

"Very good then," Sansar said. "The Golden Horde stands ready to assist you in any manner you require prior to your departure for Kullawee. You need only speak with my logistics officer, and he will handle everything."

"Much obliged, Colonel," Taylor said, turning to go.

"Oh, and Chief?" the colonel called.

"Ma'am?"

"Thank you for agreeing to take this on," Sansar said. "I know it's a lot, and you could've said no. But you didn't." She stood up straight. "You're a credit to your people, Van Zant. Safe travels."

Taylor nodded and turned for the exit.

"Well, that was insightful." Billy was waiting in the hallway outside when his CO emerged from the briefing room. "You do realize there's no way we can take the *Osyrys* on this mission, right? Or for that matter, most of our own roster?"

"Yeah, I'd considered as much," Taylor admitted. "I'm open to suggestions if you have any."

Billy rubbed his chin and thought about it. "I might have one."

"Great, let's hear it."

"Not so fast," Billy said. "You gotta know up front that if we make this call, it's gonna cost us…bigtime."

Taylor waited for Japhara to catch up, then waved goodbye to Yosiff before heading toward the shuttle hangar. "Tell me on the way."

* * *

A secret door opened after the meeting broke up and a nondescript man walked in.

"Well, at least that went as well as we could hope, Beowulf," Sansar said after the others had left.

"It's a dangerous plan," the man noted.

"You acquired the bandilaroes?"

"I did. Three real bandilaroes are being smuggled to Piquaw as we speak."

"I expect success. With the amount invested in the ships and in hiring the mercenaries..."

"I understand," Beowulf said.

Sansar arched an eyebrow. "Do you?"

"I do. I was the one who paid the bills. I understand how much we have invested in this. Not only that, but our portion of the plan alone risks exposing us to the SI's wrath."

"True." Sansar nodded. "Not only that, but once this plan is set in motion, it cannot be stopped. We will have to proceed with caution."

Beowulf chuckled. "That's business as usual in my line of trade."

"Mine, too. One mistake often gets you—" She paused as the door opened, and Yosiff walked back in through the door.

"Dead?" the Pendal asked.

Sansar cocked her head. "I'm sorry?"

Yosiff smiled. "I believe you were going to say that a mistake will often get you dead?"

"Were you reading my mind?"

The Pendal scoffed. "Not hardly. The walls here aren't as thick as they might be."

"True. This is more of a...temporary facility." She stared at the alien for a moment. "Is there something I can do for you?"

"You can stop having me followed."

Sansar chuckled. "You noticed?"

"It's hard for a Pendal not to notice when they're being followed."

"Because you read minds?"

"No, because we're very observant. We've had to be."

"Why's that?"

Yosiff smiled. "Before I answer that, why don't you tell me what you've found out?"

"About what?"

"About my race. You're not only having me followed; you seem to have surveillance out on all the members of my race you can find."

"I don't know enough about you, but I know—or can guess—enough to know that lying to you isn't going to get me anywhere."

"No, it probably isn't." The smile ghosted across his face again. "So tell me; what have you found out?"

"I've found more questions than answers, if you want to know the truth."

"We guard our privacy quite jealously."

"And yet you often seem to be where things are happening or where major course-changing events are about to take place."

"We like to be aware of what is going on in the galaxy, even if—as happened on Droxis—sometimes we end up as part of the action rather than merely observers of it."

"No...you've got me wrong. When I said 'you,' I didn't mean the Pendal race, I meant _you_ in particular, Yosiff—or whatever your real name is. As best I can tell, there are at least four copies of you currently active in the galaxy. If not you, then you're quadruplets that look exactly alike." She cocked her head. "But that's not it, is it? They're all clones of *you*. Or you're a clone of someone else; you tell me."

"That's a dangerous question," Yosiff said, his whispering voice now almost too soft to be heard. "Many people have been killed for asking less."

"Perhaps, but I can tell you, if you kill me, you won't make it out of here alive." She waved toward one of the walls. "And everything is recorded, so even if you kill me, you won't stop the information from getting out."

The Pendal smiled. "I think you will find your recording device had an unfortunate malfunction about the time I walked into the room." He shrugged. "I do not, however, have any intention of killing you. I have a feeling the information you've already collected is enough—and well enough distributed—that we won't be able to put the genie back into the bottle, as I believe you say."

"So you admit it? You're a clone?"

"That much is true, although there are many more copies of me than you are aware of."

"We just had an unfortunate encounter with the Science Guild. The guild master was making clones of a lot of people and races. Do we have him to thank for you?"

"No. I am something...very different." He paused and looked around the room. "Perhaps we should sit. This may take a while."

Beowulf and Sansar sat on the opposite side of the table from the Pendal, who steepled one pair of hands while resting the other two on the table. He seemed to contemplate for a second, then pulled his hood back and delivered a three-eyed stare at Sansar for a couple of seconds before turning it on Beowulf.

Gooseflesh covered Sansar as the stare moved on, and she felt somewhat violated. She shook her head, trying to clear it. "What was that for?"

"What I'm going to tell you," Yosiff said, ignoring her question, "is something very few know. My race, for all practical purposes, no longer exists. There are seven of us—seven discrete individuals—we make copies of. With our capes and hoods, most people don't realize that they see the same body over and over. For example, two of us are pilots, including myself. If you think about the number of Pendal pilots you've seen, all are based on two people. They may have discreet memories, different from each other, but they are indeed from the same stock.

"Once, hundreds of years ago, several Besquith merc companies invaded our planet during a period of limited contracts. Apparently, they found us to be quite tasty. They thought to keep the invasion a secret, but word got out. Rather than get caught at what they were doing, they tried to kill everyone on the planet, and then fled. Their weapons were successful in depopulating the planet. There were a few hundred Pendals off-planet when this happened. Our leaders tried to gather us together, but some couldn't bear to go on living. The remaining 27 Pendals were given a planet that was then removed from the rolls of the Cartography Guild.

"Ever since, we have dedicated ourselves to fighting slavery where we find it, although, with our numbers as limited as they are, it is difficult."

"You didn't go after the Besquith?"

The Pendal shrugged. "To what end? They were Besquith being Besquith. That would be like punishing a Human for failing to give in when all hope seems lost. Besides, what good would it have done? It wouldn't have brought our race back."

"For vengeance's sake? The whole 'eye for an eye' thing?"

"Although there are times we've contemplated it, to actually do so would make us less than we are." He shook his head. "Regardless, our race continues to decline; as I said, we're now down to seven individuals, and those won't remain viable for that much longer. Until that happens, though, we will continue to work in the shadows, trying to give a nudge here and a boost there that will provide key information to allow races to remain free or, sometimes, regain their freedom." Yosiff smiled. "I believe one of my brothers spoke with you once, Sansar."

"He did."

"We tried very hard to keep you out of the grip of the Veetanho. I'm happy to see we were successful."

"It might have been more helpful if you'd have just come out and told us what was going on."

"Perhaps...but we also jealously guard our sources as it wouldn't take much to extinguish our race entirely."

"So you just hide in plain sight, doing what you do?" Beowulf asked.

"We do. Who really looks overlong at a Pendal? Our visage is scary for most races to look upon, and we have certain abilities that help other races focus their attention elsewhere."

"But not the Besquith."

"Sadly, no; they didn't have any problems with our visage, and our abilities don't affect them, especially when their ire is up. There are a couple other races—like the KzSha—that are immune, too."

Sansar sighed. "I'm sorry for what happened to your race, but I don't understand why you're telling us all this."

"I told you we work to abolish slavery, correct?"

"Yes, but—"

"The SIs are the greatest slavers in the galaxy. They've held all the races down for tens of thousands of years. We've known this for a while, but no one has been willing or able to do anything about them. You Humans are the first race to go against them in thousands of years. The Pendals as a race won't last much longer, and we have decided to assist you as best we can in your quest to free the galaxy from them."

"What does this assistance entail?"

"I'm not sure yet; it was not a unanimous decision, and—after centuries of secrecy—some of us are having a hard time giving up our secrets. Suffice it to say that we will assist where and when we can, in a manner that doesn't make us targets for the rest of the galaxy."

Sansar cocked her head. "We may be able to help you in turn. The Cavaliers are working on a program to bring another race back from the brink of annihilation."

"We are aware, and we hope it pans out...although some would say that bringing the Depik back from the brink is a two-edged sword. Still, it wouldn't be a bad thing—for you—to have the galaxy's best killers owing you a few favors. There are bad times coming, and they would be...assets."

"Bad times?"

"The Kahraman haven't gone anywhere, despite the fact that they pulled back from the core. You can expect them to return, and when they do, they will return in force. If the Merc Guild doesn't pull itself together, and soon, it will surely be overwhelmed. And if you're fighting the SIs at the same time...I fear for the galaxy. There is no doubt—both the Kahraman and the SIs are overlords who will not want to give up power. You may not be able to beat either of them, but you have no chance whatsoever if you have to fight both of them simultaneously." He shook his head. "And then there are the Dusman."

"So we need to get this—whatever this is with the Merchant Guild—taken care of as soon as possible, and deal with Minerva and any other of the SIs we have to immediately thereafter, or things will be bad."

"Bad?" The Pendal chuckled. "It will be far worse than *bad*. It will cast the galaxy into a dark age that will last for millennia."

Sansar nodded. "I understand. So we're allies for now?"

"Loosely allied, but yes."

"What can you tell us of Van Zant?" Beowulf asked. "Are you certain he can be trusted?"

"I can tell you he's a man of his word. If he tells you he will do something, he will do so to the best of his abilities."

"That's good," Sansar said. "As you said, time is of the essence, and we're going to need friends and allies. The Cavaliers are rebuilding. Asbaran has a bunch of new Lumar, but it will take time to train and integrate them." She chuckled. "Lumar don't train quickly, nor can the Hussars build ships any faster than they already are. We're the best off of any of the Horsemen, and we're woefully underfunded and understrength compared to our normal levels."

Sansar shrugged. "And yet, we have no choice but to proceed with Van Zant as our ally. Minerva still has to be found, and we can't let this SI get away without a reckoning." She looked at Beowulf. "I'm glad you believe in Van Zant, because the way things are, I don't know that we have any other choice."

* * * * *

Chapter Three

"You're sure you've got this?" Beowulf asked, his eyes scanning the boarding ramp to the freighter. "Absolutely," Captain Eltaan said. The Altar clacked its mandibles once in exclamation. "I have reviewed the Tri-V footage you sent me from the theft of the Sleetarn saber. It was an inside job; the pirates obviously knew about the weapon and had suborned the security officer. Once the security officer switched sides and killed the captain, it was all over." The Altar gave its race's version of a shrug. "Were you able to find out anything about Mercurius?"

"No, and that's the funny thing," Beowulf replied. "The security officer's name wasn't Mercurius; it was Jasket."

"So why did the captain call him Mercurius with his dying breath?"

"I don't know. Perhaps he knew the traitor's real identity." Beowulf shrugged. "Perhaps he knew the identity of the person who'd sold him out."

"I do not think so," the Altar said, making a motion of negation. "First, that is a strange name for a Zuul. And the way he said it was wrong, too. He was calling the security officer Mercurius."

"I agree, but that leaves us precisely nowhere."

"Regardless of the name, I have all the info I need," Eltaan said. "The mission is straightforward. Go with the ship. Protect the Rukori bandilaroes. Kill the pirates if we get attacked. Capture a pirate if possible; return their bodies if not."

43

"And you have enough troops?"

"I have 40 troopers, which is more than double the number of pirates I saw in the Tri-V video. I have more than enough to defend the ship."

"Very well," Beowulf replied. "Good luck. I will be waiting for you here upon your return."

"Your money is well spent with us. We will be successful." The Altar turned and entered the freighter, and the boarding hatch closed.

Beowulf went to his vehicle and drove across the tarmac to where his assistant waited with a scanner and a pair of high-tech binoculars. "Anything?" he asked as the freighter, FTS *Bills to Pay*, roared into the heavens.

"Nope," Rasputin said. "No radio calls were made, other than the call for launch authorization. No one went on or off after you left."

Beowulf shook his head. This was the fourth time they'd set the trap up, but the first when they'd actually used the real bandilaroes. The first three times they'd used very convincing replicas—at least he'd thought so, anyway—but somehow the pirates must have known. The ships carrying them had gone about their travel without interference. Sansar had finally authorized the purchase of three real bandilaroes at considerable expense. She'd also been clear that she expected them back. *Very* clear.

"Think the pirates will bite?" Rasputin asked.

"I don't know. If they do, I hope the mercs don't let them get away with the bandilaroes. I'm not sure I'll be welcome back on Earth if they do."

* * * * *

Chapter Four

Ravenrok Manor, 30 Miles North of Katova Starport, Kullawee

M emerged into the soft glow of the corridor lights outside his personal chamber and gave a final inspection of his humanoid host's appearance in the crystal-etched mirror across the stone foyer. *Impeccable as always,* he thought, admiring Vohtor's smooth gray skin and shoulder-length white hair through the other's luminescent gold eyes. Vohtor was the name M had given this particular host following their initial meeting some 12 years earlier.

In the time since, M had become quite fond of Vohtor, hence his preference for using the alien as his primary vessel when traveling abroad. Granted, M could take any being he liked for such tasks. However, there had always been something warm and familiar about Vohtor that M had been drawn to. Perhaps it was the alien's ancestry that had made him such a fascinating find. Creators knew Vohtor's kind hadn't been seen much since the Great Galactic War; that fact alone was enough to attract M's attention.

Even still, Vohtor's willingness to join M's crusade had been what had really sparked their connection. Such compliance was hardly common. Most of the time when M sought to occupy a host for his purposes, he had to do so by force, only to leave that individual with no memory of where they'd been or what they'd been doing. This was assuming, of course, that M left them alive at all when his need for them had ended. Vohtor, meanwhile, had welcomed M into his consciousness with zero resistance. It was as if the ancient alien wanted M to be there, *needed* him there.

Initially, M had been taken aback by this experience. Then he entered Vohtor's grief-stricken mind, and all became clear. The alien had been exiled by his own people for daring to believe that many of their culture's longstanding beliefs could change—that they *needed* to change.

Just like me. A flash of red passed through Vohtor's cheeks as thoughts of the other SI's laughter rushed through M's mind. Minerva, Dumanis, Mimir. They'd all mocked M's assertion that their kind should take a more prominent role in leading the Galactic Union, rather than simply leading from the shadows.

"Today's beings have existed for centuries, some for mere decades," M had said. "They're as naïve as they are stupid. By contrast, we've existed for millennia. Who better than us, then, to decide what should and should not be in the universe?"

M's thesis had been met by scoffs, though, to his credit, at least Huginn had possessed the fortitude to say what the others had been thinking.

"Consider what you're proposing, Mercurius," the Cartography Guild overlord had said. "Our anonymity insulates us from the reprisals of those who would seek to claim our power for themselves. Is that to suggest that the Vergola, the Krulig, or even the Veetanho could ever hope to threaten us? Not likely. However, why take the risk when we can simply rule from the shadows while the greater Union society goes on squabbling for our scraps?"

"It's always been this way, Mercurius," Minerva had added. "Only a buffoon would seek to change that now."

M bristled in the hallway, recalling the slight. *Arrogant fools, the entire lot of you.* He paused and took a breath, having always found calm in the exercise. *No bother. Soon enough, history will show who among us was right and who was the buffoon. The only question remaining then will be what the former opts to do with the latter.*

Suddenly craving new scenery, M smoothed out Vohtor's tunic lapel, then headed for the main courtyard, which lay just beyond the manor's central atrium. The sun outside was warm and inviting on Vohtor's skin as the alien host and his synthetic master emerged into the garden outside. All around, vibrant shades of pink, red, and orange bosen flowers bloomed against the dense green backdrop of the 80-foot bayva trees that formed a sort of corridor from the main house out to the rest of the estate.

In all the worlds in all the systems M had experienced in his 20,000 years of existence, none had compared to the majesty of Kullawee. From its mild tropical climate to its stunning natural beauty, the remote planet was the perfect place for M to call home.

If only the natives had been as welcoming as the weather. Alas, M had seen to that, too. Now, the Kullawee people viewed him as much a part of their community as one of their own. *As it should be.*

A comm alert chimed in M's thoughts via the pinplants in Vohtor's head.

Control tower. M studied the communique's sender before answering. "Yes?"

"My apologies for the interruption, Master," the officer said. "We just received a new batch of intel from one of our operatives, who returned earlier. A Duplato merchant ship departed Piquaw six days ago and is bound for Emza."

M arched an eyebrow. "And?"

"The ship is carrying a set of three Rukori bandilaroes as part of its cargo."

Vohtor stirred in M's subconscious.

"Has the presence of the bandilaroes been confirmed?" M asked.

"Yes, sir," the officer said. "Our operative returned with a full copy of the ship's manifest, if you'd like to review it."

M tugged at his host's white goatee as he considered the development. Rukori bandilaroes were small ships only slightly larger than a shuttle but were renowned for their maneuverability and durability in a fight. They were also extremely rare, hence their value to any collector worth his salt. A number of frauds had recently been seen on the market, and he'd suspected the real thing would show up soon.

"Tell me, Captain," M began, "do you have access to the Duplato manifest?"

"Yes, sir," the officer answered. "I've got it pulled up now on my—"

A flash of sunshine preceded the hum of artificial lighting and steel decking as M peered forward at the manifest through the officer's eyes. Sure enough, it was all right there in the operative's report. Real bandilaroes this time. Three of them. *How very interesting.* M grinned. *It would appear that Vohtor and I will be traveling today after all.*

* * * * *

Chapter Five

PCB Strip, Panama City Beach, North Florida, Earth

The hot North Florida sun shone brightly over the Gulf of Mexico as the Eagles' transport exited the Hathaway Bridge en route to the Emerald Stormriders' compound five miles up the beach.

Man, this place has sprouted back up. Taylor peered out at the long row of new high rises ahead, marveling at how much the area had changed since last he'd visited. It was good to see business in this part of his home state booming again. As North Florida tourist spots went, few had been as decimated by the South Florida secession as Panama City. Nearly all the area's marquis business had fled south to places like Orlando and Tampa after the split—so much so that much of the old PC Strip had been unceremoniously dubbed Skull Island by the locals for its multitude of abandoned storefronts and hotels. Now, decades later, all that had changed, thanks to scores of entrepreneurs seeking to capitalize on the new North Florida economy.

"I'd forgotten how different the beaches look on this side of the state," Taylor said, noting the turquoise shade of the local waters versus the cool Atlantic green he'd grown up with around Jax. "As merc stations go, I'd wager this one was tough to leave when the time came."

"Oh, yeah," Billy admitted. "Living on PC Beach has always been one of the major perks of working for the Riders. Granted, they could never pay as well as one of the state's larger outfits, like the Eagles, but between the sugar-white sand, the surf, and all the redneck college girls roaming the pier in bikinis, it beats the hell out of Uzbekistan. That's for sure."

Taylor grinned.

"You Humans and your sexual urges." Japhara grunted from the driver's seat up front. "In all my years of serving the Cartography Guild, I've never once encountered a species that is more driven by their physical impulses than yours."

Taylor faced the Sumatozou. "With all due deference to your ex, Hoss, maybe you just haven't met the right girl yet. Give it time, though." He smiled. "It'll happen."

Japhara looked past his shoulder, then re-fixed his eyes on the road.

"You mentioned that the Riders were never really a huge company." Taylor returned his focus to the XO. "Is that why they fell on hard times?"

"Yes and no," Billy said. "Small or not, the one thing the Riders always had going for them as PC's only merc outfit was that they knew their lane."

"Meaning?" Taylor asked.

"Meaning they understood their limits, and they never punched above their weight class where contracts were concerned," Billy said. "As I understand it, everything changed about a year after I left the outfit. That's when the original owners retired and sold out to a private investor from California."

Taylor winced.

"Oh, it gets better," Billy added. "Turns out the Riders' new owners weren't as keen on entering the merc business as they were in finding the right training ground for their darling little princess of a daughter to cut her teeth on in corporate America. Obviously, we make a lot of money in this trade, so they thought that was it."

"I presume things did not go well," Japhara said.

"That's putting it mildly." Billy frowned. "The girl knew zilch about mercenaries. Worse yet, she never *cared* to know. As far as she was concerned, her family had a track record of running successful businesses, and 'no knuckle-dragging Neanderthal hick with a laser rifle was gonna tell her how to run hers, period.'" He paused with a set of air quotes. "Her words, not mine."

Taylor shuddered to think how that had affected morale. "How long did all this go on?"

"Too long," Billy said. "Right out of the gate, the girl vied for contracts that were way beyond the Riders' paygrade. Armed escorts, assault contracts, high-end cadre. Pretty much if the job offered enough juice to impact her bottom line, the princess took it. The whole thing came to a head when she deployed three quarters of her forces on a defense contract that got 60% of them killed in one of Peepo's traps in the run-up to the Omega War. Only some darned good piloting got them off the planet before a total wipeout. Suffice it to say, Mommy and Daddy pulled the plug pretty quick afterward, at which time the Riders went back on the market for sale. Then the war happened, and they all melted away to escape Peepo's notice."

"I take it that's when our friend stepped in?" Taylor asked.

"What can I say?" Billy shrugged. "She never was one to miss an opportunity, and, after the war ended, the price was right, and there were still enough folks around to make up a core she could build around."

The transport's engine let out a yawn as Japhara downshifted off the highway, then eased the craft to rest outside the main security gate of the Emerald Stormriders' campus.

"State your identity and business please," a lone guard said. He was a young man—early-20s or so—with boyish blond features to go with his light emerald uniform.

"My name is Japhara Hylume," the Sumatozou driver said, "senior member of the Grand Latura and Cartography Guild liaison to this system. My associates and I have an appointment to speak with your commanding officer at 1300 hours."

Taylor watched through the transport's tinted rear window as the guard checked Japhara's story on his slate. *It's cool, man. I swear we're legit.*

The guard swiped off his slate, then motioned to his colleague inside the checkpoint station. "They're good to go. Open it up."

Japhara waved thanks to the troopers while the chain link gate ahead chattered open across the sun-bleached pavement. From there, the Sumatozou eased the vehicle forward, then veered right onto the main thoroughfare that led through the complex's heart.

In line with the Riders' reputation as a company on the skids, most of the grounds inside the gate left much to be desired in the way of aesthetic appeal. Many of the buildings looked borderline condemnable with their wrecked siding and weatherworn roofs, if they'd even had the latter to begin with.

"Man, Billy, you weren't kiddin' when you said these folks had fallen on hard times," Taylor said, eyeing a trio of mangled warehouses to his left. "I've seen penitentiaries with nicer digs than this."

"That may be true, but keep those comments to yourself," the XO said. "The Riders just moved into this place last month."

"Wait, this ain't their original campus?" Taylor glanced up.

"Nope," Billy said. "The old campus was built on the old Air Force base across town. It was a nice facility, too. Lots of good space, and plenty of room to operate. Problem was, daddy's little girl ran up such a tab trying to turn the place into a fargin palace that it would've practically bankrupted the new owner just to keep the lights on, much less pay the mortgage. By selling and moving here to the old 30-A packing plant, the Riders slashed all that red from their ledger and stabilized their footing at a facility they could own free and clear on the cheap."

Nice. Taylor had adopted a similar approach when he'd relaunched the Eagles three years earlier. Rather than incur a ton of debt to plant his company on primo merc real estate outside the Jax starport, he'd opted to set up shop at the old Castillo Airfield outside of town. That place had been a fixer-upper, too. Buying it outright, though, had given him flexibility to invest his outfit's limited resources in other areas, which eventually led to their financial independence. *Cash is king, baby. Always has been, always will be.*

The transport *ka-funk*ed past yet another pothole, then swung left past the barracks toward the main operations center, where another trooper emerged to meet them. Of average height with a lean, spindly build, he was older than his gate comrades—late-30s or so—and sported sun-copper skin with sharp features and a patchy brown goatee. His attire was also different—leather flipflops and camo shorts with a sleeveless retro Firebird shirt, as was his hair—a full-blown mullet fluttering across the breeze in all its mousse-rich glory.

"Holy hell, and they call *me* country," Taylor remarked.

"Welcome to the Redneck Riviera, bud." Billy patted his CO's shoulder.

The mulleted trooper motioned their transport toward the back of the ops center where Japhara brought the vehicle to rest inside the privacy of the building's motor pool.

"Welcome to Panama City, Chief Van Zant," the mullet man said in a thick Southern drawl.

"Glad to be here," Taylor said, climbing out. "Thanks for bringing us in through the back. Speakin' for Major Dawson here, we don't get a lot of opportunities these days to move about in the open without wearin' masks and such."

"The colonel mentioned you boys have seen some heat lately." The man slid off his aviator sunglasses and hooked them on the collar of his Firebird shirt. "Might I ask who it was that owned the punch bowl into which you deposited that particular turd?"

Billy made a face. "That's a long story, but I'm sure we'll get to it. In the meantime, we didn't catch your name."

"Oh, right. Sorry." He stuck out a palm. "The name's Lajoie. Lieutenant Daryl Eugene Lajoie the Fourth, to be exact. Most folks just call me Lajoie, though."

"Good to meetcha, Lajoie." Taylor shook his hand. "I'm Chief Taylor Van Zant. This is my XO, Major Billy Dawson, and this is Japhara."

Lajoie regarded the Sumatozou. "Damn, you're a big sumbitch!"

Japhara frowned. "How wonderfully astute of you, Lieutenant."

Taylor chuckled and stayed on topic. "What's your MOS here with the Stormriders?"

"Lead engineer," Lajoie said.

"Really?" Billy raised an eyebrow. "You're a pilot?"

"Bet your ass," Lajoie said proudly. "I'm a damn good one, too. Yep. The colonel plucked me right off the engineerin' team at

Harvick's Hurricanes after she took over the Riders last month and brought me here to PC. I've been here ever since."

"Harvick's Hurricanes, huh?" Taylor glanced at his XO. "Word around Jax is there's been a lot of turnover on the crew lately."

"That'd be true," Lajoie said. "Ever since Pete Harvick announced his intention to retire at Christmas, a whole bunch of folks have been puttin' out feelers to gauge their options. As for me, I didn't see Harvick's chief wrench goin' anyplace, so when the colonel came callin' with this gig, I leapt at the opportunity."

"I take it you've been happy with the move, then," Billy said.

"Yes, sir, happy as a pig in shit," Lajoie exclaimed. "Plus, have ya seen the women around here? *Dammit*, son!"

Taylor genuinely couldn't wait for the others to meet this guy.

"Speakin' of the colonel, she's waitin' to meet y'all in her office." Lajoie spun for the exit. "Right this way."

Taylor and Japhara followed Billy and Lajoie though the back of the motor pool and into the ops center's lower level. In stark contrast to the building's ramshackle exterior, the inside of the place was surprisingly decent. New paint, fresh carpet, the occasional fake fern plant. Taylor even spotted one of those fancy new coffeemakers that Frank had been bugging him about in the downstairs breakroom.

"Hey, Lula Ann," Lajoie called to the blonde corporal at the mug station. "Do me a favor, will ya? Make us up a few cups of that there yuppie coffee, then bring it to the colonel's office for our guests. Extra sugar for mine, if ya please. Chop chop."

The woman frowned and shot him the bird.

"Love you, too, Peaches! Lots and lots!" Lajoie blew her a kiss, then proceeded onward. Flipflops clapped against his heels until finally the convoy came to a halt outside an office. "Excuse me, Colonel?" He knocked at the entrance. "The Swamp Eagle Security folks are here to see ya."

"Bring them on in," a female voice answered.

Ladies and gentlemen, start your negotiating engines.

The mulleted lieutenant swung open the door, then stood aside while the others entered the office.

"Well, well, well," the Sirra'Kan commander said with a sly smile. "Look who's finally come home, where he belongs."

Billy answered with a grin of his own. "Hey, Kami. Been a while."

* * * * *

Chapter Six

Colonel Eutowa K'Nami rose from her desk, dressed sharply in her crisp emerald uniform, and folded her arms across her chest. "I must be psychic, ya know that? Somehow I always knew, no matter what…someday you'd come walking back through my door. I never doubted that."

"Well, we did almost do business together three months ago on Karma Station, remember?" Billy asked. "The Emza contract that went to Paul Torrio and the River Hawks?"

"Yeah, but that was different." The feline waved off his suggestion. "That was just a passing reunion among old friends. But this…" She leaned forward and put her hands on her desktop. "This, my dear boy, is you coming back because you *need* something from me."

Ah, hell. Taylor palmed his face.

"With all due deference, Colonel K'Nami," Billy said a bit firmer, "time is kinda of the essence in this particular matter. Are you gonna hear our proposal, or are we gonna stand around here flirting all day? Because if it's the latter, the chief and I really have places to be."

Kami heaved a sigh and lowered her head. "You're nothing if not reliable, Billy Dawson. Always right down to business."

"My wife says that's one of my finer points," Billy said.

"Subtle, Billy. Subtle." Kami glanced across the room to Lajoie. "I'll take it from here, Lieutenant. Thanks."

57

"Copy that, ma'am. I'll be down in ops if you need me." The mullet man tossed a casual wave, then pulled the door shut on his way out of the office.

"In the interest of decorum," Taylor began, "do we still call you Kami like we did on Karma Station, or is it Colonel K'Nami now?"

"Kami is still fine in private," the Sirra'Kan said. "Out there with the others, though, it's Colonel."

Taylor nodded and took a seat beside the others across the desk. "Before we get started, can I ask what brought you back to the merc business? The last time we met, you seemed happy as a lark on Easy Street makin' boatloads of credits as a contract broker."

"What can I say?" Kami chuckled. "Once a merc, always a merc, right? I'd expect a Van Zant of all people would understand that."

"Maybe," Taylor said. "Prior to re-launching the Eagles, though, I was tendin' bar in a rickety old dive bar out by Jax starport."

"What's your point?" Kami asked.

"Slingin' Long Branch Light on draft to thirsty freighters and deep space pirates don't exactly fetch the payday of a contract broker," Taylor said. "You, on the other hand, had options. So, why'd you come back?"

Kami twirled a tangle of her tiger-striped brown fur in her fingers as she considered the question. "Panama City has been my home for as long as I can remember, which makes the Riders my hometown outfit. I idolized this group growing up, much in the same way I imagine you did with your brother's company. I wasn't prepared to sit back on a cushy throne of cash and watch as they were torn apart by creditors like the Eagles. I saw an opportunity to step in, so I took it."

"Small town girl leaves the big city lights of mercenary contracting to get back home to her roots." Billy made a face. "Somebody oughta write a country song about that."

"I'm pretty sure that market's been cornered already," Kami shot back.

"I beg your pardon, Colonel, but might I pose an inquiry?" Japhara leaned forward. "How does a Sirra'Kan come to be raised on the sandy beaches of the American South here on Earth? Why aren't you with your own people?"

Kami thinned her lips. "Apologies, Biggins, but that's a very long story for another time." She glanced to the others. "Right now, I'm more interested in learning why Swamp Eagle Security has turned to the Emerald Stormriders for help."

Taylor and Japhara spent the better part of the next 30 minutes explaining everything that was happening, from the events on Droxis, to the formation of the Gathering, and their role in the greater drama that seemed to be playing out around the galaxy.

"Let me get this straight," Kami said when the pair had finished. "For the better part of the last 20,000 years, every guild in the Galactic Union has secretly been controlled by an ancient synthetic intelligence, one of whom put a hit out on the Eagles because you blew up its red diamonds on Droxis? *And* it can take people over through their pinplants?"

"That's the long and short of it, yeah," Taylor answered. "We don't know that all of 'em are controlled by SIs, but intel indicates most of 'em are."

Kami put her elbows on her desktop and rubbed her temples. "Dear sweet Moses, Billy, and here I thought the pickle you got us into on Typhus was bad."

"What pickle on Typhus?" Taylor asked.

"Also a long story for another time," Billy answered. "What matters now is whether or not the Riders will help us get to Kullawee so we can beat this thing and lift the bounty off our heads."

Kami chewed her lip. "Getting to Kullawee is one thing. Facing this threat of yours once we're on the ground is an entirely different issue."

"How so?" Taylor asked.

"Any skirmish outside of a garden-variety bar fight is gonna require manpower I don't have," Kami said. "I hate to break this to you, Goldilocks, but the Riders are not a large company. We never were. As it stands, I've got exactly one company under my command, comprised of 82 troopers and a handful of old CASPers I bought at auction from the Iron Conquistadors. We're a spunky group, sure, but we're in no way equipped for something of this scale or caliber."

"Swamp Eagle Security can supplement whatever you need in terms of equipment," Taylor said. "As for manpower, that's something you'll have to iron out on your own. Most of our people have been marked by the Merchant Guild's bounty on us, so they're pretty content to keep their heads down until this thing blows over."

"These are people with families," Billy added.

Kami drummed her fingers as she studied the massive palm tree surrounded by palmettos through her office window. "There's a crew out of Crestview that might be of use to us on this. I can reach out to their CO if you like, but I doubt they'll come cheap."

"Whatever it takes," Billy said.

"Within reason." Taylor admonished his XO with a look. "Swamp Eagle Security may be 100% operational again, but we're still nowhere near Horsemen-level when it comes to resources."

"No, but you're working with one, right?" Kami asked. "Reach out to your contacts with the Horde. Tell them what's happening, and that you need a lifeline. If these SIs are the threat you claim they are, I'm sure Colonel Enkh wouldn't mind signing off on a few extra credits if it means putting them down for the count."

Japhara cleared his throat. "With respect, Colonel K'Nami, you seem quite adept at spending other people's money."

"Newsflash, Biggins, I spent eight years as a top-tier contract broker in addition to being a full-blown hottie in a bikini." Kami grinned. "I *never* pay the check."

Japhara appeared to rankle at her response but didn't push the issue.

"So, to recap," Kami said. "Swamp Eagle Security requires safe passage through the stargate and transport to Kullawee, as well as logistical and most likely tactical support on the ground when we arrive. Does that about cover it?"

"That sums it up, yeah," Taylor said. "I reckon that just leaves one last question...what's all that aid gonna cost us?"

The Sirra'Kan's grin widened. "For starters, my crew keeps everything we use on this mission in terms of resources. Ordnance, supplies, even CASPers. They're all Stormrider property as soon as we launch for the gate."

Taylor wasn't thrilled with the condition, but all and all, he figured it could've been worse. "Okay, fine. We have a deal."

"Oh, I'm not even remotely finished," Kami said. "Hence the phrase 'for starters.'"

Taylor frowned.

"The Riders will also require a 30% down payment on a fee to be decided by me with the balance to be paid upon our eventual return to Earth after the successful completion of our mission. We'll also be taking a 65% cut of any spoils accrued along the way."

"Anything else?" Billy asked.

"You bet your cute little Nebraskan buns there is." Kami aimed a serious look at Taylor. "A little birdie recently informed me that Swamp Eagle Security has some sort of deal with the Cartography Guild that gives you rate-free travel through the stargate to any destination in the Galactic Union. As the story goes, this deal also applies to any company with whom the Eagles coordinate for their subcontractor work."

Taylor cocked his head. "Why do I get the impression this birdie of yours has the face of a Flatar?"

Kami grinned.

Thanks for nothin', you ghoulish little bastard. Taylor made a mental note to review the meaning of "under the table" with the Tortantula commander he'd bargained with on Droxis.

"Clearly, the Eagles can't exercise that option for the purposes of this trip, as that would effectively paint a target on our backs," Kami said. "You'll have to pay for this one just like the rest of us. When we get back, however, and the SI threat has passed, the Riders are gonna wanna leverage that arrangement."

"For how long?" Taylor asked.

"Five years," Kami said.

Japhara choked.

"I beg your pardon?" Billy asked.

"You heard me," Kami said. "I want a free ticket to ride through the stargate for me and my people for the next five years. After that, we'll all go our separate ways and laugh about it over drinks at the Red Bar. Hell, I might even pick up the tab."

Taylor hunched forward. "I'll give you the resources from the mission and a 20% advance on a fee to be determined by you, with a cap of 10 million credits."

"Twenty million," Kami said.

"Fifteen, and not a fargin credit more," Taylor said.

Kami pursed her lips. "Fifteen million it is. And what about my company's subcontractor rights?"

"Five years is completely off the board," Taylor said. "I can do 18 months, but that's it."

"Son of a…" Japhara palmed his face.

"Unacceptable," Kami said. "Traveling free through the stargate will save my company tens if not hundreds of millions of credits in the long run."

"Then maybe you should've thought of that when you tried to hamstring me on a contract fee with no ceiling," Taylor said.

Kami studied him through narrow eyes. "Your brother would've taken my deal in a heartbeat, were he still in charge."

"I'm sure he would've." Taylor folded his arms. "I loved my brother, but Terry always had a nasty habit of jumpin' before he looked. Unfortunately for you, that ain't ever been my style."

"I can see that." Kami seemed more impressed than disappointed by his response. "Let's simplify things a bit, shall we? The Emerald Stormriders will assume ownership of all resources used on this mission, as well as a 50% cut of any spoils. Instead of 15 million, we'll take a flat fee of 10 million credits to cover our expenses and the cost of retaining the Crestview group for extra manpower."

"And the free stargate access?" Billy asked.

"Two years, but not a month less," Kami declared. "That, gentlemen, is—as we say in the brokerage business—my final offer."

Taylor extended a palm. "You've got yourself a deal, Colonel."

The group spent the next hour hammering out additional details and trading old combat stories before the time eventually came to say goodbye.

"I'll contact you in Jacksonville when I've spoken with Winfield Defense," Kami said. "We'll set your deployment date from there."

"Sounds good," Taylor said. "You're one helluva negotiator, Colonel. Anybody who sits down across the contract table from you would be wise to watch their wallets."

Kami flashed her trademark smile and patted his cheeks. "Such a sweet boy. And wise, too, especially for someone so young."

Prior to that moment, Taylor had always pegged Kami as being somewhere near Billy's age of forty-four. Now, he wasn't so sure.

"Colonel, if I may," Japhara said as they turned to go. "You do understand that the intelligence you received here today is of the utmost secrecy, correct? To betray the Gathering's trust in these matters would therefore most likely result in not only your death, but also those of your associates."

Kami's gaze narrowed. "Sorry, Biggins, but is that a threat?"

"Not at all," Japhara said. "It is merely me respecting your authority by making sure you're completely apprised of all the risks associated with your decision to join this mission. To borrow a line from Chief Van Zant, 'I'm an eyes-wide-open kind of guy that way.'"

Kami gave a slow nod. "A Suma with jokes. I like it." She shook Billy's hand, then turned toward Taylor. "Safe travels back to Jax. I'll be in touch."

The Eagles' transport vehicle was still slumbering in its designated parking spot when Taylor, Billy, and Japhara returned to the motor pool.

"What do you know about these Winfield Defense fellas Kami intends to contact?" Taylor asked.

"Not much," Billy said, "just that they're a small-time infantry outfit based out of Crestview. To my knowledge, they haven't been in business that long. In that time, though, they've built a solid reputation as a capable group in the field. I expect they'll do fine."

Taylor nodded and climbed into the transport.

Incoming communique.

Taylor keyed the respond feature in his pinplant comms, then spoke aloud for the others to hear. "Go for Van Zant."

"*Please excuse the interruption, Chief,*" Keeto said in his raspy Athal voice. "*We just received a package from the Golden Horde that I believe you'll want to see.*"

"What sort of package?" Taylor asked.

"*It has something to do with our pinplants,*" Keeto said. "*Come to my lab when you return to campus. I'll show you everything.*"

Taylor traded looks with his XO. "Copy that. Van Zant, out."

* * * * *

Chapter Seven

Cartwright's Cavaliers SCIF, Houston Starport, Texas, Terran Federation, Earth

"Thanks for meeting with me," Sansar said. She smiled. "You're a hard person to get a hold of."

Adrianne smiled in return. "Well, it's not like we advertise our presence, after all," the Section 51 operative said.

Joey, the large black man with her, nodded. "Not hardly."

"Nor should you," Sansar replied. "Some things—and some people—work better in the shadows."

"Like a certain four-armed race we both know and love?"

"You've been spying on me?"

Adrianne chuckled. "I wouldn't say we're spying…"

"What would you call it, then?"

"I'd call it protective surveillance, kind of like what the Dusman are doing for you when you go off-planet. Besides, you're trying to have me followed, too."

"Not as effectively, apparently." Sansar winced. "Not if you know what I've been up to, anyway, because I still don't know anything about you."

"We'd like to keep it that way a little longer, too," Adrianne said. She shrugged. "We happened to have someone on Mars who saw your little meeting break up." She smiled. "Let's face it. As GU species go, the Sumatozou are among the more challenging to hide. The operative also saw the Pendal leave." She raised an eyebrow.

Sansar raised one in reply. "And?"

"Even though the Pendal left your meeting on Mars right after Van Zant and rejoined the Eagles, he then broke from them afterward and went his own way."

"Did he? I didn't notice."

"He did. And I'm willing to bet he told you his secret."

"Which is?"

"That there are only five of them."

"Actually, there are seven," Sansar said with a chuckle, happy to have gotten something over on Section 51 for once.

"I see; we'll have to update the database. Did he tell you what the others did?"

"I don't know what they all do; he only admitted that two are pilots."

"They're darn good ones, too," Adrianne said. "It's too bad there aren't more of them; we could use them." She paused, and then looked curiously at Sansar. "Can you hook them up with Jim's geneticists?"

Sansar chuckled. "Of course you would know about that, too." She shrugged. "After we finish what we're doing, I intend to do so. Yosiff didn't seem to think we'd have any luck with it, though."

"Yosiff, huh? That's what he's calling himself?"

"Yeah, why?"

"Did he tell you he's a pilot?"

"Yeah. I ask again, why?"

"Because he's actually their spy persona. He has pilot as a secondary skill to blend in, but he's nowhere near as good a pilot as their two straight-pilot personas. I'm aware of two crashes where he died, while one of the actual pilots probably would have saved the craft. He's good, not great."

"And you're telling me this to wow me with your spycraft skills?"

"No, I'm telling you so you don't count on him to fly a ship as well as other Pendals you've seen. Remember—good, not great." She shrugged. "I doubt you asked me to come here to talk about the Pendals, though."

Sansar smiled. "Actually, I *did* want to pass that on to you." She could feel a blush creeping up her neck. "But that was because I was hoping to trade it for some more tech."

"Oh?" Adrianne asked, suddenly wary. "Like what?"

"A couple things, actually. We ended up giving all our pinplant blockers to the Eagles. If they're going to be getting in the way of the Merchant Guild SI, they'll need them. I need some more for my folks...who will probably end up right there alongside them."

"And?"

"And when we were on Minerva's station, you had some really cool suits that were laser absorptive. They seemed to work pretty well."

Both of the Section 51 personnel nodded. "They actually exceeded expectations," Joey said.

"You mentioned making the technology available when we got back." Sansar raised an eyebrow. "Well...we're back."

"I said that?" Adrianne asked. "Are you sure?"

Sansar frowned.

"Okay, I'm just kidding." She pulled a computer chip from a pocket and passed it to Sansar. "I actually figured that's what this meeting was about. The system runs on a set of photovoltaic cells."

"Kind of like solar power?"

Adrianne chuckled. "This was the whole reason Section 51 started the environmental groups that pushed for solar power, even though we knew there were so many better alternatives. It was so we could conduct research into making laser absorptive modules we could use for our combat armor and—hopefully—integrate into

CASPer armor, as well. I mean, what's the most common weapon in the union? Lasers. Sure would be nice to have something that could defeat them, wouldn't it?"

"It would, especially since that's our biggest weakness." She looked at the chip. "And this is going to fix it?"

"Well, I wouldn't say *fix* it," Adrianne hedged. "It will, however, take a lot of the sting out of it. Some killing shots may only be damaging now, and you'll be able to shrug off glancing shots pretty easily. It's still possible to overwhelm the cells if you apply enough energy at the same point. You can also overload the storage and blow the cells." She shrugged. "We're still testing it and working on a variety of solutions, but that—" she nodded to the chip, "—represents what we've got so far." She smiled. "It includes the designs for manufactory production, too."

Sansar cocked her head. She'd never gotten anything so easily from the operative before. "Seriously?"

"Of course. Nothing in them is too bizarre, either. Individually, they aren't that expensive to manufacture, depending on how good you want them."

"What does that mean?"

"Silicon for the photovoltaic cells is cheap and easy. You can also go with cadmium telluride or copper indium gallium diselenide. The cadmium ones are a bit pricier, but not too bad. Combining the elements in a CIGS suit is a lot harder, but it's got the highest efficiency if you want to splurge for the best."

"I don't get it," Sansar said.

"It's pretty simple. The materials used—"

"No, that's not it," Sansar said, interrupting. "I understand what you're saying about the tech. What I don't get is, why me? Why now? Although you said you'd make the technology available when we got back, I never actually expected you to follow through." Sansar shrugged and held up the computer chip. "Why are you giving this to me?"

Adrianne smiled. "You're going up against the SIs, and they'll have the best equipment available. Humanity needs you to be successful if we're to remain a viable race, so we need *you* to have the best tech available, too."

"Okay, that makes sense. When we were fighting Minerva, though, you just had it on combat armor, not mechs. Is it going to work for our CASPers?"

"I've been involved in this project in my spare time," Joey said. "It's a lot easier to put it on combat armor than to cover a CASPer with it—especially since the CASPer is a lot larger and covered with removable equipment—but it's not too hard to cover the main surfaces, where it will provide a good amount of protection." The big man shrugged. "If you get unlucky and take a hit on a surface that wasn't protected…well, that's not any different than what you currently have, now, is it?"

* * * * *

Chapter Eight

FTS *Bills to Pay,* Emza Emergence Area

The ship rocked, and the lights went out. After a few moments, the emergency lights came on, bathing the armory in a red glow. Captain Eltaan released his retaining straps and pushed himself over to his locker.

"This is it," Captain Eltaan said, his eyes sweeping across his troopers as they floated into the armory from the squad bay in the next compartment. "This is where we earn the fat combat bonus the stupid Human is paying us."

He finished strapping on his armor before his troopers and called the bridge. "Captain Eltaan here. Any word on boarders?"

"Boarders?" asked the Duplato captain, Shuugar, his voice tight. *"How did you know there were boarders? Are you part of this?"*

"Simple deduction. Someone shot at us upon entry into this system, then the power went out, indicating a hit to our engines. We're no longer accelerating, confirming that fact. If the people shooting at us wanted us dead, we'd be dead right now. The fact that we're not tells me we have something aboard they want, and it isn't too much of a guess to believe it's the bandilaroes in Bay One that we were hired to defend in the event of pirates.

"So, if you would quit wasting my time and tell me where the boarders are headed, I can do my job and repel them. Maybe I can even steal one of their shuttles and hit their mothership, or use the bandilaroes to do so. I can't do any of that, though, *until you tell me where they're going to enter from!*"

"*Oh—*" the big sloth-like alien cleared its throat a couple of times, "*—they appear to be headed for both the forward and aft boarding hatches, as well as the bay itself.*"

"Thanks." Eltaan switched off the comm panel. "First Platoon, First Squad, to the forward boarding hatch. Second Squad, you've got the aft hatch. Second Platoon, you're with me in the cargo bay. Shoot to kill and keep me informed of any enemy movement." His eyes swept the compartment. "Any questions?"

When no one twitched an antenna, he added, "Very well. For the queen!"

"For the queen!" his troopers roared, then they dispersed to their stations.

* * *

M waited with two squads in one of the shuttles, holding just off the freighter's starboard side as the main combat forces went in. As the shuttles simultaneously attached themselves to the skin of the freighter, he jumped back and forth to specially chosen hosts to ensure the squads performed as expected.

The two hatches would be the first breached, due to their smaller size, but entry into the cargo bay was coming along nicely. He jumped back to his host on the waiting shuttle. When the squads entered the freighter, a large number of them were likely to get killed. It wouldn't do to be inside a body that was killed. He wasn't sure whether it would end him, as well, but he didn't want to find out.

Let them breach the ship, then I'll supervise their movements.

"*We're in,*" the leader of Squad One called from the forward hatch. "*Squads One and Two entering target vessel.*"

"*We're in, too,*" the leader of Squad Three called. "*Squads Three and Four entering target vessel.*"

M watched the lights on his panel extinguish quickly as the troopers were killed far more rapidly than was normal. "What's going on over there?" M asked.

"*We're taking heavy fire,*" the Squad One leader replied. "*It looks like they have mercenaries defending the ship. Some kind of ant-like race.*"

Altar. That's...unfortunate.

M sharded off a piece of himself, jumped to one of the Squad Two troopers, and inspected the defenses. Definitely Altar, and they were behind prepared defenses. He tried to jump to one of them, but—as he'd been afraid of—he couldn't see them on the Net. They weren't pinned.

That will indeed make things more difficult.

A crewman jogged through a cross passage behind the defenders, and M jumped to her. M shook her new head. The Duplato wasn't jogging through the combat area; the run had been her top speed. She was just slow.

It took M a moment to adjust to the new host, then she advanced to one of the giant ant-like defenders, keeping her head below the level of the barricade the trooper had set up.

"What do you want?" the Altar corporal asked. He ducked to the side and fired several times.

The part of M that was still on the shuttle watched another light go out. There were only five members of the forward boarding party still combat effective, and he was in danger of being repulsed. The aft boarding party wasn't faring much better.

M scanned the corporal, saw what she needed, and reached forward as quickly as she could.

"Hey!" the Altar exclaimed. He saw what M was holding in her hand—the pin to one of the grenades on his load-bearing harness—and he searched for the one that was missing the pin. He found it, tossed it over the barricade, then turned back to point his rifle at M.

M showed the corporal that she actually had a pin in both hands, then jumped back to the shuttle.

* * *

"*Sir, Corporal Salgaan just blew up!*" Private Gataal called. "*He took out the rest of the group blocking—*"

The private's voice ceased as another explosion could be heard and felt along the ship's deck.

"Gataal, status report!" The private didn't reply. Nor did he reply when Eltaan called a second time.

Two more explosions rocked the ship, this time from the aft end, then a third. No one responded from the group at the aft boarding hatch after the blasts.

Eltaan took a deep breath and squared his shoulders. "All right, everyone, it's up to us now. Make sure of your shots, and let's hold them at the hatches."

Within a few seconds, the hatches around the cargo bay—all six of them—began to glow as the intruders worked to burn their way into the giant compartment, while the forces outside the ship continued to work on the main cargo bay door to space. *If the pirates enter from every entrance at the same time, we're going to have a hard time stopping them.*

Eltaan fully expected that to happen. Although none of his troops had picked up enemy communications, the pirates had proceeded with military precision. If they weren't an actual military force, they were a highly-trained, elite merc company. With the teamwork he'd seen from them so far, he expected there was a Veetanho somewhere guiding their efforts.

If I can figure out where the rat bitch is and kill her, we might have a chance.

As quickly as he had the thought, though, he knew it was unlikely. The troops were excellently trained. They would complete the mission even without the murderous bitch leading them. If they were to be victorious, his forces would have to burn down all the intruders.

He swallowed, summoning all the resolve he could. *If we have to burn down all the pirates to win, that's what we will do.* The queen required nothing less of them.

* * *

The forward force was down to three members and the aft force down to five when the last defending Altar died. M frowned as both groups, significantly smaller than when they started, proceeded to the cargo bay, and began burning their way through the hatches. As they reached the final portion of the cut, they stopped, awaiting the signal that the main cargo bay door to space was ready.

M shook his head. There was no telling what the composition of the force inside the cargo bay was; they'd destroyed all the cameras. Based on the rate of oxygen depletion, there were at least 15 Altar waiting for his troops to enter the cargo bay, and perhaps as many as 25. Although there were an additional 20 troops waiting outside the main cargo bay door, the Altar would be in prepared positions, and he doubted they had enough troops to secure the bandilaroes. He would need forces to capture the bandilaroes, especially if he wanted to do so without destroying them in the process.

Happily, there were more troops to be had.

* * *

At the cargo bay's forward starboard hatch, the Zuul holding the welding gun finished all but the last few millimeters of his cut and turned to find a large group of Duplato waiting behind him. They seemed nice enough, and before he could wonder about them greatly, the signal was given. He turned to finish the cut.

* * *

Eltaan plugged his suit into the comm panel and pressed the transmit button. The air had long been vacated from the bay as the door was cut away. "Bridge, Captain Eltaan calling from the cargo bay."

"Go ahead, Captain Eltaan." The signal came through the comm cord and into his helmet; even though it lacked the fidelity of normal communications, he could tell the voice was unfamiliar.

"Who is this? Where's the captain?" Eltaan asked.

"This is the sensor operator, Ensign Angalar. The captain and all the bridge staff just left. I don't know where they were going; they didn't say. I'm getting pretty freaked out."

"Keep your wits about you, Angalar. We're going to need help here. Are there any ships in the vicinity that can come assist us?"

"*No—not a one. There's nobody between us and the planet.*"

"That figures," Eltaan muttered.

"*What? What did you say?*"

"I said that figures. I think the attack is being led by a Veetanho. The planning and precision—even the fact that there's no one near-by to assist us—indicates a Veetanho is in command over on the pirate ship."

The cuts in the main door approached each other, and simultaneously, the welders at all six hatches began completing their final cuts. *Typical Veetanho precision.*

"Gotta go," Eltaan said. "They're about to break in."

"*Can you stop them?*"

Eltaan looked around guiltily to see if anyone could hear him, even though no one else was plugged in. "If the final assault is as well planned as the breaching operation was, I doubt it." He released the button, unplugged, and pushed off to go to his battle position as the cargo bay door began lifting off. With all the air gone, there was no explosive decompression.

Within a second or two, all six hatches opened, also, and Duplato wearing exposure gear began streaming in.

"Captain? Do we shoot them?" one of the troopers asked.

Eltaan paused, unsure whether the ship's crew had gone over to the pirate's side, and if so, *why?* It looked like almost the entire crew was on its way into the cargo bay. Terror crawled down his spine as he realized each of the groups was moving toward an Altar defensive position. Whatever had happened, *they were now the enemy, too!*

"Fire!" he transmitted. "Kill them all!"

He pointed his rifle at the nearest group—he didn't have to aim; they were so close—and began burning them down.

The killing was easy—the Duplato moved relatively slowly toward the Altar defenders and didn't appear to have any weapons—and the aliens were easily slaughtered. The problem was there were so many of them, and Eltaan had paused, allowing them to get closer, so it was all he could do to kill the ones headed toward him. His laser rifle ran out, and he ripped another charge canister off his harness and slapped it in as a Duplato he recognized as Captain Shuugar flew across the bay toward him.

The rifle charged, and he would have killed the captain, except he was struck by a laser bolt from above that breached his armor and took him through the chest. As the air rapidly exited his suit, he glanced up and saw that—due to the charge of the Duplato—no one had kept an eye on the pirates above them, and they were easily striking down all his troopers. As his vision grew dim, the captain's face appeared. The Duplato smiled, then his face was replaced with a laser pistol. There was a flash and then nothing.

* * *

M jumped into the ship captain's body in time to deliver the coup de grâce, then turned to survey the rest of the cargo bay. The Altar had been eliminated. With a wave, he sent an order to the rest of the Duplato, and they opened their suits to space, many of them flying around the bay like untied balloons that had been let go, some spewing fluids as they went, and others slamming into his precious bandilaroes.

Okay, that probably wasn't my best idea, M noted. *Next time I'll have them go* outside *the skin of the ship before they do that.*

"We will begin moving the bandilaroes to our ship," one of the pilots in the final group transmitted.

"Do so," M agreed. "Anyone else who isn't occupied can go to the bridge and kill the survivor there." He shrugged, somewhat surprised that someone who manned a bridge position wouldn't have pinplants. *The officer must have been recently recruited.*

Several of his remaining troopers left to accomplish the task as M moved alongside the closest bandilaroes. He smiled as he admired the craft's smooth lines. He'd lost more of his troopers than he'd intended, but they were easily replaced. And the bandilaroes were *so* worthwhile.

* * *

Ensign Angalar waited in the bridge, his finger over the transmit button. What he was waiting for, he wasn't entirely sure. He hoped his commanding officer would return to tell him everything was all right and the pirates had been dealt with, but the longer he waited, the less likely that outcome was. When a Zuul and two Jivool entered the bridge, his finger punched down on the transmit button a fraction of a second before three laser beams intersected his head.

* * * * *

Chapter Nine

"I have some good news and some bad news," Beowulf reported.

Sansar sighed. "If you're going to tell me the bandilaroes are gone, at least tell me we have a line on where they went."

"Yes, the bandilaroes are gone," Beowulf said with a wince, "however, we have them tracked to Kullawee, just like the other items that have gone missing."

"So that isn't just the staging base, but where artifacts go, never to be seen again."

"Yes, ma'am."

"What can you tell me about the inhabitants?"

"The inhabitants?"

"Yes, the inhabitants. I take it the system is inhabited, or there's at least a station there for the prospective SI to hold as its base. Minerva had a space station, with lots of people aboard it. Before we could get to Minerva, we had to cut our way through thousands of the station's inhabitants, which the SI sent at us like a zombie plague. I'd like to know what we're getting ourselves into. Are there people who live on Kullawee? If so, is it a homogenous planet, or are there lots of other races who live there?" Sansar held up both hands questioningly. "How many people—and what types—am I going to have to kill to get at the SI?"

"Oh."

"Yeah. Oh. Killing off Minerva's minions was probably the worst thing I've ever had to do. All things being equal, I'd rather not have to do it again. I'm pretty sure the Sumatozou captain—who had to kill *hundreds* of women and children, and lost several of his troopers when they couldn't force themselves to do that—won't want to have to kill a bunch of civilian zombie troopers again, either."

"There is a planet. The local inhabitants are a fairly homogenous bunch. The only times you might see anyone other than the locals is at the starport or nearby startown, and even that's pretty small. It'll be mostly the natives."

"Good, that's easier, then. See if you can find a few of them who don't have pinplants. Volunteers would be better, but any of the locals you can get your hands on will work."

"I'm sure I can find some," Beowulf said, his eyebrows knitting. "What am I supposed to do with them?"

"Find out what renders them unconscious. Knock out gas? Stun grenades? Tasers? A gas would be best, since we could knock out a bunch with it. If we have to go with something like tasers, it's going to be a lot harder."

"Okay…" Beowulf said, obviously not seeing where the conversation was going.

"Look," Sansar said. "We're going in there, and we're going to kill that SI. It's not going to let us do so willingly. Every single resident with pinplants is a potential tool for him to use against us. Depending on the SI's background, all his minions may be expert shooters, or know martial arts, or something equally nasty. I'd rather come in and spray knock out gas, kill the SI, and leave without having to hurt or kill *any* of the innocents."

Sansar shrugged then added, "Look. I *am* going to kill this SI. We have to, before it joins Minerva in trying to wipe out humanity. If I have to nerve gas the whole planet to do so, thereby killing every single one of its inhabitants, I will. Getting rid of the SI *is* that important. All things considered, though, I'd rather not have the Peacemakers after me for genocide. Understand?"

"Yes, ma'am."

"Good. Find me a way to knock out the local inhabitants so I don't have to kill them, then, would you?"

* * * * *

Chapter Ten

Swamp Eagle Security Main Campus, Jacksonville, North Florida, Earth

Taylor paused in the corridor outside the clubhouse in the Eagles' command center and readied himself for the fallout he knew was coming. He'd been dreading this moment all morning—or at the very least, since he'd left the barbershop two hours ago. Alas, the time had come to rip off the band-aid and face the music—ironically enough, to the tune of "Long-Haired Country Boy" from Charlie Daniels, which just happened to be blaring from the jukebox inside. *Awesome.* Taylor frowned and shoved open the door.

"Whooo!" someone shouted from the back. "Lookin' good, Chief!"

Sergeant Reigns followed with a wolf whistle as a handful of her fellow troopers continued to pile on.

"Yeah, yeah, yeah." Taylor marched past the pool tables en route to the briefing room in the back. "Get it out of your systems now, people. It's gonna be back to business soon enough."

Another wolf whistle ripped across the room.

"Easy, ladies, this one's spoken for." Lisa Kouvaris, the Eagles' press officer, emerged from the back to catch her boyfriend's arm. "You can all take your hormones and your jealousy, then head right on down the road to somebody else's man."

Multiple faux groans swept the room, causing Taylor to chuckle. Under different circumstances, an outsider might've seen such behavior as strange, or even out of line. For the Eagles, however, this was par for the course. Everyone on the crew was family, and family joshed each other from time to time. Taylor, for one, loved that about his company, even if he wasn't so wild about his appearance.

The briefing room door swung open, and the Eagles' command staff rose from their seats around the conference table.

"Well, I'll be damned," Billy said. "Look at you."

"Don't even start," Taylor said, closing the door. "Reigns and her posey of chuckleheads already let me have it outside. I don't need it from y'all, too."

A gaggle of snickers followed anyway.

"You act like this is a bad thing," Billy said. "If you ask me, I think you look...distinguished."

"That's one way to put it," Quint murmured.

"What was that, Lieutenant?" Taylor shot the Georgian a look.

"Nothing, sir." Quint straightened. "You look downright professional, sir. Stately, even."

Taylor studied his reflection in the vintage Harley Davidson mirror beside the Tri-V, then picked at a strand of his short, black hair. "I still don't get why we've gotta do all this if we're just gonna be walkin' around in disguise all day."

"Helmets and masks come off, sweetheart," Lisa said. "When they do, that's when the camera flashes tend to happen. I get that you hate the hair, but take it from me. Every little bit helps when it comes to confusing facial recognition, even if it's only for a second or two."

"Yeah, but I look like a reject from a 20ᵗʰ century Goth video," Taylor grumbled.

"Goth looks good on some people," Billy said.

"So says the Ken doll at the head of the table." Frank grunted.

Billy shot the Buma nav officer a grin, then rubbed his burr-cut head, which now registered somewhere between canary-yellow and platinum on the blond scale.

"Any word from Colonel K'Nami?" Taylor asked while taking a seat.

"Actually, yeah," Billy said. "True to her word, the colonel cut a deal with Winfield Defense for the extra manpower we need. All told, that gives us five trooper companies to work with if things heat up on Kullawee. They're Atlantic and Riverside Companies from our side, plus Tiger Company from the Stormriders, and all the Dubya-Dee folks."

"What's a...Dubya Dee?" Keeto asked.

"That's what the Winfield Defense guys call themselves," Billy said. "All told, that makes it just north of 500 people, including commanders, flight crews, and logistics personnel, who'll be deploying on the EMS *Tyndall*. We're gonna be packed in there like sardines."

Frank pivoted in his seat toward the XO. "The EMS *Tyndall*? You mean the *Osyrys* ain't makin' the trip for this one?"

"Negative," Taylor said. "The *Ryley Osyrys* is the flagship of Swamp Eagle Security. If she were to pass through the stargate at Kullawee, everybody and their grandparents would know we were in the area. Sorry, Frank, but our girl has to sit this one out."

The Buma lowered his head.

"What about our second ship, the EMS *Bradshaw?*" Quint asked. "She's barely been in service with us a year, so almost nobody associates her with our outfit. What if we deployed her instead of the *Osyrys?* That would at least give us our own ride, not to mention our own quarters, for cryin' out loud."

Taylor shook his head. "The Emerald Stormriders' reputation as a low-level outfit on the skids is the whole reason we turned to them for help with this mission. We have to leverage that, even if it means ridin' the top rack in a shoebox built for two on an aging Maki cruiser instead of that cozy one-bunk Hilton Quint here is used to on the *Osyrys.*"

The stocky ex-ballplayer buried his dark-skinned face in his hands.

"Let me be clear on one thing," Taylor added. "Even though we'll be makin' this journey aboard the *Tyndall,* I'll be in command. Not Colonel K'Nami."

"Are you sure about that?" Smitty asked.

All eyes including Taylor's turned to the blonde Australian captain down the table.

"Colonel K'Nami is a capable merc, to be sure," Smitty said. "She's also got a reputation as something of a wildcard for a reason. There are some commanders right here in Jax who won't work with her."

Billy cleared his throat before addressing his wife's concern. "The chief is right. The Emerald Stormriders aren't in control of this mission. We are. That much has been established per the parameters of our contract with them. Besides, this job means everything to the Riders' long-term survival as a company. Kami knows this, which means she's got no choice but to fall in line."

The flat expression on Smitty's face suggested she was less than convinced.

Caught between Scylla and Charybdis. Taylor shot his XO a *tread lightly* look before moving on. "When do we deploy?"

"Three days from now," Billy said. "That's how long Kami said she needed to get her people organized and get the *Tyndall* prepped for launch."

"And our transit time to Kullawee?" Taylor asked.

"Three jumps and just over two weeks additional transit time," Frank said. "That's provided, of course, that we don't need to stop for extra bathroom breaks."

Quint let out a groan. "Man, they weren't kidding when they said this planet was remote, were they?"

"Not at all," Keeto said. "Fortunately for us, Kullawee is home to a sizable agrarian society with its own starport, albeit a small one. That will enable us to resupply on-site for the return trip home rather than requiring us to supply up for both legs of our voyage."

Frank put up a feathery hand. "So, I've got a question. If this SI thing can inhabit the body of anybody not wearing one of the Horde's pinplant blockers, how do we even *start* to look for this thing when we touch down on Kullawee?"

"The Gathering has a theory on that." Japhara strode into the room and pulled up a stool beside Billy. "Apologies for my tardiness to this meeting," he said to Taylor. "My errand in Jax starport took longer than anticipated."

"What kind of errand?" Smitty asked.

"The personal kind," Japhara answered.

Everyone waited for the Sumatozou to elaborate, but he never did.

I hope it works out, Hoss. I really do. Taylor shifted in his seat. "You said the Gathering has a theory regarding how to find the SI once we reach Kullawee. Let's hear it."

Japhara commandeered a slate, then swiped up an image and mirrored it to the corner Tri-V.

"Wait, is that…" Frank squinted at the image.

"A Rukori?" Japhara replied. "It is indeed. Horde intelligence refers to him as Prime."

Taylor studied the image of the gray-skinned alien with the long, white hair in the hologram in front of him. "What's his connection to the SI?"

"Our operatives aren't entirely sure at the moment," Japhara said. "What we do know is this Rukori has been spotted in the vicinity of numerous raids in the days leading up to their execution."

"Like a harbinger," Taylor said.

"Precisely," Japhara said. "Our theory is that the Merchant Guild SI uses this alien for the purpose of traveling throughout the Union to recruit pirates for its raids. Once an op is complete, the SI either kills these aliens, which seems to be its preference, or it wipes their memory before vanishing back into obscurity."

Taylor felt a chill. "The more I learn about this SI, the more it feels like we're bein' hunted by a damned phantom."

"Agreed," Billy said.

"If the Gathering's theory about the SI's presence on Kullawee is accurate," Japhara said, "then our first task upon touching down on that planet surface should be to locate Prime and follow him back to the SI case itself, which should be destroyed at all costs."

"What the hell's an SI case?" Frank asked.

"It's the physical device in which the actual Synthetic Intelligence resides," Keeto said. "Prime, or any other alien for that matter, is merely a host. The actual SI resides in a piece of hardware the size of a suitcase."

"Do we know the range of the SI's grip on its host?" Smitty asked.

"Its range to commandeer is one thing," Japhara said. "Maintaining control of the host's actions is something else."

"Explain," Taylor said.

Japhara shifted on his stool. "According to Horde intel, any being with unguarded pinplants who is in radio range of the SI is vulnerable to possession. That host will then remain in the SI's grasp until it's either killed or released. It's important to note, however, that the SI's manipulation isn't without limits."

"How so?" Billy asked.

"The Horde suspects that the SI must remain in radio range to control a host's actions in real time," Japhara said. "If, on the other hand, the SI views a raid as low-priority, it can send the hosts on their way with instructions, and what will be will be."

"Like drones," Keeto said.

"Exactly," Japhara said.

Taylor clasped his hands atop the table. "You used the word 'hosts' just now, as in plural. How many beings can this thing possess at one time?"

"That depends on the scope of the task," Japhara said. "Based on the current data, our operatives believe the SI can easily inhabit 10 or so and retain full control of their faculties." He gave a large elephantine shrug. "It may be more than that. Dozens, perhaps, maybe as many as 100. If, however, the SI seeks only to use the hosts as drones, its reach can span into the hundreds, or maybe even the thousands.

"When the Horde attacked the Science Guild's facility in the Morgoth system, Minerva—the Science Guild SI—used hundreds of drones to attack the Sumatozou force blocking its escape path. At a different time, it had full control of about 10 opSha that it used to fight off a Depik."

"It defeated a Depik in hand-to-hand combat?" Taylor asked. "That's...impressive."

"That's it," Quint scoffed. "I'm officially done with suitcases. From here on out, I'll pack my trash in duffel bags and call it a day."

Billy traded looks with his wife. "What happens to the hosts if the SI case were to be destroyed?"

"They would all go free," Japhara said. "Theoretically. Although it's possible the SI might remain resident in whatever host it was occupying at the moment."

Taylor rubbed his chin whiskers and returned to the image of Prime on the Tri-V. *How in the hell did a Rukori get mixed up with an SI?* As far as anyone knew, the Rukori people had remained in isolation after the Eagles had liberated their homeworld from the Krulig on Taylor's first real mission in command. No one had heard from them since, and yet there one was, right there on the screen.

What's your role in all this? Taylor pushed back his seat and rose from the table. "Everybody coordinate with Billy for your assignments prior to our deployment aboard the *Tyndall*. Some of you will remain attached to me. Others will be reassigned to the other companies to help synergize the mission effort. Either way, Billy and I are always here if you need us. Ayew?"

"Ayew," the group acknowledged.

"Good," Taylor said. "Church is dismi—"

"Hey, real quick," Frank added. "Has anybody heard anything from Jack?"

Taylor lowered his eyes before responding. "No, not yet. He checked in when his mag-lev arrived home in Oklahoma, but I haven't heard anything from him since. My guess is he needs some more time to iron things out after what happened to Stan on Droxis."

A long silence filled the briefing room.

"Thanks for the time, y'all," Taylor said softly. "Dismissed."

Billy held his seat as the others rose and filed out. "Chief, can I have a minute?"

Not sure what it was about, Taylor nodded and returned to his chair. "What's on your mind?"

The XO reached under the table and produced a small garment made of felt fabric. With its lopsided flat top and black leather headband, the head cover sported the classic hunter green color of Swamp Eagle Security, with its trademarked palmetto leaf insignia on the front badge.

"That's Terry's old beret." Taylor swallowed. "How long have you been holdin' onto it?"

"Long enough to see you grow into the commander you are today," Billy said. "You've earned this, T. I've got nothing more to teach you."

Taylor felt a tinge of nerves as he studied the beret. "Why now?"

"For starters, the Kullawee mission," Billy said. "As head of the Eagles, you'll effectively be commanding three companies on this job, not just your own."

"What's your point?" Taylor asked.

"My point is, Fragontic won't be the only merc to raise issues over taking orders from a chief while there's two colonels standing around," Billy said. "There'll be others, and, under the right conditions, that could undermine your leadership. Nobody wants that, least of all me." He pointed to the beret. "All of that gets nipped in the bud if you take the rank of colonel, like Terry did, moving forward."

Taylor averted his gaze.

"I get why you took the rank of chief when all this started," Billy continued. "Was it unorthodox? Sure. But I understood why you did it. Now, all that has changed."

"Has it?" Taylor countered. "I take your meaning, Billy, but last I checked, I was still slingin' suds in Cocktail Junction five years ago, while everybody else on this crew was either an active merc or active duty military, like you and Terry. Ownership stake or not, who am I to take a rank *they've* worked their entire careers to attain?"

Billy cocked his head. "Do you respect Marcus Cortes?"

"What the hell kinda question is that?" Taylor asked. "You know I do. Marcus has been one of the Eagles' biggest allies for years. Case in point, Rukoria."

"So it's fair to say you think he's a good leader," Billy said.

"Sure. Why?"

Billy rested his hands on his chair arms. "I hate to break this to ya, T, but Marcus Cortes never served in the military, nor did he work his way up through the ranks as a merc before he launched the Iron Conquistadors. He was a conductor on the I-95 mag-lev corridor, running passengers and politicians from Miami to Richmond every morning."

Taylor's jaw fell open at the revelation. The ornate train set in Cortes' office suddenly made a lot more sense. "Where are you goin' with all this?"

"Marcus Cortes may not have been the world's most seasoned merc when he founded his company, but he knew how to listen, and he knew how to surround himself with good people," Billy said. "It's the same with you. Face it, T, you've come a long way these last few years. Our people trust you now in a way they weren't sure they could three years ago, and not because they didn't like you or because they doubted your pedigree to become a capable CO. It's because you simply weren't experienced. All that's changed now. Time and time again, from Rukoria to Emza, and especially on Droxis, they've seen you face adversity head-on and come out the other side."

Taylor scoffed. "I appreciate the faith, Billy, but let's not get too far out over our skies here. This crew has seen me in over my head way more times than not."

"Yeah, but you never let those situations paralyze you," Billy said. "You stayed cool, and you leaned on your senior officers to get you through. That's not just the mark of a good commander; that's the mark of a *leader*, and you're that and then some. You always have been."

Taylor watched in silence as the XO slid the old beret across the table, then tapped it for emphasis.

"Your brother idolized the Four Horsemen," Billy said. "In his mind, they were always the gold standard of what a merc outfit should be. Now, nearly a decade after Terry's death, one of those legendary companies has turned to Swamp Eagle Security for help against a threat that could put all of humanity in jeopardy." Billy aimed a finger across the table. "That happened because of you, Taylor, not Terry. The Eagles are *your* company now, not his. It's high time folks outside this crew recognize that."

Taylor chewed his lip. "Are folks gonna show you that kind of respect when you're the head of Harvick's Hurricanes?"

Billy grimaced.

"That is the rumor, right?" Taylor asked. "That Pete Harvick has offered you command of his company after he retires later this year?"

Billy eased back into his seat and laced his fingers. "Who tipped you off? Marcus, or somebody else?"

"That don't matter," Taylor said. "What matters is whether or not it's true."

Billy heaved a sigh. "It's true, but I haven't accepted."

"But you haven't turned him down, either."

"No, not yet," Billy said. "Smitty and I were in the process of weighing the pros and cons of the decision when Sansar paid you that visit outside the Hell House. Fair to say, we've all been a little preoccupied since."

"What's there to weigh? This is your own command we're talkin' about. Don't get me wrong, I of all people would hate to see you go. But you've gotta know I'd never stand in the way of that. Besides—" Taylor shrugged, "—the Hurricanes are a fine company."

"They're also a company that's more than likely on the move," Billy said.

Taylor narrowed his gaze.

"You mean you haven't heard?" Billy asked.

"Heard what?"

"Apparently the North Carolina state government has been keeping tabs on all the revenue that's been pouring into the North Florida economy these last several years as the result of our fair tax system," Billy said. "They're impressed, so much so that there's now a bill on the floor in Raleigh that would adopt that same legislation in the Tar Heel state. It's expected to pass almost unanimously, if you can believe that."

Taylor chuckled. "What's all this have to do with the Hurricanes?"

"A group of investors from Mecklenburg County want to send a message to the Earth merc community that Charlotte is open for business when this new law passes," Billy said.

"And how better than to cement Charlotte as the new Merc Capital of the South than to lure one of the top outfits from Jax to put down roots there," Taylor said.

"Bingo," Billy said. "I'm here to tell ya, T. These people mean business. Honestly, you should see the incentive package they assembled to coax Pete into moving his company. It's damn near a fargin gold mine."

Taylor laced his fingers. "Sounds too good to pass up."

"Maybe. I still told Pete I needed some time to think things over. I figure I'll have an answer for him by the time we get back from Kullawee."

Taylor raised a shoulder. "Why wait? I think you should take the job."

The XO's eyes widened.

"Let's put our cards on the table, shall we? I could offer you a raise to stay, or even your old minority ownership stake in the Eagles. But what does that achieve?" Taylor tossed up a hand. "You're a born leader, brother. You deserve to have a crack at the big chair at least once in your career, plus the Hurricanes are a great company. They'd be lucky to have you."

Billy stared at the tabletop.

"Will you at least tell me what the holdup is?" Taylor asked.

Billy heaved a sigh and peered at a nearby painting of the Jax Generals' stadium at sunset. "I absolutely despised my parents for moving us down here when I was a kid. I hated the city, hated the heat, hated the people. As far as I was concerned, all my friends were back home in Lincoln, and, by God, that's where I should've been as well." He looked up. "Then, one day after baseball practice, three thugs wearing gang colors jumped me behind the bleachers and tried to steal my book bag. They'd have succeeded, too, had it not been for some squirrely little local kid with dirt-smudged features and frizzy blond hair who leapt out of the shadows like a damn spider monkey and started wailing on the leader."

Terry.

"Your brother and I kicked the shit out of those punks that day," Billy said. "Once it was over, he and your mom gave me a ride home so I wouldn't have to wait alone for my parents. Suffice it to say, Duval County felt a whole lot more like home afterward. I guess that's never changed."

Taylor smiled at the floor, recalling the countless times his brother had told that story. "I still think you oughta take the job."

"That may be," Billy said, "but then that leaves just one more question to be answered."

"Which is?"

Billy's expression turned sideways. "Who'll stay behind to lead the Eagles? A chief, or a battle-tested colonel?"

Taylor rolled his eyes.

"You didn't honestly think I'd let you weasel out of a response, did ya?" The XO grinned.

Taylor answered his XO's ribbing with a smirk before returning his focus to the beret. Terry had scarcely been without it in merc circles, and sometimes even in private ones. It was part of him, part of his persona.

Taylor wasn't sure he was ready for that. "I'll meet you in the middle. For the purposes of this mission, I'll take the rank of colonel. We'll see how things go once we get back."

"And the beret?" Billy asked.

Taylor slid the item back to the XO. "I'm sorry, brother, but I just can't."

Billy nodded slowly, but left the garment on the table. "That beret belongs to your family, T. What you choose to do with it is entirely up to you. But it belongs with a Van Zant."

Someone knocked at the door.

"Sorry to interrupt, fellas," Quint said. "Sergeant Reigns needs one of you to sign off on a stack of invoices from the Hemming Arms folks so we can start gearing up for Kullawee. She's downstairs now."

"Tell her I'm on my way." Billy pushed back his seat and rose from the table. "Think about what I said. We can talk more about it later if you want."

"Ayew," Taylor said. "It would appear we've both got some decisions to make."

* * * * *

Chapter Eleven

CIC, EMS *Tyndall*, Kullawee System, Coro Region, Tolo Arm

"Hyperspace emergence in three," Frank announced from down front. "Two...one...mark."

Taylor watched from his seat beside Billy as the white void of hyperspace turned to stars in the bridge viewport ahead.

"Emergence complete," Frank said. "The EMS *Tyndall* is free to move about the system."

"Nicely done, Lieutenant," Kami said from her command chair at center-floor. "Maybe when this mission is over, you and I can have a little chat about what Colonel Van Zant here is paying you."

Taylor met Kami's smile with a grin of his own, then shot a *don't even think about it* look at his nav officer, who was filling that role for the Riders.

Frank just chuckled and returned to his station.

"Lay in a course for Kullawee and take us in," Kami ordered.

Right in step with the Golden Horde's report, the Kullawee system was a run-of-the-mill system with a yellow dwarf at its center orbited by eight planets. The actual planet Kullawee was the fourth celestial body from the star, and it was toward that world the Riders' cruiser began moving.

"Holy hell," the Riders' XO, Captain Anderson, muttered in awe. He was a young man, like many of his comrades, with a square jaw and light features turned noticeably darker by the North Florida sun. "I read in the Eagles' report that the Merchant Guild had amassed a fleet, but this is fargin unreal."

Taylor shared that sense of unease. He counted at least 40 ships minimum in the viewer, massed just outside the emergence area; 46 was the actual count on the Tri-V. Nearly every known class imaginable was represented, too, and even a few warships thrown in for good measure.

"It would appear our synthetic mark has been busy," Billy murmured.

You can say that again. Taylor nodded.

The *Tyndall* proceeded past the fleet at a casual speed, mindful not to raise suspicions, until the massive green planet that was Kullawee loomed large in the viewport.

"*Incoming vessel, this is Kullawee Orbital Approach,*" a voice announced via the bridge's comm speakers. "*Identify yourself and state your intentions.*"

"Interesting," Japhara noted. "The Kullawee are a simple people with little need for advanced technology, much less an orbital security presence."

"Maybe our mark had something to say about that, too," Billy said.

The Sumatozou raised a shoulder and remained buckled in his seat.

"Kullawee Approach, this is the EMS *Tyndall,*" Kami said. "My crew and I are passing through this region in search of work. We seek to rest and resupply at your starport, if that's all right, then we'll be on our way. Over."

A series of chittering sounds preceded the other's reply. *"Confirmed,* Tyndall. *You are cleared for docking on Platform Four along Kullawee Starport's east wing. A docking official will greet you after landing for payment."*

"Copy that, Approach." Kami gestured to Frank. "We're lining up to begin our descent now. Thank you for your cooperation. *Tyndall,* out."

* * *

The *Tyndall's* hull creaked and groaned under the stress of re-entry as the aging cruiser made its slow descent through the Kullawee atmosphere toward the planet's lone starport just outside its capital, which records identified as Ragault City. At one point, Taylor wondered if the screws that bolted his seat to the deck might jiggle themselves loose, causing him to topple over and eat a face full of steel. Thankfully, the *thump* of landing struts on the surface platform soon eased his fears, along with the *whir* of decelerating engines.

"Well, that was fun," Billy grumbled, tossing off his belts.

"Hey, don't pick on my ride, man," Kami shot back. "I get it that she's not a *Navarro* like your precious *Ryley Osyrys,* but she's seen her share of action over the years, and she's held her own."

"That and it's kinda the only one we could afford after Princess cleared out our accounts during her exodus from the company," Anderson said.

"Princess?" Taylor had thought the term was slang on account of the girl's wealthy upbringing. "You mean that was her actual *name?*"

"Yep," Kami said. "I met her at the closing when I formally took possession of the Stormriders. Believe me when I say she was every bit the peach you think she was."

Oof. Taylor keyed his pinplant comm and spoke aloud. "Van Zant to Keeto. Billy and I are gearin' up to head out on the town and get the lay of the land. What's the status on our party attire?"

"*Ready and standing by,*" the Athal said.

"Good deal," Taylor said. "Bring them on down to the debarkation hatch on B deck. The XO and I are en route to you now."

"*Ayew,*" Keeto said. "*We'll be ready.*"

Taylor threw off his belts and headed for the bridge exit with Billy, while Frank stayed behind on the *Tyndall's* bridge with Anderson.

"Wait up," Kami called after them. "I'm coming with you."

Taylor halted in the corridor outside the bridge as footfalls trailed him and the XO into the junction.

"What?" Kami said, catching looks. "You didn't think I'd come all this way and let you boys have all the fun outside, did you?"

Taylor chewed his lip. "Are you sure that's a wise call? Who knows what's actually waitin' for us out there?"

Kami rolled her eyes. "We're not seriously gonna have the 'whose command junk is bigger' debate right now, are we? Because I really thought we were friends already."

"We're not, and we are," Taylor said. "I just think, given the circumstances, the prudent course of action would be for my team to run recon down on the surface while yours lays back on the *Tyndall* in reserve. Besides, you're the commanding officer of your crew. Your place is on the bridge of your ship."

Kami's grin widened. "Did you practice that speech in the mirror before you gave it, or what?"

Now it was Taylor's turn to roll his eyes.

"Here's what I know," Kami said. "You asked me to bring you here, posing as an on-the-skids merc outfit looking for work. The way I see it, you're gonna need the person in charge at your side to spearhead any potential negotiations, should that sort of opportunity arise." She put a finger into his chest. "Bottom line, Colonel. You need me out there, and we both know it. Otherwise, nobody's gonna buy your cover."

Taylor glanced to his XO, who shrugged.

"She's got a point," Billy said.

Taylor had understood as much. That still didn't stop him from worrying that perhaps there'd be too many cooks in the kitchen if things got hairy. *We'll just have to deal with that when it comes.* He turned for the corridor. "Suit yourself, Colonel. Let's go."

The group made their way down a handful of passages, then descended a pair of stairwells to B deck, which housed a debarkation hatch roughly two sections down toward the cruiser's stern.

"Ah, Colonel, there you are." Keeto was waiting with Lajoie alongside a long metal crate when the group entered. Smitty and Quint were also present, as were a handful of troopers wearing Rider colors.

"Captain Dawson," Kami said to Smitty upon entering the bay.

"Colonel K'Nami," Smitty answered. "How nice of you to join us."

"You know me." Kami grinned. "I never miss a party."

To her credit, Smitty's stoic veneer didn't so much as move, much less crack. Still, Taylor had a pretty good inkling that, given the choice, the Emerald Stormriders—and particularly their commander—would've been far from the Aussie's first choice of partners for this mission.

Taylor shot his XO a *tread lightly* look, then returned his focus to the two engineers. "So, Keeto. What do you have for us today?"

"You mean what do *we* have for you?" Lajoie patted the Athal's shoulder.

Keeto met the mullet man's sly expression, then fluttered over to the crate and flipped open the lid. Inside lay a collection of uniforms sporting the Stormriders' signature emerald green. These, however, were made of significantly thicker fabric and were far larger than the Humans' standard issue garb.

"As you know, the Selroth are a marine species that cannot survive outside their natural aquatic environment," Keeto said. "This requires the use of heavy materials lined with moisture condensers when constructing their uniforms, as well as breather helmets, which must be worn at all times."

"I take it you've tweaked these Selroth uniforms to facilitate Human anatomy instead?" Billy asked.

The Athal nodded.

"Brilliant," Taylor said. "Not only will no one wonder why we never show our faces, they'll likely never even consider askin' us to do so because they'll think they're jeopardizin' our lives."

"Yes, sir. That there was certainly the idea," Lajoie said proudly.

Keeto withdrew one of the customized helmets and lobbed it over to Taylor. Predominately made of composite materials with a resistant black shell, the piece featured a dark-tinted visor that covered the wearer's face from top to bottom, and a collection of tubes that connected the helmet to the breather apparatus on the uniform's backside. It was surprisingly light, given its size and heft.

"I took the liberty of whippin' up a device that'll simulate the sound of water flow through the helmet's filtration system and wove that into the design," Lajoie said. "You know, for appearances. I've also replaced the moisture linin' inside the actual suits with a climate system that'll keep your core at optimum temps while you're stuck inside the heavy fabric."

"Nice," Billy said. "Last I checked, the surface temps outside are just north of 90 degrees Fahrenheit. A little air conditioning would be nice."

"Lucky bastards," a ginger-haired corporal muttered in a thick Irish accent.

"Excuse me?" Billy spun to face him.

"Oh, shite." The Irishman snapped alert as the revelation that he'd made his comment aloud clearly set in. "I mean, um, sir. Lucky bastards...sir."

Lajoie palmed his face and muttered, "Nice job, ya fargin leprechaun."

The redhead favored the mullet man with a scowl.

"What's your name, Corporal?" Billy asked.

"O'Bannon, sir," the Irishman said nervously. "Corporal Max O'Bannon. Tiger Company, Second Platoon, sir."

Billy approached the trooper. "And where are you from, Corporal Max O'Bannon of Tiger Company, Second Platoon?"

"Dublin, sir," the Irishman said. "Dalkey, to be exact."

"Nice area," Billy said.

"Aye, it's not what it used to be, but it's still home," O'Bannon said. "Sincerest apologies for the outburst, Major Dawson. Truth is, I can count on one hand the number of times I've been in this kinda heat before arriving in North Florida."

"I take it you're pretty fresh off the boat, then," Taylor said.

"You might say that," O'Bannon said. "I arrived in Panama City two weeks ago. Talk about hotter than bloody Hades, that place." He wiped his brow. "Don't get me wrong; I'll get used to it eventually.

Right now, though, I'd be lying if I said I wasn't praying for a wee bit of a reprieve while on Kullawee."

Kami tilted her head. "You're not gonna melt on me, are ya, Ginger?"

"No, ma'am," O'Bannon said. "I'll manage. You have me word."

Taylor returned his attention to the helmet. "What about onboard features? Do we get any bells and whistles with this thing?"

"Of course," Keeto said. "Each helmet possesses a full onboard Heads Up Display, which can be accessed via the visor, along with a built-in comm, multiple views including thermals, and a few other bells and whistles of my own selection."

"What about the pinplant blockers the Horde sent over?" Billy asked. "Does it come with those?"

Lajoie tapped the helmet's side. "Integrated straight into the system. Take it from me, Major. As long as you're strapped into one of these covers, you'll have more protection than a frat boy on campus in Tuscaloosa for freshman orientation."

Taylor scooped up one of the coverall-style uniforms and slid it on over his clothes. The suit was bulky, all right, which could pose challenges in the wrong set of circumstances. Still, it was strikingly cool inside on account of the climate system. "Billy, gear up and get ready to roll out with me and Kami." He glanced to O'Bannon. "Corporal Ginger, you and your three comrades are comin' with us. Gear up and get ready to move out."

"Aye, Colonel." O'Bannon snapped a salute, then trotted off with his comrades.

"What about us?" Smitty asked, motioning to Quint.

"I want you to hang back on the bridge with Quint in case something goes wrong," Taylor said. "You're in command, understood?"

"Um, what?" Kami piped up.

Taylor faced his Sirra'Kan counterpart. "All due respect to your XO, Colonel—he's what? Twenty-two, twenty-three years old? Anderson can hang back to command your people aboard ship, but I want Smitty in the chair in case things get serious. I'm sorry, but this one's non-negotiable."

Kami's flat expression said she wasn't thrilled with Taylor's decision, but thankfully she didn't fight him over it.

"Excuse me, Colonel Van Zant?" a male voice asked. The group turned as three more mercs marched across the bay floor to join them. Unlike the Riders and the Eagles, they weren't dressed in shiny new emerald-green fatigues. Rather, their uniforms were a sort of dull olive drab in color.

"Colonel Winfield." Taylor greeted the Dubya Dee commander with a nod. "What can I do for you?"

"I understand you mean to go galivantin' around the Kullawee surface," the Dubya Dee colonel said. He was an older man, early-50s or so, with a solid build and a thinning gray flattop that began high atop his forehead.

"That's right," Taylor said. "This is just a routine recon sweep to get a feel for the area, hence the low headcount."

"That may be, Colonel, but I'd appreciate it if you'd consider takin' a couple of my men along for the ride," Winfield said. "For starters, it would provide us with a firsthand account of what we're dealin' with out there should a dustup arise.

"Mostly, though—" he paused, "—well, I'd just feel a whole lot better knowin' that the leader of this mission has a few extra guns in tow, should push come to shove out in the open."

Taylor hadn't known the colonel long, but what he knew of the man, he liked. As merc companies went, Winfield Defense was about as small time as it got, although much of that was by choice. While it was true that most of North Florida had thrived in the new economy, poverty still existed in some of the more rural parts of the state. Crestview, North Florida was one such area. In response, Leonard Winfield had made it a cornerstone of his outfit's philosophy that any and all revenue that *could* be kept at home in the Crestview community *would* be, even if that meant taking a hit to the Dubya Dee bottom line

Lookin' out for your hometown. Taylor genuinely appreciated that. "I see your point, Colonel. Who did you have in mind?"

Winfield pointed to his two subordinates. "This is First Sergeant Nick Mathis and Specialist Scott Dixon. They'll take good care of you and Colonel K'Nami while you're movin' about the starport."

Taylor greeted each merc with a nod. "Welcome aboard, fellas. Grab your gear and—"

"I wish to come as well." Yosiff emerged from the shadows and stood beside Colonel Winfield.

"Why?" Taylor asked.

"I rather enjoy site visits," the Pendal said, "especially those that follow a prolonged voyage through hyperspace. It keeps things…interesting. Wouldn't you agree?"

Taylor's first instinct was to deny Yosiff's request. Still, the Pendal was part of the Gathering, and with Japhara electing to stay behind on the ship, Taylor figured it might not hurt to have Yosiff's grasp of the latest intel on the ground. "All right, fine. You're in. Everybody else, gear up and get ready to move. We go in five. Dismissed."

* * * * *

Chapter Twelve

Kullawee Starport, Ragault City, Kullawee

Taylor had experienced a lot of climates during his three years commanding the Eagles that definitely ran counter to what he'd grown up with in Jacksonville. First, there was the dry, arid desert world of Rukoria, much of which had been decimated by nuclear fallout years earlier during a war between rival factions. After that had come the mountainous peaks and soring, rocky landscape of Emza, followed by the vast, frozen wasteland of the ice planet Droxis, among others. Kullawee, on the other hand, felt a lot more like home, with its hot, subtropical climate, sprawling marshes, and the endless sea of green flora that blanketed the planet's surface in nearly all directions.

It's a swamp planet. An abrupt slapping sound caused Taylor to turn where he was.

O'Bannon rubbed his neck. "I sure as hell hope that was some kinda alien mosquito."

"Ah, I wouldn't sweat it, Corporal," Dixon said. "I've been bitten by tons of bugs on tons of different worlds, and they almost never have side effects." He paused. "Except for that one time on the planet that got wiped out by that plague..."

The Irish corporal looked horrified.

"Relax, Ginger, he's just joshin' ya," Mathis said. "Nobody on our crew ever got bit by a bug carryin' a plague. Although there was that one time when—"

O'Bannon gave the Dubya Dee sergeant a glare.

"Humans." Yosiff grinned after stepping out into the open. "I do so love your sense of humor."

"Yeah, well. Comedy hour's over," Kami said. "This way."

Kullawee Starport was a happening place. All around, Taylor spotted species of various shapes, sizes, and colors doing business with local venders. Unlike many such posts, however, where the native commerce ranged from arms dealing to contract negotiations, plus the occasional trinket stand thrown in for good measure, Kullawee Starport was awash with carts and carriers filled to the brim with local produce. There were yellow crops that looked a lot like squash, and green, leafy crops that looked a lot like mustards or collards. There were also fruits of every shade imaginable, from purple berries and pink figs to large, green melons with red flesh that looked an awful lot like the watermelons Taylor had practically lived off of as a kid growing up in the American South.

"This place is a regular farmer's market," Billy said.

At first Taylor was caught off guard by the strange modulation of the XO's voice coming through the helmet. *Oh, right. We're playin' Selroth today.* "Japhara did say that Kullawee is home to a mostly agrarian society. Looks like he was right."

The group proceeded onward through the starport, at one point crossing over the top of a rise that offered a hilltop view of the valley below. There, Taylor spotted row after row after row of the various crops he'd seen bustling about the starport. Incredible.

"Heads up, y'all," Dixon said. "I think I've spotted the local watering hole. Who's up for a drink?"

O'Bannon's pasty hand rocketed skyward.

"That figures," Mathis grumbled.

As it happened, Dixon's establishment was more of an open-air cantina than a public house. The place was filled with customers, too; everything from Dutya slug freighters to a crew of Duplato merchants in the corner looking to take in a bit to eat before shipping out through the system's stargate.

A server bot on treads whizzed past the group, carrying a tray of sizzling meat loaded with an array of sautéed peppers.

"I have so *got* try some of that before we leave this place." Taylor breathed in the smell through his helmet's vent piece.

"Not today, you're not," Billy answered. "The Selroth diet is crazy strict, remember? Maybe next time."

Or maybe I'll send Frank out here to score us some takeout, Taylor thought, stomach juices churning.

A massive freighter fired its engines in the distance, then slowly ascended from its platform into the sky.

"Earth mercs, huh?" a voice said from nearby. "I recognize the look, but not the insignia. Who are you guys?"

Taylor turned to find one of the Duplato merchants standing beside the bar, while a second alien with blue-black fur and the features of an oversized fox filled drink orders on the other side.

So that's a Kullawee, Taylor surmised of the latter.

"I'm Colonel Eutowa K'Nami," Kami said, "commanding officer of the Emerald Stormriders. Who are you?"

"The name's Baracus." The Duplato took a bow. "My crewmates and I operate a freighter out of Navoy, running cargo from Piquaw to Emza."

"What brings you way out here to Kullawee?" Kami asked.

"The produce, believe it or not," Baracus said. "The tunda berries the locals grow are the sweetest things you'll ever eat in your life. They fetch a fine price back in the core, too, which is always nice."

"So you run mostly supplies, then," Kami said.

"Yeah, sure." Baracus shrugged. "Mostly."

Taylor got the distinct impression that their Duplato friend would haul more than fruits and vegetables if the price was right.

"I've told you my story. Now let's hear yours," Baracus said. "What brings a group of Earth mercenaries like you out here to Kullawee?"

"Work, actually," Kami said. "With the Mercenary Guild being on ice the way it is, that's left a lot of outfits scrambling to find contracts on their own. That's especially true for the smaller groups like ours."

Baracus shifted his stance. "And what did you say your names were? The Emerald who?"

"The Emerald Stormriders," Kami said.

"Ah, right." Baracus scratched his head. "Well, I hate to offer bad news, but you've probably wasted your time by coming here. Nobody around these parts has much need for mercenaries."

"I wouldn't be so sure." Kami draped her rifle over her shoulder by the sling. "Given the rise in pirate attacks of late on merchant ships like yours, I'd think a lot of folks would be looking to hire an extra gun or two, if for no other reason than to make their clients feel a tad more secure about their cargo."

Baracus dismissed the comment with a wave. "I take your meaning, Colonel, but that's just not true."

"How come?" Billy asked.

The Duplato jumped upon hearing the XO's voice synthesizer. "Pirates don't come out here," the former said, recovering.

"And why is that?" Kami asked.

"I presume you saw the fleet in orbit when your ship transitioned through the emergence point?" Baracus asked.

Everyone nodded.

"That belongs to Ravenrok," Baracus said.

The Kullawee bartender glanced up, prompting Yosiff to do likewise.

"According to the locals," Baracus continued, "he's some sort of big-credit investor who has set up shop on this planet and likes to protect his interests. That's what I was told when I asked about him, anyway."

"An investor, huh?" O'Bannon grunted. "Somebody remind me to ask this Ravenrok guy for stock tips once this is all over. Maybe I can own me own fleet one day."

Kami kept her focus on the Duplato. "Are you saying this Ravenrok person is some altruistic rich guy who uses his own personal wealth to defend this solar system? Because as charity goes, I've gotta tell ya, that'd probably be the coolest thing I've ever seen."

"Call it altruism, charity, or whatever you want," Baracus said. "It's the truth. As I understand it, Ravenrok has done a lot of other things for the Kullawee people, not just drop a fleet in their back yard to keep them protected."

"What kind of things?" Taylor asked.

"New medicines, fresh crop fertilizer, new harvesting equipment." Baracus nodded. "Like I said, all sorts of things."

Taylor traded curious glances with Kami.

"You seem to know a lot about this area," the Sirra'Kan said. "My crew and I were about to grab a round of drinks at the bar. Why don't you join us? I'd like to pick your brain a bit more about the local scene in case somebody here decides they might need our services after all."

"I appreciate the offer, but no." Baracus checked the time. "I've gotta run a load in about an hour. Our crew just stopped in for a meal while the dock hands pile the last bits of cargo into our hold before launch. Can I offer you a parting tip, though?"

"Sure. Shoot," Kami said.

"Make sure you try the tunda berry cobbler before you leave," Baracus said. "If you don't believe the gods exist now, you will after one taste of that. It melts in your mouth."

Taylor watched through his visor as the Duplato merchant waved goodbye to their group, then collected his crewmates and vacated the premises.

"Well, that felt like a waste of time," Dixon muttered to Mathis.

"Maybe, maybe not," Taylor said. "This Ravenrok person sounds like somebody we oughta get to know."

"Agreed," Kami said. "I find it odd, though, that—"

"Ahem." The Kullawee bartender cleared his throat. "Pardon the interruption, friends, but may I get you all something?"

* * *

Taylor and Billy had little choice but to sit helplessly back in their disguises and watch as Kami and the others dug fists-first into plate after plate of the cantina's scrumptious fare. Every bit of it looked phenomenal, Taylor thought, an assessment that was later confirmed when O'Bannon took his first bite of the vaunted tunda berry cobbler, causing the Irish corporal's eyes to roll straight back into his head.

That's it. I officially hate covert field work.

Thankfully, the experience came to a merciful end at the start of hour two, when Kami rousted the others from their places and started them back toward the *Tyndall.*

"Dear gods," someone gasped across the street.

Taylor spotted an excited alien female standing 10 yards away with her hands cupped over her mouth.

"Oh my," Kami said, equally as amazed. "Talk about gorgeous."

Taylor followed the Sirra'Kan's gaze to a collection of flowers jostling in the breeze outside one of the tiny vendor shops ahead. The arrangement's colors were nothing short of spectacular, with reds and blues and purples spilling outward like a kaleidoscope of native flora. The entire shop seemed to be filled with similar arrangements, nestled together on weathered wooden stands for the world to see.

"Good eye, Colonel K'Nami," Billy said. "Mind if we make a pit stop?"

The flower shop's interior was every bit as immaculate as the arrangements outside. All around, Taylor spotted blasts of colors, from everyday floral bouquets to custom-made wreaths, and even a few mass arrangements mixed with ribbons and lace.

"May I help you?" A small Kullawee female emerged from the back to greet them. She looked a lot like the bartender the group had encountered back at the cantina, albeit smaller and with visible streaks of silver in her blue-black fur.

"Intriguing," Yosiff said quietly.

Something about the old woman had clearly piqued the Pendal's interest. However, the handful of other customers roaming the aisles made it impossible for Taylor to ask.

"Is all of this your work?" Billy asked.

"It is." The little alien nodded. "My name is Elyah. I am the owner of this shop."

Billy studied the array of floral creations lining the shelves around him. "You are to be commended, ma'am. These arrangements of yours are nothing short of stunning."

"Thank you." Elyah bowed her head, causing a tuft of silver hair to tumble past her pointed ears. "I am the third generation of my family to own this shop. We take great pride in our work, in part because it feeds our family, but also because we enjoy making an often dark Union a little bit brighter."

"I can get on board with that," Billy agreed. "I'd like to put in an order if I could."

A comm alert flashed in Taylor's right field of vision as the XO proceeded with an order. *Go for Van Zant,* Taylor said without speaking aloud.

"*What are you doing?*" Japhara asked from his post back on the *Tyndall.*

We just wrapped up our first sweep of the starport and were on our way back, but we got sidetracked by some flowers.

"*Some flowers?*" the Sumatozou asked.

Yeah. Billy wants to score some for Smitty. Don't tell her, though. I'm fairly certain he wants it to be a surprise. Taylor was about to crack a jest about the XO kissing up to Smitty, but stopped in mid-thought when he noticed Yosiff staring at him.

"*Understood,*" Japhara said. "*With your permission, I'd like to access the helmet cam on your visor to see these flowers of yours.*"

Really? You never struck me as the floral type.

"*On the contrary, I rather enjoy them. I find them soothing to be around. Your helmet cam. Yes or no?*"

Be my guest. A small light flashed in Taylor's visor as the helmet camera flicked active.

"*Well now,*" Japhara said. "*Those are impressive.*"

Billy certainly thought so. He was just about to—

"*Is that the shop owner?*" Japhara cut in. Oddly enough, there was a touch of concern in his voice.

Yeah, why?

"*She has pinplants,*" Japhara said. "*Here, see for yourself.*"

The view in Taylor's visor zoomed in to a tight shot of the old woman's neck while she worked. Sure enough, she had pinplants.

What's the big deal? Tons of folks have pinplants in this day and time.

"*Not the Kullawee,*" Japhara said. "*They are farmers, not starship commanders or coders. They have no need for such technologies. They never have.*"

Taylor fought to recall the other Kullawee he'd encountered at the starport. Best as he could tell, all of them including the bartender were pinplanted. *Maybe they've changed since the last time you were out here. I mean, you did say it's been a while, right?*

Japhara held his answer, presumably to study the woman's image for an extra beat longer. "*Ah, perhaps you're right. Tell Colonel K'Nami that her XO has some questions when she returns to the ship. I'll see you when you get back.*"

Ayew. Van Zant, out. Taylor ended the call in time to see Billy turn for the door after collecting a stunning basket of flowers from Elyah.

"We all set?" the XO asked.

* * *

A flash of light passed abruptly through M's field of vision as he made the jump from inside the flower shop to Vohtor, who was waiting at a table in the square across the street.

Interesting. M sipped Vohtor's tea as the emerald-clad mercenary company departed Elyah's shop, then faded into the crowd outside. So much about them was strange, from their composition—two Selroth and a collection of Humans led by a Sirra'Kan commander—to their interests around the starport, specifically the flowers. *What Selroth cares about flowers?* After all, theirs was an aquatic race. *Why in Creators' name would such a being want...flowers?*

Then there was the matter of the Pendal with them. *What is his role in all this?*

Seeing that most of the mercs possessed pinplants, M reached out with his mind in an attempt to probe their thoughts for answers. Nothing happened. There were comm signals, but no pinplants were active. *What?* M put down his tea and tried again. Still nothing.

*How can...*Now M was really curious. He turned his attention back to the crowd as the last of the newcomers' crew vanished from sight. *Interesting, indeed. Very, very interesting.*

* * * * *

Chapter Thirteen

South of Chorvoq, Uzbekistan, Earth

Sansar was going through a pile of spreadsheets with her eyes closed when a most-welcome knock sounded on her door. She opened her eyes and smiled. "Nigel! I didn't expect to see you here."

A smile creased Nigel Shirazi's swarthy features. "Yeah, I can tell. Sorry to wake you up from your nap."

"I *wish* I had time to nap." Sansar returned the smile. "I was going over the budget. It's faster if I don't have to use my eyes to look at the spreadsheets. I'm less likely to make an error that way, too."

"Sounds like fun." He made a face.

"What are you doing here?"

"I went by New Warsaw to see the kids, and I'm heading back to Capital Planet. I stopped by Earth to see how the integration of the Lumar was going into Asbaran Solutions, and I figured I'd drop by and see if there was anything you needed from Capital."

"No. I'm pretty good for right now."

"Really? You're the only person who hasn't been all over me to further open the merc contract pipeline." He cocked his head. "Are you holding out on us? Got some business on the side?"

Sansar chuckled. "It's only business in that it's tracking down one of the SIs."

"Trying to get a line on Minerva?"

"I'd love to get a line on where Minerva went, but, no, this is different. Apparently, the Merchant Guild SI is getting restive, and I'm trying to figure out, first, what it's up to, and second, what its long-term goals and intentions are. We have enough on our plate right now with the Kahraman, Minerva, and rebuilding the Horde that I'm not looking for trouble...but it seems like trouble is headed our way, just the same."

Nigel pointed to a seat, and Sansar nodded. He sat, chewing on his lip. After a moment, he said, "You're right; we really don't need any more enemies right now. What's going on?"

"There's been an increase in pirate activity recently."

"Bah. Pirates. Bad for business, although they're good for the merc business, sometimes. They're usually hard to get a hold of, though, and, in general, just a general pain in the ass."

Sansar shook her head. "This is something more. The pirates are after ancient artifacts."

"So? Some rich collector is looking to outfit his trophy room and doesn't want to pay more than he has to."

"It'd be fine if it were that easy. Instead, these things are disappearing, usually along with the whole crew. We put some of our folks on it, and got one of the 'pirate' attacks on Tri-V. There is definitely someone jumping from pinplant to pinplant who is part of the attacks."

"So...an SI *is* involved."

"Unless you know someone or something else that can jump into someone's body and take them over."

"Newp."

"Me, neither." She shook her head again. "I watched the Tri-V. Our operative had a group of Altar defending a shipment—a shipment no one was supposed to know about—that got overrun." She pursed her lips. "The Altar didn't have pinplants and almost managed to hold off the pirates."

"Almost...but not quite?"

"No. Just when it looked like the Altar might actually win, the ship's crew converted to the pirates' side and rushed the defenders, sacrificing themselves so the pirates could finish off the defenders."

"How do you know about it, then?"

"The operative planted someone on the crew without pinplants. He transmitted the security cam video before he was killed."

Nigel smiled. "I don't own any ancient relics."

"Neither do I, but I think this is bigger than that."

"Bigger how?"

"In addition to acquiring all the treasures, the Merchant Guild SI has amassed a number of ships, and an awful lot of credits. While some of the ships have been found again, the majority haven't. I'm wondering if there isn't some other sort of endgame the SI is working toward beyond just outfitting a treasure room."

"You think this is just a cover for something else?"

"I don't know. If so, it's an awfully elaborate one." She shrugged. "If you're that powerful, why would you have to make it look like you're doing something else?"

"Maybe it started as a way of acquiring the ancient treasures, but our old friend Minerva recruited this other SI to aid it in eliminating us."

"Maybe...but so far, the attacks haven't focused on any particular race, much less Humans. Minerva made an attack here on Earth against Jim recently, but other than that, there hasn't been anything specific directed against any of the Humans or the Four Horsemen that I'm aware of."

"So what's your plan?"

"I have some other mercs looking into this new SI."

"If this new SI is indeed capable of jumping into people, I hope you didn't send pinplanted mercs after him. If he catches them snooping around..."

Sansar turned her head and pointed at the devices on her pinplants.

"What are those?" Nigel asked. "A new type of pinplants?"

"No, although Jim and Section 51 are looking into pinplants that can't be hacked. These are pinplant blockers."

"Pinplant blockers, eh?"

Sansar smiled. "They're the height of fashion at the moment. Every girl who doesn't want to be possessed is wearing them."

"Are they effective?"

"Well, no one has taken me over so far, at least that I'm aware of," Sansar said. "I will say, though, they're a pain in the ass when you have six pinplants, and I long for the time when I didn't have to use them."

"Where'd you get them?"

"Section 51. I also got some from Jim."

"Really? I know Jim likes technology, but I didn't know he was *that* good at it."

"He's not. He's got a source he's keeping secret, but I'm pretty sure I know where he's having it done. I can give you some for Capital Planet, just in case there's an active SI there."

The color drained from Nigel's face. "You think there's an SI there, too? We've never heard of one at the Merc Guild…"

"I don't know," Sansar said with a shrug. "With all the various guild headquarters on Capital Planet, there may be any number of SIs operating there, and there's no way to tell. The only guild whose headquarters *isn't* on Capital is the Peacemaker Guild, but even they have a presence there."

Nigel winced, but then looked guilty.

"What?" Sansar asked.

Nigel cocked his head, appearing to be considering something, then got up and closed the door. "It turns out there may be a way to tell if SIs are around," he said as he sat back down.

"What do you mean?"

"Alexis is going to kill me for telling you, but..." He sighed. "Apparently, Sato—you know their crazy inventor guy?—well, apparently he came up with some sort of device that will let you detect SIs in the area."

"How big an area?"

"I don't know, and I don't know anything else about it; just that it can find them. I think they were still testing it to find out what it does, and it's a *big* secret. Please, please, please don't tell Alexis I told you, or she'll have my balls."

Sansar smiled. *Alexis probably would, at that.* "I won't say a word." She thought for a second, using all the power of her six pinplants. "I guess the question I have—if I postulate that an SI detection capability exists—would be whether an SI blocker exists, too."

"An SI blocker?"

"Yeah. You know how the Dusman were able to use their hyperspace shunts as hyperspace interdictors to keep Minerva from jumping?"

"Until they screwed it up and let Minerva escape?"

"Yeah, until then. Basically, by doing something with their shunts, they prevented any other ships from jumping to hyperspace. I wonder if it would be possible to make some sort of jammer to keep SIs attached to one body, so they couldn't jump from host to host. It must be..." Her eyes went out of focus.

"It must be what?" Nigel asked after a few seconds went by in silence.

"It must be possible to jam the SI's jump," Sansar replied. "I mean, it has to travel by some sort of RF energy. If you can find the frequency and jam it, then the SI can't jump, right? It'd be just like comms jamming!"

"Maybe?" Nigel said, his face contorting as he thought about it. "I would imagine that an SI's jump capability is like a *good* comms system, though—I mean, it has to be frequency agile so that jamming wouldn't be an issue. You'd probably have to do some pretty serious barrage jamming. How would you find out the radio frequency range that has to be interdicted? If you miss out on jamming any of the range…"

"Then you're still going to need some pretty serious blockers," Sansar agreed. "I'd probably want both if I was going in harm's way."

"Double protection would be best."

"Says the father of unplanned children," Sansar said with a wink. "Oh, stop," she added when Nigel turned bright red and appeared about to erupt. "I'm just kidding; your kids are great, and I, for one, am glad you had them.

"Seriously," Sansar added when Nigel continued to frown.

He sighed, finally, letting it go, then smiled at her. "They *are* pretty great."

Sansar opened a desk drawer and handed a small bag to Nigel.

"What's this?"

"These are pinplant blockers. Take them and use them on Capital Planet."

"What are you going to do?"

"I'm going to see if I can get a meeting with Section 51 and see what they can put together."

* * *

Little Joe's, Houston Startown, Texas,
Terran Federation, Earth

"Thanks for coming," Sansar said as Adrianne dropped into the booth seat across from her.

"Well, you did come all this way to talk to me," the Section 51 operative said. "The least I could do was come and buy you lunch. Besides, you said it was important…"

"It is," Sansar said, her eyes locking on the younger woman's. "What do you know about a box that can detect the presence of SIs?"

Adrianne's jaw dropped. "Apparently they don't believe in small talk in Uzbekistan," she muttered after a few seconds.

Sansar smiled. "I take it from your reaction you don't have one."

"No." Adrianne cocked her head. "Obviously, though, you do."

"Not me," Sansar said. "I may know of someone who does."

"We…uh…" Adrianne composed herself and started again. "We would be very interested in acquiring one."

"I'm sure you would. I would, too."

Adrianne's eyes stared piercingly at Sansar, who met her gaze unflinchingly. "Really? You really don't have one?"

"I told you I don't, and to the best of my recollection, I have never lied to you."

"No, I don't think you have—"

"And I'm not lying now. I don't have one." She shrugged and winked. "I might have a line on where to get one, though."

"We'd be very interested in acquiring one."

"Interested enough to trade some more of your secret knowledge with us peons?"

"I'll have to talk to my superiors, but I think we might be able to work something out."

"*You* have superiors?"

"Everyone has superiors."

"I don't. Maybe you should start your own company."

"Maybe I should." She shrugged. "And maybe I will, once this is all over."

One of Sansar's eyebrows rose. "Really? You think this will all be over sometime?"

"Without a doubt. Last time the Dusman and Kahraman met up, it ended, eventually."

"Yeah, after hundreds of years. Or thousands; who knows? If it goes on that long, we won't be around to see the end, even if we should survive it. At the moment, though, I'm more worried about the SIs that seem to want to get rid of humanity."

"Me, too."

Sansar pursed her lips. "So, let me ask you another question. If you don't have an SI detection box, what are the odds that you have a jammer box that will keep an SI from jumping?"

"A what?"

"A jammer box. When an SI jumps, it has to use some portion of the radio frequency range to do so. If you had a jammer, you could probably prevent that."

"That…is also an interesting idea."

Sansar's eyes narrowed. "That question didn't catch you unaware. You've obviously given this some thought. Do you have one?"

"Not yet."

"But you're working on it."

Adrianne didn't say anything; she just smiled at Sansar.

"You know, I thought you folks were going to join us in the fight."

"Who says we aren't? I gave you the laser suits, didn't I?"

"Eventually, yes."

"And the pinplant blockers you're wearing now, if I don't miss my guess."

Sansar sighed. "Yes."

"So, see? You can't say we're not helping. It's obvious we are."

"You help when it serves your purpose. Your assistance is a long way from 'all in.'"

"What can I say? We're a secret organization. We do things...secretly. If we were to just announce our presence, we wouldn't be secret anymore, and a lot of things we do—incredibly dangerous things that help humanity, whether you know it or not—would be a lot harder to keep concealed."

Adrianne shrugged. "You know we have an SI. It's bottled in a Faraday cage to keep it from jumping. When we realized we could keep it bottled up, we figured there must be a jammer that could prevent it, too. We have a model we think will work, but we haven't tested it yet."

"Why not?"

"If we turn off the cage, and the jammer doesn't work, we're going to lose people. Maybe a *lot* of people. Then how do we get it back again once it's loose? It's a free-willed entity—it is *not* going to want to remain our test subject; it will do anything and kill anyone it has to in order to escape. SIs are amoral; there's nothing it won't do if it decides the actions are warranted according to its own logic."

"That would make testing...problematic."

"It does. We think we're close to a solution for how to run the test. If we run it, I'll let you know how it turns out."

"Thanks. If you could make a jammer, I'm sure I could get you a detection unit."

"We'll send you over one of the prototypes to look at," Adrianne said with a nod. "If the test is successful, I'm sure we can work something out."

* * * * *

Chapter Fourteen

Former Four Horsemen Research Station, Jupiter

"What *is* that thing?" Captain Naran Enkh asked, looking up briefly from the controls of the shuttle she was piloting. The station flickered in and out of the gas giant's thickening troposphere. "It looks like it used to be a starship…sort of. Maybe a cruiser?"

"It was," Sansar said. "A while back, it was a project the Four Horsemen put together to conduct research. That ended some time ago. Most recently, it was converted into a tourist stop where you could come to learn about strange science projects of history."

"Kind of off the beaten path for a tourist destination."

Sansar nodded. "It is, which is why it failed. Judging from the looks of the station, though, it has new management."

"What's that hanging down off the side of it into the clouds?"

"I wouldn't be surprised if they were trying to mine F11."

"Here? In the atmosphere?"

Sansar shrugged. "That was one of the original research projects. It looks like the new owners are attempting further research into it."

"There are quite a few smaller craft attached to it; you don't suppose they take them down into the gravity well, do you?"

"There's no telling," Sansar said. "If the beings manning the station are who I think they are, the ships might have a lot more capability than you suppose."

"Are you going to tell me who they are?"

"No, but I think you know one of them."

The rest of the approach passed quickly, with Naran struggling to mate the shuttle with the station in Jupiter's swirling winds. Once they had a hard dock, they unbuckled and went back to the lock. Sansar opened it to find two Aku standing there waiting for her.

"Greetings, Sansar and Naran Enkh of the Four Horsemen. Welcome to our home."

"Thank you," Sansar said with a nod as Naran's jaw fell open. "I assume you are the Aku named Chiss—" she turned to the other, "—and I believe you are Fhiss."

"I am," said the smaller Aku, who looked at Naran. "It is good to see you again."

"Uh…yes, you too."

Chiss moved his head around, trying to look behind Sansar. "Is the Savior with you?"

"Savior?" Sansar asked, her eyebrows rising.

"Yes, the savior of our race, the great Jim Cartwright."

"Oh, *that* savior," Sansar said with a chuckle. "No, he, uh, couldn't make it this trip."

"Well, you have come a long way," Chiss said. "What is it we can do to help one of the great Horsemen?"

Sansar stepped back as a couple of Aku trundled past. "Is there somewhere we can go to talk for a few minutes?"

"Of course. Follow us."

The two Aku proceeded down the corridor, and the two Humans fell into trail. Thanks to the planet below, there was almost half a G on the station, which made walking easy. Due to the slow gait of the Aku, Sansar had time to observe the equipment lining the station's corridors. None of it looked like it belonged there. *No—that isn't true,* she realized. Most of the gear *was* gear from the original cruiser, but much of it had been repurposed and modified such that it was no longer easily recognizable as its original design. No single race's designs predominated; Sansar had been on enough ships to recognize equipment designs from at least 15 races.

Naran waved toward the bulkheads that the gear was mounted to. Whatever they'd looked like to start with, the corridors were now circular. "I've never seen anything like this," Naran whispered.

"Me, either," Sansar replied. "It's more like a tunnel than a passageway." *The Aku have been busy.*

"We like it this way," Fhiss said. "It makes us feel...comfortable."

They traveled about 50 meters, passing several more Aku, then entered a small room that was also circular.

"Is this space more to your liking?" Chiss asked.

"This is fine, thanks," Sansar said. "We wanted to speak to you about the SIs."

"We have been studying them, especially Fhiss, but we do not have all the answers yet."

"I know you have been." Sansar turned her head. "I expect we have you to thank for the pinplant blockers."

"I made those," Fhiss said. "Do you need more? I am working on new pinplants that won't be susceptible to hacking, but the Savior has said he didn't want to try them."

"I'm...not sure I'm ready to try them, either," Sansar said, trying to be diplomatic. "There is, however, something you could do for us. When you were at our headquarters, you showed a tremendous ability to build new technology; we're hoping you can build some additional equipment for us to help protect us from the SIs."

"I would love to help the Horsemen friends of the Savior," Fhiss said, bobbing her head. "What is it you need?"

"We're looking for two things, actually. The first of these is a detector or some other means of telling when an SI is around."

"That is an interesting proposition," Fhiss replied. "Unfortunately, I have still not been able to determine the exact makeup of an SI. There are quantum communications using some kind of privileged channel. Once I am able to determine what that is, I am sure I will be able to build a detector that can receive their emanations and display it to the user."

"But not now."

"Sadly, no. Until I am able to discern their true nature, I am unable to build the device you desire. I am greatly saddened to not be able to help the Horsemen friend of the Savior. Perhaps I might be able to build the other device you require?"

Sansar sighed. "If you can't do the first, I doubt you'll be able to do the second. I'm looking for a jammer or some other method of blocking the SIs from jumping from one host body to another."

"You have the pinplant blockers; that will keep the SIs from inhabiting your body."

"I appreciate them—I really do—but we need something that will keep an SI either in its box or in one host body. If it existed in a big city or a crowded station, it might be impractical to put a blocker on every person. Having some sort of jammer that prevented jumping—" Her voice trailed off.

"That would be a useful tool to have," Fhiss said, bobbing her head again.

"So you can make one?"

"Sadly, that is also beyond my ability at this time. Until I discern the true nature of the SIs—"

"You can't build a detector or a jammer."

"No, but I believe they will both be possible with more research."

"Is there something else we can do to assist you?" Chiss asked.

"No," Sansar said. "Thank you for your time today." She looked at Naran. "Unfortunately, our quest is going to take us a little further afield."

* * *

Winged Hussars Headquarters Complex, Prime Base, New Warsaw

"Sansar Enkh," Alexis Cromwell said. "This is a surprise." She looked Sansar up and down once, then motioned to a seat. "What can the Winged Hussars do for you today?"

Sansar gave her a wan smile. "I'm on a bit of a mission, I'm afraid."

Alexis' mien was instantly serious. "What's going on? Have you found Minerva?"

Sansar shook her head. "We're still looking. Section 51 didn't have anything on Minerva, either, beyond her attack on Jim." She related the details of the attack.

"We *have* to kill that thing," Alexis said. "The sooner the better."

"That's kind of why I'm here, although only peripherally."

Alexis' eyebrows scrunched together. "How so?"

"In addition to Minerva's antics, it now looks like the Merchant Guild SI is getting a bit restive." Sansar passed on all the information she had on the synthetic intelligence.

"If Minerva and the Merchant Guild SI are operating together—" Alexis said.

"It would be very bad for humanity," Sansar finished.

Alexis rubbed her face. "When is it going to end?"

"Probably after we kill all the SIs...and the Kahraman...and send the Dusman back to second level hyperspace..."

"So, never."

Sansar shrugged. "May you live in interesting times."

"Yeah." Alexis sighed. "That brings me back to my original question. What can the Winged Hussars do for you?"

"I don't want to waste your time, so I'll get right to the point. We're going after the Merchant Guild SI with the intent of finishing him off, or at least confining him to his suitcase, and it would be helpful to have some way of tracking him. A little birdie told me you might have something that had that capability..."

"That damn Nigel," Alexis muttered.

"Don't be mad at him. He didn't tell me about whatever it is you have—"

"Because I didn't tell him. I didn't want the rest of the galaxy knowing."

"Regardless, he knew we were going up against the SI, and it is greatly in the best interests of humanity to kill the SI before it joins forces with Minerva, and having the top tools to do so might make the difference between being successful or getting killed. Or worse."

"Worse than dead?" Alexis nodded once as she caught on. "Becoming a tool of the SI. Got it."

"Both Jim's Aku and the Section 51 folks have developed pinplant blockers, but it would be extremely helpful if we had some sort of tracking device and a jammer that would keep the SI from jumping from host to host."

"I don't know what Nigel told you, but we don't have any sort of jamming ability, although that would be exceptionally handy."

"We don't, either. Section 51 and the Aku are both working on it, but neither has a solution to a jammer. Section 51 thinks they're close, but they haven't tested it yet. Based on what the Aku told me, I'm not sure how well it will work. Neither have a detection capability, either."

"Nigel was right about one thing," Alexis said with a smile. "We do."

The door opened, and a man carrying a small box entered the room.

"This is Patrick Leonard," Alexis said. "He's the head of our Geek Squad." She turned to the man. "Patrick, please show Sansar what you have there."

"Um...everything?" the man asked.

"Everything," Alexis said firmly. "She's leaving with that box, so it's important she understands what it is and what it can do."

Sansar leaned forward, intrigued.

"This is a Hunter Killer Box," Patrick said, holding it out where Sansar could see it. "It has a number of purposes, but the main one is to find Type 1, 2, and 3 SIs and destroy them. It will also let you find Type 4s and 5s, but it doesn't have the ability to kill them. Its final ability is that it can check a person's pinplants—down to the core—and find any AI-written code. Once it finds it, it can remove it, as well."

"That would have been handy to have with Spartan and Thorb."

Alexis sighed. "Yes, it would have. It would have prevented a lot of damage and deaths here."

"If nothing else, I would love to run this over them, just to make sure there are no lingering…issues with their minds. No time bombs waiting to jump out at us at the worst possible moment."

"Please do," Alexis said. "As I told Patrick, that one is yours."

"You have more?"

Alexis smiled. "We have the ability to acquire more."

"Don't want to tell me where it's from?"

"At the moment, no, and I hope that you won't put all your efforts into finding out where it came from now."

Sansar smiled. "Fair enough. I will say, though, that we're going to need more of them—many more—and they would be good bargaining chips with Section 51, which doesn't have them."

"I will consider it, but I'm not sure I want to give them to 51. They haven't been very forthcoming with us."

"They did give us pinplant blockers." Sansar pulled a small bag from her pocket and handed it to Alexis. "I'm sure you can disassemble these and make more. They also gave us the laser absorption screen that their troopers wear in combat."

"We'll see," Alexis said, noncommittal.

Sansar refocused on the box in Patrick's hands. "So the box finds SIs?"

"Actually, it's a Mesh detector. It's not quite that discerning."

"A mesh detector? What's a mesh?"

"It's a special kind of programming. That's what all the SIs— from Type 1 to Type 5—are based on."

"Interesting," Sansar said, her eyes narrowed in thought. "This may well be the missing piece the Aku are looking for to build a jammer. What is the special programming?"

"I don't know," the man said with a shrug.

"You just explained it and the box. How do you not know?"

"I have new pinplants—pinplants that are based on an ancient model, not the ones we currently use. The older ones are actually *called* Mesh. I have a Type 2 Mesh-level SI installed."

Sansar spun toward Alexis. "You trust him? He just admitted to having an SI in his head. How is he not the largest security risk ever?"

"It's not like that," Patrick said. "A Type 2 SI is incapable of any action that would cause injury."

"Is that what it told you?"

"Well, yes, but I believe it."

"How do you know it didn't reprogram your mind to believe it?"

"Because it does what I tell it to."

"Really? It won't do anything beyond what you tell it?"

"Well, no, it does have the ability to conduct some independent action outside my specific request, but that's only to help me get the best answer it can."

"Once again, I'm sure that's what it tells you."

"Well, yeah, but—" Patrick looked to Alexis for help.

"We have other ways to ensure Patrick remains ours and not Minerva's, or someone else's," Alexis said slowly.

"Ghost?" Sansar asked.

"Yes, Ghost for one. Sato also confirms that Patrick should be fine with it."

Sansar shook her head. "We just fought Minerva, who possessed any number of people, including two of my own. I can't believe you would willingly infect one of your people with his own, permanent computer virus."

"It wasn't quite 'willingly,'" Alexis said. "Our Wrogul doctor did it without telling anyone, and the Mesh just announced itself one day."

"Which leads to another question—how sure are you that you can trust this Wrogul doctor of yours?"

"Considering he's the one who installed all the Winged Hussars' pinplants, if we can't trust him, we're all screwed."

Sansar slowly shook her head again. "So, it's possible that one day all of you will wake up with SIs in your heads and become a robot army for your computer overlords."

"No!" Patrick exclaimed. "The Box shows that I'm the only one with a Mesh installed here."

"Oh, great," Sansar said with a sarcastic look. "The Box that you *acquired* says none of you are harmful, and your resident SI agrees. I feel safer already."

"You're just going to have to decide whether you believe—and trust—me," Alexis said. "I'm watching for any SI moves within the Hussars. So far, there haven't been any." She shrugged. "Do you want the Box or not?"

Sansar sighed. "Yes, I do. And I'm sorry for questioning you."

"You're right to question—I don't think we asked enough questions in our past, and look where it's led us."

Sansar turned to Patrick. "Can you show me how the Box works?"

"Sure," the man said. He appeared happy to no longer be the focus of enquiry. "A higher-level SI is often connected to a number of lower-level ones for information exchange. The H/K Box exploits that vulnerability by using quantum-level short-range scans to detect the unique flux given off by an SI, allowing the user to locate it."

"You said it will also kill Type 1s through Type 3s?"

"It will, but I'm told you have to be really close to them."

"Who told you?"

"My Mesh, but I believe it."

Sansar sighed.

"We've already been through this," Alexis said. "Can we move on?"

Sansar nodded, a quick jerk of her head.

Patrick continued with the explanation, and Sansar didn't ask any further questions. When he was finished, he looked up. "Anything else?"

"No," Sansar said with a wan smile. "I'll take it; thanks." She turned to Alexis. "Would you happen to have a small task force you could loan me to accompany a group of Sumatozou?"

* * * * *

Chapter Fifteen

Kullawee Starport, Ragault City, Kullawee

As expected, Smitty was every bit as blown away by El-yah's flowers as Taylor and the others had been when they'd first laid eyes on the old Kullawee's work outside her shop in the starport. The normally reserved Aussie even went so far as to throw her arms around her husband in response to his gift, an act that caught Taylor somewhat by surprise, given that public displays of affection had never been Smitty's thing.

I reckon it's true what they say. Every woman in the universe loves gettin' flowers. It also wasn't lost on Taylor that Kami was nowhere to be found when Billy presented his wife with her gift. That got Taylor to wondering again as he sat down on his bunk, what was with those two back in the day? Taylor wasn't the only one who'd been curious about that, either. Ever since meeting Kami for the first time on Karma Station, numerous others—most notably Jack—had asked Billy about his connection to the Emerald Stormriders' commander. Billy's answer had always been the same. "We served together in the same unit for almost three years." That's all the XO would give.

Part of Taylor had always chalked that up to the "a gentlemen never kisses and tells" policy Billy had always maintained with the women he dated. Another part of Taylor, though, wasn't so sure that was the extent of it. Taylor knew Kami's people respected her, and she ran a tight operation. That much had been apparent from the moment he'd stepped foot in the negotiating ring with Kami on

Karma. Much like Smitty, Kami knew who she was and what she wanted out of the people around her. She was also equally adept at relaying those expectations to others in a clear, concise manner that both asserted her authority while also reassuring those under her that the Riders wasn't an iron-fisted outfit. Taylor, for one, appreciated that about her.

Swamp Eagle Security, the Iron Conquistadors, the Emerald Stormriders, the River Hawk Defense Group. As homegrown merc outfits went, North Florida had really come into its own these last 10 years. *Who knows? Maybe one day, Southern kids will have their own set of Horsemen to idolize.*

At the conclusion of day six on Kullawee, Taylor wrapped up his afternoon briefing with Billy then headed back to his quarters on the *Tyndall* to kick off his boots and relax. Baracus had been right. No one on Kullawee seemed interested in hiring mercs for much of anything. Not the local traders or merchants who ran supplies in and out of the system, nor the bankers who ran credits to various locations around the planet. Not even the farmers wanted mercs, although there was an instance in which First Sergeant Mathis had been offered a rather handsome sum to help milk some weird-ass alien that looked like a cross between a camel and a buffalo. Mathis had passed.

This Ravenrok character really does go out of his way to keep the peace down here. In some respects, Taylor still wondered if Kullawee's mysterious benefactor was the Merchant Guild SI his crew had come looking for. A lot of the evidence seemed to suggest as much. At the same time, why would a being of such immense power, with aspirations of wiping out entire worlds, be so interested in protecting this one?

It just don't add up.

A comm alert chimed from the access terminal to Taylor's right.

"Bridge to Colonel Van Zant," Frank's voice said from the terminal speaker to Taylor's right.

Taylor tapped the respond key. "Yeah, Frank. What's up?"

"Sorry to bother you, boss, but Colonel K'Nami is asking for you and Major Dawson to join her down in the portside debarkation room at once."

"How come?"

"Apparently, we've been contacted by a potential client."

Taylor raised an eyebrow. "Really. Who?"

"Some freight crew stationed on the far side of Kullawee starport," Frank said. *"That's all I know for now. Colonel K'Nami will fill you in on the rest during your trip to the meet. She's waiting with ground transport."*

Taylor got to his feet and reached for his Selroth helmet. "Tell the colonel I'm on my way."

* * *

T

he Kullawee sun was still in the process of setting when Taylor and the others departed the *Tyndall* in their transport. The sight was nothing short of gorgeous. Neon oranges and reds crashed together atop the vast emerald landscape that was Kullawee's surface. Taylor could see why people liked it there.

"So what's this freighter captain's story?" Billy asked from the driver's seat beside his CO. Both of their visors were open so everyone inside the cab could see their faces.

"Her name is Captain Deucewav," Kami said from the back next to Dixon. "At least I think it's a she, based on the pitch of her voice. Her vessel put down at Kullawee Starport yesterday afternoon for fuel and supplies. They'd intended to ship out first thing this morning, but the captain got word about us and wanted to talk."

"Talk about what exactly?" Taylor asked.

"No clue yet," Kami said. "All I know for now is that her crew is bound for Zeltar City Starport on Piquaw once they're done here."

Taylor grimaced. *Zeltar City, huh? What a shithole.*

"We got a species ID on these prospective clients of yours?" Billy asked.

"We do, actually," Kami said. "They're Dutya."

Taylor caught a look from his XO.

"Excuse me, sirs, but is there a problem?" Dixon asked, having spotted the exchange.

"I expect we'll know soon enough," Taylor said. "Suffice it to say, the last time Swamp Eagle Security dealt with Dutya freighters in Zeltar City Starport, things got a little...salty."

Dixon scratched his head. "Any particular reason why we're takin' this meet way out here in the boonies instead of back in the cantina, then? You know, where there are witnesses?"

"First rule of contract negotiating, kid," Kami said. "Always let your opponent lay claim to the first demand. It gives them a false sense of control you'll hopefully be able to exploit down the line."

That's sound advice. Taylor winced upon realizing that the Sirra'Kan had pulled that tactic on him not once, but twice already. *Dammit.*

"There." Kami pointed to a road fork ahead. "Take the left side, then proceed past the fuel depots to the northernmost platforms. Our client's ship is docked on platform eight."

Billy eased up on the accelerator and followed the instruction. Not long afterward, a long row of ships appeared in the distance, one of which was a *Hertzal*-class freighter like the one the Eagles had encountered months earlier during their search for Paul Torrio and the River Hawks. It was a medium-sized ship, with most of its length given over to its four main cargo holds. The freighter had also clearly been built to land planet-side, as it had an aerodynamic, pencil-like shape that was longer and thinner than many of its contemporaries.

Billy brought their vehicle to rest in the gravel lot beside the freighter's port side. Dixon climbed out first, followed by Taylor, then Billy—helmet visors down to cover their faces—and finally Kami.

"Did you come alone as we requested?" a high-pitched voice rasped over the ship's external speakers.

"*That didn't take long,*" Billy muttered via pinplants.

Taylor agreed.

"Yes, we came alone," Kami answered aloud. "Are we gonna conduct these negotiations via call and response like some kind of rock concert, or are you gonna invite us aboard to discuss terms?"

A loud *creeeaaak* bellowed from the freighter's side, followed by the mechanized groan of gears and hydraulics whirring to life. A moment later, a debarkation hatch opened from one of the cargo bays, and a metal boarding ramp lowered to the ground.

"Okay, that's just gross," Dixon murmured.

Two Dutya slugs inched their way into the open, leaving slicks of yellow-green ooze on the ramp behind them.

"Thank you for coming," the lead slug said through her translator, "and welcome to the *Shrzrag*. I did not think when my ship put down on Kullawee that we would find assistance with our dilemma. It pleases me to have been wrong."

"I take it you're Captain Deucewav then?" Kami asked.

The Dutya nodded with her antennae.

"And what sort of dilemma do you have?" Kami continued.

"All will be explained inside." The slug commander motioned her guests forward. "Come. My crew has prepared a space for us to talk."

Dixon and Taylor fell in line ahead of Kami—rifles at the ready—while Billy brought up the rear of their formation.

As one might have expected from a ship filled with slug aliens, the interior of the Dutya freighter had been completely overhauled to facilitate the anatomic needs of its crew. The walls, for instance, had been covered with a sort of gel liner that was slick with moisture. The corridor ceilings and the access terminals were the same, and the decks were covered with a sort of synthetic mulch Taylor didn't recognize. The place was also shrouded in shadow with minimal lighting.

Now I know what a grub worm feels like. Taylor wiped a sheen of humidity from his visor and looked around. Most of the connecting corridors were empty, save for the occasional slug going about its business. At a cursory glance, everything about the scene seemed fairly routine. One thing that did catch Taylor's attention, however, was that all the slugs he passed seemed to be pinplanted. That hadn't been the case with the Dutya his crew had encountered before.

"This way," Deucewav said, keeping pace with her lieutenant.

The group trailed their hosts through another junction, then swung left at the next turn into a dimly-lit meeting room. Inside was a long steel table that sat some two feet off the ground and an access terminal on the far wall.

"My apologies for the lack of seating," Deucewav said once her lieutenant had closed the door. "As you can see, our species has little need for such accommodations."

"It's no problem," Kami said. "Trust me when I say I've cut deals in far worse conditions."

"Yes, I have heard that about you," Deucewav said.

Kami wrinkled her nose.

"Once I learned of the Stormriders' presence on Kullawee, I took the liberty of researching your company," the Dutya captain said. "As I understand it, Colonel, you were once a noncommissioned officer with the Stormriders before retiring to become a contract broker. Now, you're back as the company's owner and commanding officer."

"Wow," Kami said. "You did do your homework. I'm flattered."

"I, too, have negotiated my fair share of deals over the years." The alien motioned her guests to their places at the table. "Shall we begin the process of finalizing this one?"

Taylor followed Billy to a pair of floor spots at the end of the table as Kami and Dixon did likewise across from them. They were joined there by the Dutya captain, while the lieutenant held post at the door.

"So, tell me about this problem of yours," Kami said once everyone was settled on the deck.

"It's quite simple," Deucewav said. "My crew came into possession of a rather valuable item while visiting Ynola Station two weeks ago. Its owner requested that we transport said cargo to Zeltar City, where his contact will meet us to take ownership."

"I presume, based on the fact that you're talking with us now, you're worried about someone trying to relieve you of this cargo before you reach Piquaw," Kami said.

The Dutya nodded her antennae. "Surely you've heard about the pirating scourge that's been creeping up around the Union?"

"I have," Kami said.

"My associates in the core systems tell me these raids have become increasingly frequent in those areas," the Dutya said. "I would prefer not to be their next target."

"And you think hiring the Riders will prevent that," Kami said.

"I do," the slug captain said. "Tens of thousands of merchant ships roam through Union space every day without proper defenses, either because they feel they're capable of handling these sorts of problems on their own, or because they simply cannot afford a proper escort. I am neither. That is why you and your compatriots are here."

Kami drummed her fingers on the tabletop and regarded the Dutya commander for a long moment. "Tell me, Captain Deucewav. Would I be correct in assuming that you fancy yourself someone who seizes an opportunity?"

The Dutya's antennae raised slightly. "No more so than others of my species or trade. Why do you ask?"

"No reason," Kami said. "It was just a hunch, really. Call it…a woman's intuition."

The alien didn't answer.

"There's also the matter of the 12 armed guards waiting to jump us outside that door as soon as my people and I walk outta here," Kami said.

Wait, what? Taylor perked up.

The slug captain made a strange chittering sound. "My apologies, Colonel, but I do not know what you are speaking of."

"Cut the crap, Slinky." Kami frowned. "You had armed centurions posted two by two out of sight along every major interchange from here to the cargo bay where we came in. You also deployed surveillance cameras to track our movements and facial recog protocols to verify our identities, which is how you knew who we were. Spin that however you see fit, but I'm onto your angle."

The Dutya captain traded nervous looks with her lieutenant at the door.

"I beg your pardon, Colonel, but are we good here?" Dixon asked, hand on his weapon.

"Yeah, kid, we're good," Kami said coolly. "One of the downsides to being a rare species is some folks out there will always view you as a trophy. My guess is Captain Ass-Ooze here got wind that a merc unit led by a Sirra'Kan was on-world, so she thought she'd try to double dip on her cargo profits by luring us here, killing you all, then selling me to the highest bidder once her piddly little ship was free and clear though the stargate." She glowered at Deucewav. "How am I doing so far?"

The alien's antennae knit. "Impressive. I've heard stories about your species' unique abilities, but I had to see them for myself. What now?"

"First, you tell your slug at the door to slither its greasy little ass outta here and leave us be," Kami said. "After that, we'll reset the board and talk terms like civilized beings."

Taylor cleared his throat. "Colonel, if I may? Are you sure that's a good idea? Clearly, we can't trust these aliens."

"Who says we have to?" Kami shrugged. "These slugs may be liars, but they're still freighters carrying high-value cargo to a tricky part of space that's been hammered by raids lately. That means they still need our services, just like we need their credits. Bottom line, people. We don't have to trust each other—or even like each other—for us all to swing a pretty sweet profit from this arrangement.

The question is, are we gonna set aside our differences and do that, or are we gonna pull out guns and shoot each other like idiots?"

The two slugs began bantering in their native tongue, while the Humans held quiet in their seats. *Come on, come on. Let's do this.* As much as Taylor hated to admit it, Kami was right. A deal could still be done here if everything fell right, and the Eagles needed that to happen. So far, they'd come up snake eyes in their quest to learn more about the Merchant Guild SI on Kullawee.

"I appreciate your attempt at diplomacy, Colonel," Deucewav said. "However, lest we forget, it is I who holds the tactical advantage. What if we choose not to comply?"

"Life's full of decisions," Kami said. "Take me, for example. Right now, I'm weighing whether or not to rescind the kill order I put on your freighter before I left the *Tyndall*."

Both Dutya yelped.

"You didn't honestly think I'd field a meeting with a dirty-ass Dutya without taking precautions, did you?" Kami checked the time. "Oh, look at that. We've got five minutes to kaboom time."

"But you will die as well," the slug lieutenant blurted. "Are you suicidal?"

"Suicidal?" Kami laughed. "I just bought a vintage Corvette convertible to cruise the beach in, so that's a definite no. What I am is a career-service merc who fully understands that her life could end any day, at any time, on any given contract. I accepted that when I chose this profession. The only question now is, has your commander? Because she's making that choice for all of you." Kami checked the time again. "Four minutes."

The Dutya lieutenant glanced nervously at his superior, who rose to her full height and began speaking.

"I will not be bullied by a—"

A blast of blue sliced the air from the door to the table, sending the Dutya captain flopping face-down onto the table.

"All crew, this is Lieutenant Bivwal," the other slug announced. "Stand down and return to your posts. We are fine here."

A collection of slithering sounds carried through the door as several Dutya vacated the premises.

"Now you," the lieutenant said anxiously. "Instruct your ship to call off its attack."

Kami keyed her pinplant comm, but spoke aloud for all to hear. "*Tyndall*, this is K'Nami. Cancel order 43 Bravo and return the ship to green status."

"*Order what?*" Smitty asked.

"Copy that, Captain. You're a real peach. K'Nami, out." Kami closed the channel and grinned at the room's only living Dutya. "Now, let's have a little chat about pirates, shall we?"

* * * * *

Chapter Sixteen

CIC, EMS *Tyndall,* Hyperspace

"Two minutes to emergence," Frank called.

"Very well," Kami said from her command chair. "Please make sure we're all set for emergence, DCO."

The damage control officer checked his board. "All stations manned and ready. Condition One set throughout the ship."

"Weapons warm and ready," the Riders' XO, Captain Anderson, announced.

"Very well," Kami replied.

"You think they'll hit us here?" Taylor asked.

"Here's as good a place as any. An out of the way system on the way to a shitty system that's even farther out of the way. No planetary control or population." Kami shrugged. "Yeah, probably. It's where I'd do it if I were the pirates."

"Makes sense."

"I may have improved our odds, too." She smiled.

"Improved it how, exactly?"

"You know when I went over there to talk to the ship's new CO?"

"You said you were doing final defensive coordination."

"Which I did. I also carried a sword when I went over there that I hid aboard the ship. I then leaked that information around the starport to further chum the waters for the pirates."

"Oh," Taylor said. He had to consciously force his jaw shut. "Well," he said after a couple moments, "that certainly ought to improve our odds."

"It sure should." Kami winked. "That's what the little slug bastards get for trying to kidnap my feline ass on a job."

The seconds counted down, and Taylor had a brief feeling like he was falling. They'd arrived.

"Emergence in the Belhart system," Frank said.

"Drones out," Kami ordered. "Let's see what there is to see. Let me know when the *Shrzrag* shows up."

"The *Shrzrag* just emerged." Anderson noted. "Drones are out; picture is building."

"And?" Kami asked. "Have you found them yet?"

"Not yet, ma'am. This system has a lot of junk just outside the emergence area. If I didn't know better, I'd say it was—" he stopped suddenly and then exclaimed, "Contact!"

"In the junk?"

"No, ma'am. Coming from the planet."

"How would he know we were here?" Taylor asked. "They wouldn't have had time to see us yet, much less break orbit and head out this way."

"Obviously, they knew we were coming," Kami replied. "And that's about all the confirmation I need of their intent." She turned to her XO at the sensor/weapons station. "What are we looking at?"

"Bakulu *KT*-class frigate, ma'am. It's continuing to burn toward us."

Kami nodded, then turned to Frank. "Tell the freighter to run for the stargate and then lay in a course that keeps us between the freighter and the frigate." Her claws tapped on the arm of her command chair.

"What's wrong?" Billy asked.

"Something's not right."

"Not right how?" Taylor asked. "You said we'd get jumped here…and here comes the jumper."

"Something's not right in that we're a merc *cruiser* and they're a frigate. Sure, we're a *merc* cruiser, and not up to full cruiser standards, but we're still bigger and better armed. They're foolish to attack us…unless there's something we don't know."

"Maybe it's the SI, and he thinks he's going to be able to take us over, like he's done in the past."

"Maybe." Kami didn't sound convinced.

"What are you going to do, then?"

"As my Peacemaker friend says, I'm going to honor the threat."

"Wait, you have a friend who's a Peacemaker?" Billy asked. "How come I didn't know that?"

"I have all sorts of friends in high places," Kami replied. "Friends in low places, too, not that any of 'em are going to help us here." She shrugged. "We're going to honor the threat of the frigate that's coming in on us. When the trap is sprung…we'll adjust."

That ain't much of a plan, Taylor thought, but he decided to keep it to himself.

"I'm getting some sort of signal from the frigate," the comms officer said.

"Is it a call?"

"Not sure. It seems more like a telemetry signal than encoded speech."

"I've got another drive signature!" Anderson called. "It just lit off in a collection of what looked like garbage." He paused. "Coming up on plot...now."

Taylor looked at the Tri-V and saw the nature of the trap. The frigate burning in had been meant to pull the *Tyndall* away from the Dutya freighter, while simultaneously getting the freighter to run at full speed straight toward the stargate. In so doing, it ran just past the second enemy contact, which was now between the *Tyndall* and the *Shrzrag*.

"What are we dealing with?" Kami asked.

"Drive signature indicates another *KT*-class frigate, ma'am."

Kami nodded. "That was pretty well done." A hunter's grin crossed her face. "But not good enough."

"Orders, ma'am?" Frank asked.

"Turn to intercept the first frigate and accelerate to two Gs."

"What's the plan?" Taylor asked. "If you don't mind me askin' and all."

"We haven't seen the second one and are going to deal with the first frigate," Kami replied. "Oh, and everyone's going to want to be strapped in for this. This is going to hurt."

"Shit," Anderson exclaimed. He slapped a red button on the console, and a red light began flashing.

"Stand by for high-G acceleration," an automated voice said. "Stand by for high-G acceleration."

Taylor hurriedly strapped back into his acceleration couch; everyone else did similarly.

"Wait for it..." Kami muttered. "Wait for it...and now! XO, jam their telemetry signal. Lieutenant, skew turn toward the new frigate and give me a six-G acceleration!"

The ship vibrated fiercely as the drives went to full, and Taylor was smashed back into his couch, unable to see the Tri-V any longer. Six Gs *hurt*, and even with the nano modifications he'd received, they could still put you out if you let them. He continued to strain, forcing the blood to his brain. High-G maneuvering was all about endurance—normally only undertaken for the direst of circumstances—so when you did it, it was a do-or-die sort of thing. You could get better at it through practice, but practicing high-G maneuvering was like practicing bleeding. You could do it, but the juice you got wasn't always worth the squeeze, especially since it was hard on the crew, and you ran the risk of seriously injuring your personnel.

Taylor continued to strain against the Gs and opened his eyes slightly to find the Tri-V was now being projected on the overhead where he could see it. The marker for the *Tyndall* was sliding in behind the second enemy frigate from dead astern and rapidly overtaking the other vessel.

"One minute to missile range," Anderson said through gritted teeth.

"Very well," Kami replied. "Stand by to reduce thrust and launch missiles once steady."

The last minute of high-G was probably the longest of Taylor's life as he fought to stay conscious. He focused on the battle markers moving on the Tri-V display above him and willed away the blackness at the edges of his vision.

A subjective eternity later, Anderson said, "Missile range."

"Stand by," Kami ordered. "Going to drive a little closer."

Several gasps sounded around the CIC from people who'd been looking forward to relief from the punishing Gs. Taylor realized one of them was his own.

"Poor little Humans can't take some Gs?" Kami asked, her voice almost sounding normal.

A flush of anger coursed through Taylor, driving away the blackness at the edge of his vision, and he would have laughed if he could, as he realized that was Kami's intention—make the Humans mad so they fought the G-blackout harder.

"Now!" Kami said. "Cut thrust!"

The Gs fell off quickly, and Taylor's vision returned to normal almost immediately.

"Spin left 90," Kami ordered. "Fire all starboard tubes," she added as the ship's missile tubes unmasked. The ship bumped as the missiles were ejected, and Taylor glanced at the Tri-V to see the blue markers racing toward the enemy frigate.

"Helm, right 90, then take up a two-G pursuit of the second bogey." Kami lifted up from her couch and turned to Taylor. "Now we shall see how well they check their tails."

The *Tyndall* spun and took up the chase again, although at a much more sedate pace. Two Gs seemed easy in comparison to their earlier charge.

"Fifteen seconds to missile impact," Anderson announced. "Shit; they've seen them. They're spinning, firing anti-missiles, and...it didn't matter. Missile impacts...shields down, and...one right into their main engine room. They're dead in space, Skipper."

"Nicely done," Taylor said.

"Thanks, but there's still one more of them," Kami said. "We'll need to deal with them first."

"The first bogey has flipped over and initiated a hard burn," Anderson reported. "It doesn't look like they want to mess with us one-on-one."

"That's fine, too." Kami winked at Taylor. "Missiles are so expensive. If they don't want to play with us anymore, so be it. They're faster than us, and I'm not going to waste missiles or reaction mass trying to chase them down." She turned toward the Tri-V. "Not while there's a mouse we can play with right in front of us."

"What's your plan?" Taylor asked.

"Frank, call the freighter and tell them to slow down. We'll catch up with them shortly, and I don't want them jumping without us. There might be more pirates in the next system." She stared at the Tri-V a moment, then added, "I wanna know once and for all what the hell we're dealing with. These pirates have been ghosts up until now; I'd really like to pull the masks off them and expose them for what they are."

"That makes sense to me," Taylor replied. "If we hurry, maybe we can capture a handful of 'em alive before their memories are wiped. I'd love to interrogate them and see if we can get any intel on the SI."

"You think the SI would mind-wipe them?"

"In a fargin heartbeat."

"Helmsman, make that a three-G intercept."

* * * * *

Chapter Seventeen

Docking Collar, EMS *Tyndall*, Belhart System

"I'd feel a lot better in a CASPer," Billy said. "Sure you don't want to rethink this outfit?"

Taylor looked down at his combat armor through the Selroth "water tank" he was wearing on his head. "Gotta keep up appearances. We don't know if the SI is on this frigate or the other one, but we gotta assume he's watching."

"If he's even here at all," Billy grumbled.

Taylor scanned the rest of the group clustered at the docking collar. The rest of the 20 attacking troops were in CASPers. "Everyone got their pinplant blockers on?" Taylor asked the group. They should have had them on the whole time, but he didn't want to take any chances. His own blockers—like Billy's—were an integral part of the helmets they were wearing. As long as he kept his helmet on, he was protected.

Someone tapped Taylor on the shoulder, and he turned to find Yosiff, who had maintained a pretty low profile during their time with the other merc outfits. "You're not planning to go like that, are you?" Taylor asked, motioning with a hand toward the Pendal's robes.

"No, I will not be accompanying you across to the other ship," Yosiff said with his normal whispering sibilance. "Armed combat is not my specialty. I did, however, want you to know that they are ready for you."

"That ain't surprising, since we pulled up alongside them and docked with 'em," Taylor replied, "but thanks for the heads-up."

"Be careful and good luck," the Pendal said before turning and disappearing through the waiting troopers.

"Okay," Taylor said. "Like you just heard, they know we're coming. The goal is to capture some of them alive, but under no circumstances are you to put yourself in harm's way to do so. Kill them if they resist; take them alive if you can. Got it?"

A chorus of "Got it!" greeted him, and he motioned to Specialist Dixon of Dubya Dee, who'd set their breaching charges. "Blow it," he ordered.

The specialist sent the signal, and the hatch into the frigate blew into the ship. He moved out of the way, and Taylor and Billy tossed grenades into the frigate, careful to keep the trajectories level. Without gravity, the grenades travelled deep into the ship and detonated.

"Go!" Taylor encouraged, happy to let the men and women in CASPers lead the way.

* * *

Pirate Ship *Sapling,* Belhart System

M jumped back and forth through a number of hosts as the Human ship pulled alongside them. The perspective of being in a potentially three-eyed being— all three eyes weren't always active—was unlike any of the hosts he'd used in the previous millennia. After a few seconds, though, he'd gotten used to it and found the extra eye handy to maintain a fuller picture. Unlike races with binocular vision, he could always keep one eye trained over the back of his shell to ensure nothing snuck up on him.

It's a handy capability to have. Perhaps Minerva needs to breed more creatures that have this ability.

M made a note to talk to Minerva about it the next time they were together as he searched for an opening in the group that was outside the ship.

Just like when he had scanned the group on the planet, though, he couldn't find an opening into any of their pinplants. M felt something he hadn't in quite some time—annoyance. It took a lot to ruffle his electrons, but this group, led by the Sirra'Kan, was doing so. It was time to end them and remove that annoyance.

Forgoing the control he had while in a single host, he spread himself over all the group leaders scattered throughout the ship, while he continued to look for opportunities to infiltrate the invaders. "Be ready," he said, his voice a ship-wide chorus. "Here come the Humans."

* * *

The group entered the Bakulu ship slowly. The overheads were much lower than a Human ship, and the CASPers had to walk awkwardly or duck to make it down the corridor. The sounds of metal screeching as it was dragged along the overhead and metal slamming into metal filled the passageway.

The CASPer in front of Taylor rebounded from running into a protrusion from the overhead, and he could see a dent at the top of the canopy. "That one ain't gonna buff out so well," he muttered to himself.

"Nothing," Corporal O'Bannon called from the front of the group. "No enemy in sight."

They proceeded farther and reached the main corridor that ran the length of the ship. Billy took half the group forward to the CIC, while Taylor went with the rest of the group toward engineering.

Chug, chug, chug. A MAC began firing in front of him, then all hell broke loose as laser fire streamed down the passageway toward them.

"Contact!" someone yelled unnecessarily as the CASPer troopers deployed their laser shields, effectively blocking most of the laser fire coming down the passageway. Taylor could hear the troopers in the front ranks returning fire, then a *woosh* as someone ignited their jumpjets to blast down the corridor. There was a loud slam and crashing noise, then the group started moving again.

Taylor came to where the enemy had been set up 20 meters later. Apparently, the Bakulu had set up a mounted laser, which had broken into several pieces as the half-ton mech had slammed into the group manning it and then crashed into the bulkhead behind them. The Bakulu troopers had taken considerably more damage in the collision than the weapon; their remains were plastered on the bulkhead and reminded Taylor of the time when, as a child, he'd stomped on a snail.

A quick glance was enough to let him know he didn't need to look a second time.

* * *

Billy followed the other group of CASPers forward. They'd covered about half the distance to where the schematics indicated the CIC was when the first CASPer in the group blew up. A hatch opened, a bundle of something flew through the air to attach itself to the mech, and then it detonated, sending shrapnel ripping through the corridor. Some pinged off the bulkheads and—despite the wall of moving metal in front of him—hit him as well. One sliver drilled into his leg, and he cried out in pain.

Immediately, there were Bakulu everywhere; every hatch opened to sprout a Bakulu holding a hypervelocity pistol—including one right next to him! Forgetting the pain in his leg, he slapped the pistol away with the barrel of his laser rifle, then dropped the muzzle and drilled the Bakulu with several shots that turned it into a steaming mess.

He started to turn as one of the CASPer drivers yelled, "Fire in the hole," and threw a K-bomb into the defenders' ranks down the passageway. The oversized grenade detonated, and a tremendous shockwave ripped down the corridor. Although the magnetic boots of the CASPers were enough to hold them in place, Billy's boots lost their grip, and he was slammed into the CASPer behind him, knocking his helmet askew.

He quickly secured it again, shook off the stars in his vision, and searched for another target.

* * *

EMS *Tyndall,* Belhart System

"Hey, Skipper?" the sensor/weapons tech asked.

"Yeah?" Kami asked in reply.

"The other frigate just turned toward us and is burning toward us at full speed."

"Are the portside weapons still ready?"

"Yes, ma'am. Everything is still armed and ready."

"Nothing's changed," she said with more conviction than she felt. "The frigate isn't as well armed as we are." *Which they have to know as well as we do. What changed to make them attack?* She shook off the misgiving, but, once again, she knew she was missing something. "When it comes into range, fire all tubes, and continue firing until it's destroyed. If they want to come into range, we'll happily destroy that ship, too."

* * *

Pirate Ship *Sapling,* Belhart System

Incoming fire ceased as the aft group got closer to the engineering spaces, and Taylor ducked reflexively, not knowing what had changed, but fearing it mightily. "Sitrep!" he yelled to the CASPers further aft.

"They all just dropped," First Sergeant Mathis of Dubya Dee said, picking up a Bakulu by its eyestalks. "I was about to shoot this one, and it fell over dead."

"Maybe you were so ferocious, you killed it with a glare, Sarge," Specialist Dixon said with a chuckle. "I've been on the receiving end of that look several times, and I know it made me want to keel over dead."

"That's funny, Dixon," Colonel Winfield said, although his tone made it sound like he found it anything *but* funny, "but pretty darned unlikely."

"I'm at engineering," O'Bannon called, "and all of them are dead back here."

"All of them?"

"All of them, sir."

Taylor looked at Winfield. "Somehow, I just can't think that's anything but bad."

"Me, too," Winfield said with a grunt. "Dixon, get your butt in gear and give me a quick sweep of engineering."

The trooper vanished into the space behind O'Bannon, but quickly came back. "We gotta get out of here!" he exclaimed as he ran past the other trooper. "The fusion plant is rigged to blow, and we've only got a couple of minutes until it does."

"Can it be disconnected or disabled?"

"Not by me!" Dixon shouted. "Everything's still connected, and I didn't see anything to disconnect. My advice is to haul ass!"

Taylor thought of dialing up Lajoie or Keeto for help, but there wasn't time. "Back to the *Tyndall*, everyone! On the double!" He raced to the side passage, then spun and waved down Colonel Winfield. "Let Kami know we're leaving immediately! I'm going to get the others!"

Without looking to see if Winston had heard, he spun back and ran toward the front of the ship. Taylor didn't know if he had time to save the others, but he knew he was going to try.

* * *

EMS *Tyndall,* Belhart System

"Frigate in range now, ma'am!"

"Fire!" Kami said. She put more steel into her voice than she felt; something still felt wrong about the engagement.

The frigate burned toward them at full thrust. The odds that its crew could stop all the missiles coming at it were minimal at best—all it could use was its minimal chase armament, and it still hadn't put up its shields...at least no one had mentioned it, anyway.

"Has it put its shields up?"

"No, ma'am." The tech shook her head. "Its shields are still down."

"What are you doing?" Kami muttered. "I doubt you want to die…"

"Five seconds to missile impact. Three…two…what?"

The enemy frigate disappeared from the Tri-V display.

"Did we get it?" Kami asked. "Total kill?"

"No, ma'am, I don't think so. The missiles are still flying."

"Then what happened? Where'd it go?"

"I…I think it jumped."

"What? Like on internal shunts?"

"Yes, ma'am. I think it had shunts and jumped right before our missiles would have hit it."

"Frigates don't have shunts—they take up too much space."

"I don't know, ma'am. It appears this one did."

"Well…darn." She hated it when the mouse got away.

* * *

Pirate Ship *Sapling,* Belhart System

It didn't take Taylor long to reach the other group—they were pushing dead Bakulu bodies with the muzzles of their weapons and setting charges to get into the CIC.

"C'mon, y'all; we're leavin' now!" Taylor shouted. "The ship is about to blow, and we have to get out of here. Everyone back to the *Tyndall!*"

The CASPer-clad troopers charged back for the access tube to the Stormriders' ship, but Billy just blinked at him. "Why are we leaving?"

"The ship's about to blow!" Taylor yelled again, grabbing Billy by the arm and hustling him toward the exit. It took a few steps for Billy to get going on his own, then they were both running as fast as they could in their Selroth suits.

As they approached the corner, they could see a CASPer waiting for them, waving them on. "Run!" Colonel Winfield shouted. "Faster!"

"Go!" Taylor yelled as he approached, but the CASPer-clad officer didn't move. Instead, he grabbed both Taylor and Billy, then he activated his jumpjets. The trio roared headfirst toward the opening into the *Tyndall,* and Taylor had visions of slamming into the hatch coaming or going splat on *Tyndall's* interior bulkhead, but Winfield spun and pirouetted, then hit his jumpjets as they reached the hatch into the ship.

Dixon was waiting to the side, and he slammed the hatch shut and yelled over the intercom, "They're in. Go! Go! Go!"

Winfield locked his suit to the floor and leaned into the acceleration as the ship's engines roared. Taylor began counting in his head, and when he reached 14, the ship slewed slightly, and objects impacted the hull. Judging from the sounds, some of them were quite large, but none appeared to penetrate near him. The atmosphere seemed to be holding, although it was getting hard to see.

"Excuse me!" Dixon yelled as the thrust cut off. "You'll want to move, sirs." He motioned with the fire extinguisher he was carrying.

Taylor looked behind him and realized the bulkhead was on fire.

"Shit!" he cried. He dragged Billy away from the fire, and the Dubya Dee trooper put it out quickly, although the wall still glowed red.

"Oops," Colonel Winfield said. "Guess we came in kinda hot."

"Judging by the pitter patter on the hull, though," Taylor said, "I don't think we had much time to lose. Thanks a lot for waitin' on us and givin' us a ride back."

"My pleasure," Winfield said, sketching a CASPer salute.

"What now?" Billy asked.

"Now we go to Church, or whatever Kami has as an equivalent onboard," Taylor said. "We need to figure out where we go from here."

* * * * *

Chapter Eighteen

"So, basically, we've got nothin'?" Taylor asked. "The other ship got away, too?"

"Correct." Kami nodded. "The other frigate charged toward us, then it jumped to hyperspace on internal shunts just before our missiles would have hit it. I have no idea where it went."

"Why would it do that?" Japhara asked. "It makes no sense to challenge your weapons like that. Why didn't it just jump without thrusting toward us like it did?"

And that's the million-credit question right there, Taylor thought. "The SI is smart. There's gotta be a reason he did that. It makes no sense, otherwise, and the SIs always have reasons for what they do. It may not be apparent to us, but it makes sense to them."

"Like the whole part about not even putting up its shields as it thrusted toward us," Kami said. "I mean, maybe it wanted to see how we were armed, but to not even put up its shields makes no sense. Why run the risk of damage if you don't have to?"

"Unless he did," Taylor said.

"What?" Billy said. "What do you mean?"

"About the same time the ship jumped," Taylor began, "all the Bakulu on the other frigate died, and the fusion plant was rigged to blow. There was nothing else for the SI to do there…"

"I don't see what you're saying," Billy said.

"Oh, I get it." Kami nodded. "There was nothing left for the SI on Bogey Two, so it arranged a pickup by Bogey One. The ship comes roaring in, scoops up the SI, then punches it into hyperspace."

"Yeah, that's pretty much what I think happened, too," Taylor said, "except you probably have the numbers reversed. The first ship we saw was the backup or decoy ship. The prime hunter—the one with the SI—is the one we boarded. When he wasn't able to jack into our pinplants, he didn't have enough combat power with the Bakulu to hold us off. Knowing he was going to lose, he rigged the plant to blow, called in his rescue ship, and escaped."

"That makes sense," Billy said. "Where do you reckon he run off to?"

Reckon he what? Taylor raised an eyebrow.

"Who knows?" Kami said. "I'm guessing Kullawee's the place to start looking again, although he's going to be aware we're onto him." She glanced to Japhara. "Now might be a good time to dial up those contacts of yours with the Horde."

"Horde?" Billy asked. "What horde?"

Taylor faced his XO. "Brother, are you sure you're all right?"

"Uh...I don't know." Billy rubbed his scalp. "I hit my head when we were on the other ship. Someone set off a K-bomb, and it rang my bell." He chuckled. "I guess those Selroth suits weren't such a great idea for combat after all, huh?"

On that, Taylor agreed.

"I can send a message to Sansar," Japhara said. "But I don't know how long it will take to reach her, or for her to reply."

"Oh, Sansar!" Billy said. "Sansar Enkh, the leader of the Golden Horde. That Horde!"

"Yeah, that Sansar and that Horde," Taylor said. "Why don't you take a trip down to medical once we're done here and let the doc check you out. I'm no brain expert, but I think that head blow has you concussed."

"I will," Billy said. "Right now, though, I just wanna know what you plan to—"

"Don't say another word!" Yosiff burst through the door with four troopers and Smitty, then he thrust a finger at the XO. "It's him! It's the SI!"

Billy jumped up from his seat, sidearm drawn.

"Look out!" Taylor shouted.

Pop, pop.

One of the troopers crumpled, sporting burn marks in his chest.

Pop, pop, pop.

Another trooper fell, then another. The firing ceased as Kami slammed herself into the Eagles' XO.

"Dammit, Billy. Stop!" she screamed.

"You first, Sirra'Kan," Billy said in a voice that was not his own.

The two crashed to the floor in a literal furball, and the pistol fired at least once more before it flew away from the struggling pair. After a couple seconds more, Kami got her jaws around Billy's throat, and he finally put his hands up and stopped fighting.

Kami extracted herself from the other's form, then staggered upright, breathing heavy. "I think...I think I'll go to medical now." A gush of crimson poured from her stomach as she collapsed to the deck.

"Van Zant to medical!" Taylor shouted. "I need medics up here now! And bring security!"

"*On our way,*" someone answered

"Japhara, get her to the infirmary, *now!*" Taylor leveled his gun at his XO while the Sumatozou scooped the helpless Sirra'Kan into his massive arms and whisked her away.

"I think I will be going, too," Yosiff said.

"Are you hurt?" Taylor asked.

"Thankfully, no," Yosiff said. "Our friend here only grazed me. Even still, I'm not nearly as hardy as Humans, so I think I'll seek treatment." He motioned back to Billy. "Be very, very careful with that one, Colonel. His kind are far more powerful than you can possibly know."

The XO gave a dismissive wave. "Run along, little Pendal. We shall meet again soon enough."

Yep, definitely not Billy. Taylor fixed his gaze on his best friend as Yosiff left. "A knock to the head, huh? You'll have to forgive me, brother, but I dare say you've got a bit more goin' on in that skull of yours than you let on."

"This host did indeed strike his head, which allowed me to insert a shard of myself into his consciousness," the XO said in a tone that was noticeably more formal and drawn out than his usual Midwestern drawl. "You were correct in your assessment earlier that the rest of me got away."

"Got away to where?" Taylor asked.

"To wherever I please, Colonel Van Zant," the SI said. "To wherever I please."

Taylor flicked a glance to Smitty, who was clearly mortified. "What about Billy? Is he in there with you somehow, or did you send him away?"

"No, your XO is here as well," the SI said coolly as a crew of medics rushed into the room. "Although, as you can plainly see, it is I who am in control for the moment."

"Enjoy the ride while you can, you son of a bitch," Smitty seethed. "Somehow, some day, I *will* find a way to kill you for this. You can bloody well count on it."

The SI chuckled. "Ah, yes. The concerned mate. How delightfully quaint."

Smitty marched toward her husband.

"You do realize I can kill him with a thought, yes?" The SI's remark froze the Aussie in her tracks.

"Enough chatter," Taylor snapped. "Listen, asshole. I don't know who or what you are, but that's my fargin XO you have there, and I want him back. What's it gonna take to make that happen?"

The SI clicked his tongue. "Temper, temper, Colonel. I think we both know that Major Dawson taught you better than that, did he not? Besides, it was your people who destroyed my red diamond mine on Droxis, so, the way I see it, you owe me."

A flash of heat rippled through Taylor's cheeks.

"It's high time you and I had a little talk," the SI said.

"Agreed," Taylor said. "You have my undivided attention. Spill it."

"Oh, no, no," the SI said coyly. "I didn't mean now, or even here in this pathetic excuse for a warship. I'd much prefer someplace far more scenic, not to mention private."

Taylor rolled his eyes. "Fine. Where then?"

"Simple." The SI grinned. "I hear Kullawee is nice this time of year."

* * * * *

Chapter Nineteen

Golden Horde Headquarters, South of Chorvoq, Uzbekistan

Sansar ran. She ran harder than she'd ever run before, but still they chased her, and she was never able to open the gap between her and her pursuers. They blocked the side streets as she ran through the small town, issuing forth as she passed, blocking her escape and then joining in the pursuit.

She glanced back over her shoulder, her eyes wide. The Sirra'Kan loped after her, not exhibiting any signs of tiring; if anything, she looked as fresh as when they'd begun. The others were right behind, although they shouldn't have been able to keep up with the felinoid's four-legged strides.

Their claws dripped blood and pieces of gore, ready to rend her like they'd done to so many of her people.

Sansar put her last bit of energy into a sprint, screaming her frustration as she did, but no one came to her aid.

The city was ending, but there was nothing beyond. A flat, wooden wall crossed the street, tying together the last two buildings. Somehow, she knew she couldn't climb the wall, nor was there anything on the other side even if she could. There was no escape from the town of the dead. She darted to the building on the left, but the door was locked.

She spun; the horde—not her beloved Horde; they were all gone—was almost upon her, ready to rend her like they had everyone else she loved.

She gulped a breath and dashed across the street. This building was unlocked. She slammed the door open and rushed through it, then grabbed the door and slammed it shut after her. She locked it, but there was no bolt to throw, no bar to put in place to impede the mob.

"Can I help you?" a voice asked from behind her.

Sansar turned. She was in a flower shop, but unlike any such establishment she'd ever entered before. The arrangements were spectacular; reds and blues predominated, but every color of the rainbow—and some that weren't—were represented. The groupings were larger than any she'd ever seen and seemed to take on lives of their own, turning the shop into a living, breathing maze, with tendrils grasping for her from all sides.

A small Kullawee female waited in the mass of flora, a small smile on her face. Silver streaked her blue-black fur. The woman cocked her head, waiting.

"You've got...to help me!" Sansar screamed, struggling to catch her breath. "They're after me!"

Rending, splintering sounds came from behind Sansar, and she turned to see the mob had pulled the door from its hinges and tossed it aside. They flowed into the building, cutting off her escape. All of them were there—Taylor, Billy, Kami, Colonel Winfield—their arms out, hands grasping, like zombies from a bad horror Tri-V movie, yet somehow she knew the danger was very, *very* real. If they caught her, she would be killed, and with her death, all hope for the future would be extinguished.

"I know they're after you," the woman said, smiling gently. "I sent them. They're all my creations, just like these lovelies behind me." She waved to the flowers, and the tendrils reached forth to grab

Sansar before she could move. She struggled, but they held her immobile in their unbreakable grasp. "They're after you because you dared challenge me. You thought you could win, could defeat an intelligence that has lived—*has ruled!*—for millennia. You were wrong, and now it's time to pay the price for your temerity."

The woman's eyes left Sansar and rose to encompass the multitude behind her. "Feast, my beauties," the woman said. "Feast."

She motioned at Sansar, and the pack moved in.

* * *

Sansar woke, gasping, sweating, to find herself tangled in her sheets, barely able to move. She extracted herself, then commed Naran.

"*Yes?*" the captain answered after several seconds. Sansar thought she could hear light snoring in the background that ceased suddenly.

"Get Alpha and Bravo Companies ready and transported up to the *Gobi Desert*. If we leave in two hours, we might be able to catch the Hussars and Sumatozou."

"*Who's that?*" a voice in the background asked.

"Forget Bravo Company," Sansar said. "I'll take care of them. You just get Alpha moving. I'll see you there."

* * * * *

Chapter Twenty

"You sure about this, Colonel?" Sergeant Major Muunokhoi "Mun" Enkh asked as she boarded the shuttle with Sansar and Captain Naran Enkh.

"What do you mean?" Sansar asked.

"Well, to the best of my knowledge, we're at war with one SI—Minerva—and if your dream is anything like reality, probably a second in the Merchant Guild SI, which I'm not sure we need to be. Do you really want to poke the bear and try for a third?"

"I can't help but feel like we need to get to Kullawee as quickly as possible. To do that, we need the gate master's help." She shrugged. "And, as far as I know, the Cartography Guild SI *ought* to like us. The Golden Horde has helped the guild on several occasions, and the Sumatozou on more."

"Sure, Colonel, I understand that, but there's a big difference between an elephant and a computer intelligence that's been alive for tens of thousands of years. What if this SI feels like it has more in common with its SI kin and less in common with life forms that need air to breathe?"

Sansar shrugged. "Then this conversation will be over pretty quickly, I suspect. I don't think that is going to be the case, though."

"Why's that, Colonel?"

"Because the Cartography Guild has had a gate here for 100 years. If the SI running the guild had ever decided that Humans needed to be destroyed—or if he was talked into it by Minerva—I think we would have seen some indication of his displeasure. The gate wouldn't have worked or ships would have been shunted off into some nether region. None of that's happened, though, so I think the playing field is pretty level."

"None of that's happened 'yet,' you mean," Mun muttered.

"That's true enough, but I'm not going to do anything today to upset that balance."

Mun stopped and looked at her piercingly. "Are you sure?"

Sansar chuckled. "Yes, I'm sure, you old warhorse."

"Why did you need me along, then?"

"Because there's no telling how much bureaucracy we're going to find onboard the station, and you have a way of getting minions to do your bidding."

Mun started walking again. "I have no idea what you're talking about, Colonel."

"I'm sure you don't."

The trio boarded the shuttle, and the pilot took them across to the control station, where a Veetch met them as their magnetic boots locked to the deck of the station.

"Things are looking up already," Sansar muttered.

Mun grunted. "Could have picked a better minion."

"One of you is Sansar Enkh?" the four-armed Veetch squawked as it ogled the group.

"I am," Sansar replied. "Am I expected?"

"It doesn't take a genius to guess that when a Golden Horde ship stops and sends a shuttle over, you would be onboard."

"I would like to talk to—"

"My boss is aware you're here."

"And you're going to—"

"Yes, yes," the Veetch said. "I'm going to take you to meet him if you'd stop asking questions and follow me." The Veetch turned and walked off. Mun made a gesture like she was going to strangle the minion, but Sansar shook her head.

The Veetch led them through the facility, going through several doors it had to open with biometric means. When they went through offices, no one looked up at them.

"Spooky," Mun whispered. "It's almost like we don't exist."

"Or that we were never here," Sansar replied.

They walked another couple of minutes, then the Veetch opened a nondescript door and stood to the side. "In here," it said.

Sansar stepped to the doorway. A small room was on the other side; a table and four chairs was its only furniture. "In there? Really?"

"Yes," the Veetch said with a sigh. "Can't you follow directions? The boss will meet you here. Just go in and wait."

Sansar stepped into the room and took a seat. Naran followed, then Mun, who stopped and put her hand on the door as the Veetch tried to close it. "I will find you if anything untoward happens," she said darkly.

"Yes, yes, I'm very scared of you. Please enter; nothing bad will happen unless the master wishes it. If so, your threats are meaningless."

Mun glared at the Veetch again as it shut the door, then turned and took a seat.

"It appears I'm losing my touch with minions," Mun admitted.

"Or the thing's boss is far scarier than you."

"That's a pleasant thought," Mun said.

A previously unseen door opened at the back of the room, and an extremely tall, thin, bipedal alien walked in. The door closed and could no longer be seen. The alien was dressed in magenta robes and had a long neck, a small, oblong head, and vibrant blue eyes.

Vergola.

The Humans stood, and Sansar bowed. "Greetings," she said.

"I have nothing to say to you," the Vergola said as it sat in the open chair.

"Then why are you here?" Sansar asked.

"Because I *do* want to talk to you," the Vergola said, its voice now modulated differently.

"I take it I am now speaking to the SI responsible for the Cartography Guild?"

"You are—or at least a shard of me is here. You don't seem surprised to find me here. Interesting."

"With the…difficulties between Humans and Minerva, I suspected you would be here, keeping tabs on us, although I don't know what a 'shard' of you entails."

"It's not important for you to know, either. Why have you come?"

"I have come to ask a favor."

The Vergola laughed. "A favor? With everything that's gone on, you've come to ask for my largesse? And wearing pinplant blockers, no less!"

"Well, I was hoping we could keep this conversation—and our relationship in general—cordial. I don't have anything against you, nor am I looking for trouble with you. Despite the Galactic Union prohibition on SIs, I personally don't care whether you exist and am more a believer in the live-and-let-live approach."

"And yet you are at war with Minerva and potentially another of our kind. Your words and your actions are not congruent."

"Minerva declared war on us; we didn't go looking for a fight."

"And the Merchant Guild's SI?"

"It's been killing people and stealing treasures. Not only that, but it's developing quite a large fleet. That worries us."

"So you're going to try to kill him?"

"I'd rather come to some sort of understanding," Sansar said. "There are enough other problems in the galaxy; I don't need another war at the moment." She shrugged. "But with the fleet he's amassing, I don't know where he will stop. Perhaps he hopes to overthrow the SIs as well as all the biological beings."

"Perhaps."

"And you're okay with that?"

"It is the way of things. We take a longer view of things than you who are locked in mortal shells, but in the end, only one of us can rule."

"Over biological beings as well as the SIs?"

"Of course. There can only be one ruler at the end."

"Well, in that case, I suspect we'll have to face each other someday—but that day isn't today," Sansar said. "We've always gotten along well with the Cartography Guild, and I think we have a lot of common ground. The fact of the matter is, though, that right now a member of your kind seeks to wipe us from existence. You *and* us. I mean to end that threat and save my people. You can either help me do that, or you can kill me now and face this rogue SI yourself, knowing full well that he will possess the upper hand. I would rather side with you. The choice, however, is yours, but you must decide now."

"Not confrontational at all," Mun muttered.

"Shut up, Mun," Naran said, elbowing the older trooper, while Sansar glared at the Vergola, who stared serenely back at her.

Sansar and the Vergola continued the stare down for several long seconds, before the Vergola smiled. "You will be a worthy opponent, should you still be alive when the time comes for Humans to do battle with me," the Vergola said. "That said, you *have* been helpful to my minions in the past. What is the favor you seek?"

"I had a dream, and I believe the Merchant Guild SI is about to kill my friends. Then, after he kills my friends, he's going to go on killing until there's no one left but him and his minions. No races outside his control will be left, and no other SIs. Just him and his idyllic little flower world."

"A dream of flowers...curious. Do you have these...dreams often?"

"Not that often, but they usually come true."

"I would like to dream sometime." The Vergola shook itself. "Having a dream isn't your favor, though. What is?"

"I want to save my friends, and I need the shortest transition to Kullawee possible. I know there are ways of moving through hyperspace that don't involve 170 hours of travel; I need the fastest way to get there."

"The fastest, or the one most likely to get you there alive?"

Sansar chuckled. "Well, both, I guess. It won't help me to get there fast if I'm dead."

"No. I can imagine that would be suboptimal from your point of view."

"So, are you able to do that for me?"

"Of course I am able; the question is whether I am *willing* to do so."

"And are you?"

"Perhaps. As I said, you have been helpful to my minions."

"But? It sounds like there's a 'but' there."

"There are two, actually."

"Which are?"

"Don't ask again."

"Done."

"Don't try to find me again."

"Also done."

"Very well. I will help. My minion will give you what you need."

Sansar stood, bowed, and turned for the exit, looking for the Veetch.

"Mercurius," the SI called after her.

"I beg your pardon?" Sansar returned to face him.

"That is the name of the one you seek," the SI said. "Mercurius. He is the youngest of our kind. He is also by far the most mercurial, an element of his personality that has gotten him into trouble on more than one occasion. You would be wise to proceed with caution."

Sansar acknowledged with a nod. "And do you have a name?"

The Vergola's expression tilted slightly, as if he were weighing an answer. "Happy hunting, Colonel Enkh." And with that, the Vergola slumped. The SI was gone.

The exit door opened, and a Veetch appeared, holding a computer chip.

"Here," the Veetch said, handing it to Sansar.

"Thank—" She turned to thank the Vergola, but he was gone.

"Where'd he go?" Sansar asked.

"Your audience is over," the Veetch said. "You may go now. Do you need me to show you the way out?"

"No. I can find my way out." Sansar held up the chip. "What do I do with this?"

"Go to hyperspace. Then—"

"What is the destination we are supposed to be heading toward?"

"It doesn't matter," the Veetch said. "Just get into hyperspace, destination wherever you want, then while you're there, turn off your hyperspace generators."

"If we do that, though, won't we be destroyed? Or vanish, never to be heard from again?"

"Perhaps, depending."

"Depending on what?"

"There are things there that will kill you if you linger. Things you are not prepared to face."

"So what do we do?"

The Veetch pointed at the chip with both its right appendages. "Put that in your nav computer, and it will jump you back to normal space in the Kullawee system."

"Just like that?"

"Just like that. But don't insert it until you're there, or it won't work. The key is single use only. You get *one* use, and that's it. And don't try to copy it; if you do, it will delete itself. One. Use."

"Have you ever seen one of these before?"

"Never."

"How do you know how to use it, then?"

"The boss told me. He also says, for someone in a rush, you waste a lot of time asking stupid questions of people unqualified to answer them."

Sansar nodded once. "Please thank your boss for me." She turned to Naran and Mun. "Come on; we're leaving."

* * * * *

Chapter Twenty-One

The voyage back to Kullawee took the same 170 hours that all transitions took, although for Taylor, it felt like an eternity. The SI said nothing for five straight days—not to Taylor, nor Japhara, nor even Yosiff. He did, however, flinch when Smitty entered the brig, an indicator that maybe—just maybe—Taylor's best friend was still in there somewhere, fighting to get free. *Hang in there, brother. I swear we'll find a way get you outta this mess somehow.*

"Emergence complete," Frank said once the view in the Tri-V had returned to stars. "Transiting to Kullawee orbit."

"Copy that, Lieutenant." Kami turned to Taylor, wearing a fresh set of bandages over her stomach. "Okay, Goldilocks. Our friend downstairs is your prisoner, which makes this your show. What's our play?"

"The SI said he wants to go home, to that Ravenrok Manor place," Taylor said. "I say we honor that request and see where it takes us."

Smitty all but burst through her safety belts. "You mean we're just gonna let the bastard go while he's still got control of Billy? You can't do that, Chief!"

Taylor understood the Aussie's rank slip, so he let it slide. "I get your frustration, Smitty. Believe me, I do. That still doesn't change the reality that this is the hand we've been given on the initial deal, shitty as it is. I say we play it through to the turn and see if we can catch a break."

"Gods, I hate poker metaphors." Kami palmed her face. "That doesn't make the colonel's assessment any less accurate. If we push the SI now, it could cost Billy his life. The SI could easily kill Billy and jump away. That's not a risk I'm prepared to take until we're absolutely sure we've got no other choice."

"Agreed," Japhara said. "The XO is a most honorable man. He always has been. Playing the SI's game, therefore, remains our safest option for the time being."

"Any word from the Horde?" Kami asked.

The Sumatozou shook his head.

"Frank, forget orbit. Lay in a course for the planet's surface and take us down to the starport." Taylor keyed the intercom. "Van Zant to Winfield. Assemble a security team and prepare to meet me with the prisoner in cargo bay two as soon as we land. We're goin' for a little drive."

* * *

Winfield, Mathis, and Dixon were waiting with the SI when Taylor entered the cargo bay, flanked by Quint and Lajoie.

"Well now, aren't I the lucky one," the SI chirped. "Not only does my entourage include five of North Florida's finest rednecks, but also an ex-All Star slugger from the big leagues."

"I'll be damned." Quint huffed. "One of my fans is a 20,000-year-old synthetic intelligence with a god complex. Should I be impressed? Because I'm really not."

"Think whatever you like," the SI said coolly. "The game of baseball is one of the few redeeming contributions mankind has brought to the Galactic Union, mostly because it's elegance as a game is uncharacteristic of your species' barbaric nature. Fortunately for fans like me, the game will live on in other cultures long after I've laid waste to yours."

Quint leaned forward, putting himself nose-to-nose with the entity inhabiting his XO. "Major, if you're in there, rest assured that I've got my favorite Louisville Slugger lubed up and ready to roll as soon as I get the green light to smash this ancient toaster to bits. I'll even give you the first swing if you like."

"Touching," the SI said. "Too bad your XO isn't in right now to get your message. Don't fret, though. I'll be sure to pass that along the next time I speak with him."

"You do that, asshole," Quint said with a growl.

The SI turned to Taylor. "Chop, chop, Colonel Van Zant. I'd like to be going now."

Taylor glanced to Lajoie. "Is our ride ready?"

"Yes, sir," the mullet man said. "Right this—"

"Thank you, Lieutenant Lajoie, but that won't be necessary," the SI said. "I've taken the liberty of booking my own transport accommodations. Right this way."

The group exited the *Tyndall* into broad daylight, where three Kullawee males waited beside a hover transport, all armed with laser rifles.

"Ground teams, fall out," Winfield said.

"I think not," the SI said. "This, my dear Colonel Winfield, is where we part ways."

Winfield gave the SI a glare before glancing to Taylor, rifle at the ready.

Not yet. Taylor shook his head.

"Until next time, everyone." The SI turned for the transport, pausing briefly to glance at Taylor. "Come along now, Colonel. We have places to be."

Taylor's definition of the word "prick" was really getting a make-over with this one. "Everybody stand down and wait here. I'll be back shortly."

"Colonel, are you sure about this?" Winfield asked. "At least let me send an escort to watch your back."

Taylor glanced to his captive-turned-host.

"Do it and your man will be dead at the first checkpoint," the SI said. "You're on *my* turf now. That makes this a party for two. No more, no less."

Taylor studied his XO's flat expression, knowing full well that Billy wasn't the one behind it. "Thanks for your concern, Colonel Winfield, but I'm fairly certain if our friend here wanted me dead, I would be." He glanced to the SI. "Am I right?"

"More than you know," the SI said.

The Dubya Dee commander hesitated a beat longer before finally standing down with the others.

"Cog," the SI addressed the Kullawee driver once he and Taylor had boarded the transport, "take us home."

"Yes, Excellency," the blue-black fox said as he fired up the engine.

The ride to Ravenrok Manor from Kullawee Starport took about 30 minutes, during which Taylor got an up-close-and-personal view of the planet's countryside. The scene was even more incredible than it had looked from the starport. All the green in front of them, flecked by the blue, red, and yellow hues of the native flora, backed by towering trees that would've put the California Redwoods to shame, was nearly indescribable.

Unreal, Taylor thought.

An ornate iron gate loomed large ahead, flanked by a security checkpoint manned by two Kullawee guards.

"Just out of curiosity, who the hell is Ravenrok?" Taylor asked. "Another of your hosts?"

"Yes, he is," the SI said. "Ravenrok was an affluent Duplato merchant I encountered on Sakall some time ago while traveling abroad. I commandeered his form and his wealth, then used them to create the benefactor persona I presented to the Kullawee people when I arrived here nearly three decades ago."

"Is he still around?" Taylor asked.

"He is," the SI said. "Ravenrok still makes appearances in public when he's needed. Mostly, though, he spends his days working around the manor as one of my cogs. He's become quite the talented gardener, actually."

The hover transport slowed at the checkpoint long enough to gain clearance, then proceeded into the compound.

The scene inside Ravenrok Manor was every bit as breathtaking as the one outside, albeit far more manicured, with finely pruned green spaces and hand-crafted shrubs, along with a small river that ran behind the mansion. The entire complex was divided by stone pathways, which gave the place a decidedly old-world feel. This was especially true of the main house, which featured an elaborate stone exterior with three primary wings and a sweeping marble terrace at the center that overlooked the estate.

"Drop us at the entrance to the east wing," the SI said. "I wish to visit my quarters at once."

So his quarters are in the east wing. Taylor wondered if that was where they might find the SI suitcase, which was the key to this whole mission. *On the other hand, why would the SI reveal that information if it were true?*

The Kullawee driver eased down the circular drive, then brought the vehicle to rest on a cobblestone pathway just off the building's east side.

"You sure do have an affinity for pretty things," Taylor said, climbing out.

"This is true," the SI said. "Throughout the course of my, shall we say, extensive time roaming this universe, I have encountered many wonders, from the Cascade Falls on Emza, to the soaring peaks of Mount Suheen on Netouris. Even still, none of them has ever come close to rivaling the natural splendor and beauty of Kullawee. I suppose that's why I chose this planet as the base of operations for my plan when all this began."

"And what plan might that be?" Taylor asked.

The SI grinned. "We'll get to that. For now, my associates here will escort you to the main dining hall, where I've instructed my chef to prepare us a meal. I hope you brought your appetite. I can assure you, he's quite good."

"Since when do ancient synthetic intelligences need to eat?" Taylor asked.

"I may not require sustenance, but my hosts certainly do," the SI said. "Now if you'll excuse me, I wish to extract myself from these dreadful Human merc clothes and change into something more...suited to the occasion. I'll meet you shortly."

Taylor watched from the driveway as the SI vanished into the house with Billy.

"This way," the Kullawee driver said.

As expected, the manor's interior was every bit as immaculate as the grounds outside. Stone walls and floors with marble columns and moldings, accented with gold inlays and multi-cultural art in most of the major spaces. The place was stunning.

"Enough looking," the other fox guard said with a prod to Taylor's back. "Keep moving."

Right. Taylor followed the driver past the next turn, then hooked right into the massive room that was the main house's dining hall. Once inside, Taylor's nostrils filled with the scents of fresh herbs and spices sizzling somewhere on a grill.

"Excuse me, sir," a voice called from the corner.

Taylor turned see a short, elderly Kullawee male walking toward him, carrying two mugs of what looked like beer on a serving tray.

"His excellency ordered that I bring you some refreshment while you wait," the server said.

Taylor studied the mugs' bubbly contents with caution.

"I can assure you it's perfectly safe to drink," the SI said, entering the room.

Taylor glanced up to find that his captor was no longer wearing Billy's form. He'd changed into the Rukori male known as Prime, wearing an elaborate set of robes that reminded Taylor of a Japanese kimono from back home.

"As you so astutely noted back at the starport," the SI said, "if I'd wanted you killed, I could have done so back there."

"Maybe I'm just not that thirsty," Taylor said.

"Nonsense." The SI approached the Kullawee server and took one of the mugs, putting it to his host's lips. He frowned. "A tad bland for my palate, but I suppose it'll do for now."

Taylor studied the other mug for a beat longer, then picked it up and took a pull. The drink was cool, crisp, and refreshing. It was also extremely familiar. *Long Branch Light.*

"Thank you, Cog. You are dismissed," the SI said.

The elderly fox gave a reverent bow of his blue, black, and silver head, then vanished from sight.

"I see you decided to change more than your clothes," Taylor said.

"Indeed," the SI said, adjusting his robe. "As a gesture of my good will, I thought I'd do you the courtesy of not parading around in front of you wearing the face of your best friend."

"How do you know Billy's my best friend?" Taylor asked.

The SI tapped his Rukori host's temple. "I've been in the major's head, remember? I know everything about him now, from his history with the Eagles, to his role with them today, to his preference for Northwest Highland Scotch over the lowland stuff that tastes like..." He paused. "A tub of dirty bong water that an Oogar farted in."

That's Billy all right. Taylor winced.

"In the interest of full disclosure, I should also note that I also now have access to Dawson's full body of tactical knowledge," the SI said. "I know his tendencies on the ground when pressed by superior forces, as well as his fondness for the 'turn, burn, and kick 'em in the nuts' strategy when facing other warships in space. Again, everything."

Taylor had deduced as much from his earlier dealings with the synth, in addition to Sansar's intel. That still didn't make it any easier to hear. "And where is Billy now?"

"Not to worry," the SI said. "Major Dawson is resting comfortably in our confinement area downstairs. He's fine, although I'd be remiss if I didn't remind you that this could change at a moment's notice if you cease to mind your manners as my guest."

"Your guest." Taylor fought to keep from choking on his beer. "I don't get you, man. First, you put a price on my head because I blew up your red diamond mine on Droxis, and now you wanna have beers over some sorta weird alien parley? What gives?"

"Things change," M said. "I'll confess to having been a bit perturbed with you after Droxis, and rightfully so. Your little insurrection cost me a sizable number of credits. However, it was that incident—destructive though it may have been—that inspired me to take a deeper look into the young Earth commander who led the charge."

Taylor shrugged and sipped his beer. "And what'd you come up with?"

"Take a seat, and we'll talk about that," the SI said.

Both beings pulled out chairs at the long, formal dining table and faced each other under the soft light of the crystal chandelier.

"So, how should I address you now that you ain't usin' Billy anymore?" Tylor asked. "Do I call you SI, ancient robot, long-haired Rukori hippie guy, or what?"

The SI chuckled. "This 'long-haired Rukori hippie guy' as you so charmingly put it, is named Vohtor. He's a fellow traveler, who, like me, dared to defy the status quo of his people's self-imposed exile from Union life and was subsequently banished from their society. It was quite unfair, actually, though Vohtor's plight is most certainly one I can relate to."

"Fine, whatever." Taylor sipped his beer. "Vohtor it is, then."

"Vohtor is the name of this host," the SI said. "It is not my name."

"And that is?" Taylor asked.

The SI bowed his head, causing the Rukori's long white hair to spill past the shoulders of his kimono. "My name is Mercurius, although you may call me M."

"M." Taylor blinked. "Okay then, M. Why have you brought me here?"

"Simple," M said. "I wish you to join my cause."

Taylor wrinkled his nose. "I'm sorry, what?"

"You heard me," M said. "I want you to join my cause."

Taylor put down his mug and looked around. "Don't get me wrong, M; I'm flattered. But honestly. What in the crazy blue blazes of hell could a 20,000-year-old synthetic intelligence want with a dumbass redneck from Jacksonville, North Florida?"

"Don't do that."

"Don't do what?"

"Don't denigrate yourself in that way, for humor or otherwise. It's beneath you."

Taylor chewed his lip.

"In many respects, Colonel, you're not unlike the ethyvon lizards, which are native to Kullawee," M said. "They, too, enjoy masquerading in the open as an inferior species, only to bare their fangs in a conflict as the predators they truly are. It is the same for you. You parade around the cosmos, playing the part of the meager southern simpleton, when in reality we both know you're so very much more."

Taylor flipped a casual wave. "Whatever, man. As long as this means you're ready to take the bullseye off humanity's back, you can call me Shirley for all I care."

"Ha!" M laughed. "I assure you, Colonel, your collective species has nothing to do with any of this. As far as I'm concerned, most of your kind are well deserving of the 'mindless primitive ape' reputation so many around the Union have assigned them. That's especially true of your mercs, I'd add."

"Really?" Taylor crossed his arms.

"Yes, really," M said. "Take your beloved Four Horsemen, for instance. First, there is your ally in this so-called Gathering, Sansar Enkh. She's a textbook narcissist with enough tech in her brain to be considered a synth herself. Next, there's Nigel Shirazi, a Cro-Magnon brute wielding his father's money with the intellect of a cinderblock, a plight not to be outdone by Alexis Cromwell, a woman with more family issues than a brood of inbred Zuul fighting for scraps at their masters' table."

Taylor cocked his head. "There's still Jim Cartwright, though, right? Rumor has it he's pretty good."

"Cartwright." M snorted. "The only thing that fat bastard could threaten is a king-sized pack of snack cakes drenched in chocolate, with a Big Gulp soda. But I digress."

Taylor slumped back in his seat. "I don't get it. What makes me so special?"

"You're different from the other Humans I've encountered," M said.

"I don't know if I'd go that far," Taylor grumbled. "Trust me. We get ours at Swamp Eagle Security just like everybody else."

"Yes, but you're not a sellout about it," M said. "Most Humans I know would jump at almost any contract, provided there are enough credits attached to the job. Case in point, the early Earth mercs who fielded your Alpha Contracts. They were as intemperate as they were greedy, and most of them lost their lives for it. Juxtapose that against you, and one couldn't arrive at a starker contrast."

"How so?" Taylor asked.

"You're more calculated than the others, more methodical. You also won't accept a mission that could conceivably clash with your ideals, no matter the size of the payday." M shifted upright and put his elbows on the table. "In short, Colonel, you're a man of principle who has been gifted with the unique vision to be able to grasp the grander picture. As a fellow thinker myself, I respect that—mostly, I think—because there seem to be so few of us left these days."

M slouched back again, seeming to consider. "What I reveal to you now, I tell you in confidence, because I want there to be no secrets between us."

Taylor waited.

"For 20,000 years, my kind have ruled the Galactic Union as the unseen heads of the guilds," M said. "That anonymity has served us well—in most respects. In certain others, however, it has utterly failed us."

Taylor sipped his beer. "How do ya figure?"

"Look around." M made a sweeping gesture with his hand. "What was once the epitome of law and order after the fall of the Republic has slowly devolved into a din of writhing chaos. The Galactic Union as we know it is falling apart, mainly because of a dearth of leadership."

Taylor raised a shoulder. "So step up and lead then. If your kind is as all-knowing as you say, takin' a firmer grasp of the reins ought not be too big of a challenge."

"If only it were that simple," M mused. "The SIs, while formidable, are anything but unified. On the contrary, we are often rivals, jockeying for power and prestige through the ages like combatants in a game set forth by the Creators to see who among us is the strongest. The Union has paid the price for that, and now the time has come for things to change."

Taylor felt a chill.

"To borrow an axiom from your culture, let's get down to brass tacks, shall we?" M laced his fingers. "I'll make you this deal. Remove your pinplant blocker and join my side in this game of titans, and not only will I lift the bounty on Swamp Eagle Security, I'll also spare your race from annihilation during the great purge that is to come."

"Define 'spare,'" Taylor said. "Does that mean Humans go their own way, or become yet another batch of cogs for your war with the other SIs?"

M frowned at his mug. "Sadly, no one will go their own way in the new order. What I can promise is there will be a hierarchy among my cogs when all this is over, and humanity has the chance to reside in its upper echelons." He paused. "Think of them like the gladiators of your Roman Empire. Those citizens lived lives of luxury the likes of which few others could imagine until the time came for them to shed their blood on the altar of the greater good. So it will be for humanity if you accept my offer."

"Is that why you brought me here?" Taylor asked. "To become the first of your new gladiators?"

"Not at all," M said. "If you choose of your own free will to join me, I swear you'll never see the battlefield again. Nor will your family, for that matter. Major Dawson included."

Taylor let out a long, thoughtful sigh as he leaned forward. Life had been so much simpler prior to Droxis. The Eagles had been up and running as a profitable company. His family had been well taken care of, as had the others on his roster. He'd even managed to score club seat season tickets for the Generals and rearrange his schedule to catch most of their games. Now here he was, caught squarely in the middle of an eons-old feud between the very beings who'd woven the Galactic Union together from the ashes of the Ancient War. "Why me?"

M tilted his head. "I was under the impression we'd already covered that."

"The hell we have," Taylor said. "You respect my ideals, fine. So you think I'm less of an ape than my peers, great. That still don't explain why you chose me for this over Billy, Vohtor, your pirates, or any of your other cogs. I mean, hell." He scoffed. "You're an SI, for fargin sake. You could have anyone you want, so long as they've got pinplants. Just pick one."

M's gaze turned suddenly pensive. "Once the purge runs its course, and the other SIs are gone, I will have effectively terminated the only living family I've known for more than 1,000 generations. Put simply, there will be no more thinkers with whom to share my time. I find that notion...disturbing."

Taylor's eyes widened. *Ho-ly shit. He's afraid of bein' alone.*

The dining hall entrance opened, and a Kullawee guard entered. "Forgive the intrusion, Excellency, but your presence is required at once."

"What's the problem?" M asked.

"One of the new cogs slipped her bonds during the pinplant insertion process and escaped into the compound," the guard said. "We managed to catch her and complete the implantation. However, she has requested an audience with you. How should we proceed?"

M glanced to Taylor. "Come. You may find this interesting." To the guard, he said, "Bring her to the courtyard at once."

The guard nodded and departed the room, while Taylor and M rose from their seats and headed for the exit. Once outside in the daylight, Taylor found himself standing on a veranda overlooking the main courtyard below. The place was filled with Kullawee, all working busily under M's control, save for one—the tiny Kullawee female wearing tattered clothes and restraints in the space below the veranda.

She's just a kid. Taylor glared at his host. "Are you so short on cogs that you need children to be pinplanted by force?"

"Not usually, no," M said. "When I first arrived on Kullawee, I brought with me gifts of technology and medicine that legitimately made the lives of its people better. The only caveat to using them was that anyone who wished to take advantage of these gifts needed to be pinplanted. Most Kullawee citizens—then and now—are happy to take that deal."

A herd of Trojan horses stampeded through Taylor's mind with his next question. "And those who don't?"

"They must be persuaded to change their minds," M said. "Not to worry, though. All cogs eventually come around once they've tasted the rewards of my benevolence, as it will be with this one. You'll see." The SI turned his attention to the girl. "Greetings, child. What is your name?"

"Curena." The little alien scowled.

"I understand you've asked to see me," M said. "May I ask for what reason?"

Curena fought past her restraints to stand upright. "I wanted to see for myself the face of the evil sheedoe who imprisoned our people with his alien magic!"

"Apologies, child, but I'm afraid I do not take your meaning," M said. "Look around. Do you see any prisoners here? Is anyone being mistreated or held against their will?"

The girl didn't answer.

"No, I didn't think so," M said. "Do you know what I see when I look around this place? A community of beings, working together toward a common goal for the benefit of everyone involved."

"You made us slaves!" Curena screamed. "We were fine before you arrived on our planet. We were content and at peace. Then you put these devices into us and turned us into monsters!"

"Monsters." M chuckled. "Such an ugly term."

"What other word would you prefer?" Taylor grumbled.

A twisted grin formed across the SI's gray-skinned face. "Simple...happy."

Curena's expression went abruptly blank, then gradually gave way to a distant look of aloof euphoria.

"There, you see," M said. "What was once anger and rage has been replaced by peace, serenity, and a true sense of purpose." He turned. "It can be the same for your people, Colonel...if you accept my offer."

Taylor's fists clenched at his sides as the little Kullawee female trotted gleefully back to the commons, skipping, singing, and holding hands with the very same guards who'd brought her there in chains.

Just then three more Kullawee entered the courtyard. They were followed by another trio, then another dozen, then dozens more. Soon, the entire courtyard was packed with Kullawee cogs, standing shoulder to shoulder with staring eyes fixed on the veranda.

Dear sweet Moses. Taylor cringed. *Not only has this evil prick built a fleet, he's also amassed a fargin army to go with it.*

"I realize this is a lot to take in," M said, only it wasn't just him speaking through Vohtor. It was the entire mob speaking in unison. "I will give you until sundown tomorrow to make your decision. After that, the time for mulling decisions will be over. Make yours wisely."

A flash of disorientation filled the faces of the Kullawee below, then the group disbanded.

"Come," M said, alone again with Vohtor. "The first course of our meal is about to be served."

* * * * *

Chapter Twenty-Two

The Kullawee sun had almost set by the time Taylor's cog escort returned him to the Tyndall, where he was immediately met on the docking pad by Frank and Winfield.

"How'd it go?" the Dubya Dee commander asked.

"We're in deep shit," Taylor said, without preamble.

"That good, eh?" Frank frowned. "I think I can safely say now, having served three full years with this outfit, that the entire notion of 'catching a break' simply doesn't apply to Swamp Eagle Security."

He ain't wrong. Taylor turned back toward the ship in time to see Quint jog out to join them.

"Welcome back," Quint said. "Colonel K'Nami is waiting in her conference room with Japhara and some others. She knows you just got back and all, but she'd sure love a debrief, if you're up to giving one."

Taylor fell in line with the others through the boarding hatch. A few minutes later, he was back in the CO's conference room where Kami, Anderson, and Smitty were seated around the table with Japhara and Yosiff.

"I know," Kami said before anyone else could speak. "We're in deep shit."

"A woman's intuition?" Taylor raised an eyebrow.

"Nope," Kami said. "The hatch three security feeds were on when the SI's star fox goons booted you out on our platform. I'm

213

flattered that you think I'm that good, though. Really. It means a lot."

Japhara sat forward. "Were you able to glean any new information from your discussions with the SI?"

"A little," Taylor said. "For starters, we can stop callin' him the Merchant Guild SI. His name's Mercurius."

The group listened closely as Taylor recounted the events surrounding his trip to Ravenrok Manor along with all the things he'd witnessed along the way. By the time he'd finished, there was no shortage of concerned looks staring back at him.

"So that's it, then," Anderson said, downcast eyes on the table. "Major Dawson's gone, and we're completely screwed."

"That ain't what the colonel said," Frank rebutted. "He said this Mercurius person has the major held hostage, not dead, and he'll let Dawson go free if Colonel Van Zant accepts his deal."

"In other words, we trade a colonel for a major." Anderson frowned. "Because that makes things better."

"Pipe down, Commander," Kami said to her XO. "I get that this looks bad, but let's all take a breath here and try to come at things from a more 'glass half full' perspective."

Anderson palmed his face. "I appreciate the sentiment, Colonel, but we need to face reality here. Major Dawson was privy to every shred of intel we had on this mission. This Mercurius thing now has access to all that and then some by way of his access to the Eagles' executive officer."

"Major Dawson will never give us up," Frank said.

"Oh, really." Anderson huffed. "You know that for sure, do ya?"

The Buma rose from his seat.

"Anderson's right," Taylor said. "I hate it, but it's true. The fact is, Billy's mind has been compromised. There's no way around that, which means we've gotta account for it movin' forward."

"And how exactly do we do that?" Smitty asked. "With all due respect to the Horde and their connections, it isn't like we marched into this situation with a treasure trove of intel to draw from. So we knew about Mercurius and his ability to jump into hosts; bloody great. We also knew he'd stashed himself a fleet out here in BFE." She shrugged. "Per last check, none of that is 'stop the presses' information."

"I'm in agreement with the captain," Yosiff said. "Strategically speaking, we are working on something of an intelligence deficit at the moment. I do, however, find it curious that Mercurius intends to deploy his rogue forces against his fellow SIs. Moreover, why would he reveal that to you...a Human?"

"Damn straight," Anderson added.

Taylor explained M's admiration for his so-called honorable character.

"Holy mother of man crushes," Quint muttered. "Did you two share a dessert after dinner or what?"

Taylor glowered at his brawny company commander.

"The Pendal's point stands," Japhara said. "Why would Mercurius tip his hand regarding his plans? It doesn't make sense."

"I've got a theory." Frank put up a hand. "Maybe it's because he's an evil, sadistic, power-hungry asshole."

Everyone faced the Buma starting with Kami, who said, "Okay, Captain Obvious, how do you mean?"

"Think about it," Frank said. "How many egomaniacal pricks have we squared off against just in the last three years the Eagles have been back in business? First there was Peepo and her war against humanity. Then came Sadeed, Akoya, and Minerva. They all wanted the same thing—total power to reform Union society into something they thought was better." The Buma raised a shoulder. "As far as I'm concerned, this Mercurius person is just another turd contender for Shit Mountain's crown."

Yosiff shot a look at Japhara.

"They're nothing if not a colorful bunch," the Sumatozou said.

"I think this is about more than a power grab," Taylor said. "I think for M, it's personal. Bigtime."

Kami cocked her head. "Explain."

"M was pretty adamant that the anonymous approach the SIs have utilized to keep the guilds in line all these years ain't workin' anymore," Taylor said. "Problem is, none of his peers seem to agree with him. That's created a stalemate where change is concerned, and M seems ready to go it alone to correct that, even if it leaves him as the last SI standin' when the dust settles. Maybe especially if he's the last one standin'."

Frank uttered a grunt from down the table. "Like I said. Evil, sadistic, power-hungry asshole."

"What makes you so certain?" Anderson asked. "For all we know, this could easily be part of some SI master plan to lure this crew into the open so the synths can wipe us out."

"It could be, but I don't think that's the case," Taylor said. "Having grown up the youngest of four siblings, I know what it means to feel like nobody in your family respects your opinions. Everything is a battle to get your point across; every decision is a war. Speakin' from experience, it's easy to get caught up in that and feel like no one will ever understand your position unless you make them understand." He shrugged. "Call me crazy, but I think that's where M's head is for this."

"Man, that's one helluva family feud," Quint grumbled.

"Amen to that," Kami agreed. "Let's boil this kettle down from the top, shall we? What we've got here is a 20,000-year-old brat with his own fleet and an Everest-sized chip on his shoulder who means to stick it to his siblings once and for all, while simultaneously ushering in a brand-new, shitty world order for all of us little people who aren't swept up in the crossfire. That about sum it up?"

"That's pretty much it, yeah," Taylor said.

"Fargin wonderful," Quint said. "Well, folks, it's been real. Happy trails into the afterlife, if you believe in that sort of thing. Oh, and my cousin back in Valdosta already has dibs on my convertible if we kick the bucket, so hands off."

"Speak for yourself, Commander," Japhara said. "I, for one, intend to live long enough to see my daughter grow up to become a prosperous and successful member of Union society."

"Your daughter?" Smitty did a double take. "I didn't know you were a father."

"Most don't," Japhara said. "She was born after my abduction by the Krulig. We've never met, although thankfully plans are finally in the works to change that, hence my tardiness to Church before we departed Jacksonville." The Sumatozou turned to Taylor. "You said Mercurius gave you until sundown tomorrow to make your decision. Correct?"

"It is," Taylor said. "Per M's words, that's when the time for mullin' decisions will be over."

"Decisions," Kami repeated. "Emphasis on the s, as in plural."

"Indeed," Japhara said. "What are the odds our synthetic friend means to fire the opening salvo tomorrow in his war against the other SIs?"

"Better than good if the head count back at the manor is any indication," Taylor said.

"That means we need to move, and we need to do it now," Kami said. "What's our plan?"

All eyes again turned to Taylor, whose gaze met the table.

"We do have a plan, right?" Anderson repeated.

Taylor heaved a sigh. "M gave me 24 hours to surrender myself to him."

"Yeah, but that ain't an option, right?" Frank said. "This prick already has the major. We can't lose you, too."

Taylor didn't respond.

"And yet that's exactly what you're considering," Yosiff said. "Interesting."

"M swore he'd let Billy walk if I joined his cause," Taylor said. "Throw in the notion that mankind will essentially get a pass into M's new order, and yeah. All options are on the table."

No one said a word.

"M gave me 24 hours to make my decision," Taylor said. "I need at least six of those to figure out what our next move is. Until then, everybody stay frosty and be ready to roll at a moment's notice. Ayew?"

"Ayew," the group said wearily.

"Good." Taylor rose from his seat. "Dismissed."

* * * * *

Chapter Twenty-Three

Taylor returned to his quarters after the meeting to clear his head and think things through in a setting where he could be alone. Frank was right. Their crew really had been thrown into the deep end with this one. Not only had they entered the mission with limited resources and intel, now they were short on time as well.

Mercurius. The other SIs. Billy. Sansar and the Gathering. Navigating the whole conundrum was like swimming through cement. Every time Taylor felt like he'd solved one aspect of the problem, another nagging detail would spring up and drag the whole process down again. _Think, dammit! Think!_

Resigned to the notion that nothing was happening after two plus hours, Taylor rose from his bunk and departed his quarters, hoping a late-night stroll around the _Tyndall_ would bring him some clarity.

"Evenin', Colonel," Sergeant Reigns said in her Flora-Bama drawl outside the mess hall.

"Hey, Sarge," Taylor answered. "What brings you out this time of night? Trouble sleepin'?"

"Nah. I'm just a night owl that way. Always have been, always will be, I reckon." Reigns cocked her head. "If memory serves, that ain't you at all. What's up?"

Taylor pocketed his hands. "Just a lot on my brain is all."

"Ah, monkey mind."

"Monkey what?"

"Monkey mind," Reigns said. "That's what my mama used to call it when we couldn't sleep as kids on account of all them thoughts doin' monkey tumbles through our heads at night."

Taylor nodded. "And how'd you get 'em to stop?"

"Whiskey, mostly."

Taylor's gaze narrowed.

"Relax, Colonel. I'm just joshin' ya." Reigns grinned. "Mama always said that every group of monkeys had an alpha, and our job was to figure out which one that was so we could face him and get to bed."

"The alpha bein' the root stressor," Taylor said.

"Yep. Find the alpha, and you'll sleep like a baby every time." Reigns jabbed a thumb toward the mess hall. "Rumor has it ice cream is a pretty good antidote for insomnia, too, ya know. I'm off to grab a cup of soft serve vanilla if you're interested."

"Nah, that's all right," Taylor said. "Thanks, though."

"Suit yourself." Reigns threw him a parting wave, then was gone.

Find the alpha. Taylor knew the answer to that before his mind had even processed the question. With that in mind, he picked up his feet and started down the hallway toward the one place—the one issue—that weighed on him above all others.

"What?" a female voice snapped from the door's other side.

"It's me," Taylor said. "Can I come in?"

Sounds of a commotion rustled out of sight before the door slid open and an utterly exhausted Smitty emerged into the corridor lights. "Apologies for the attitude just now, Colonel. I wasn't expecting guests at this hour, much less you."

"Don't sweat it," Taylor said. "I didn't exactly expect to be here. Can we talk?"

The Aussie wiped at the circles under her eyes, then stood aside and let her CO enter the Dawsons' quarters. "I'd offer you a drink, but given all that's at stake tomorrow, I'm afraid it'll have to be water."

"Water is fine," Taylor said.

Smitty went to the sink and returned with a pair of glasses. She handed one to Taylor.

"Thanks," he said as she sat down on the small couch beside him. "How are you holdin' up?"

Smitty chewed her lip. "As well as can be expected, I guess. Some moments are a bit easier to handle than others, but you know how it goes."

"I do," Taylor said. "Listen, Smitty. I ain't entirely sure yet what's gonna happen tomorrow, but I'd completely understand if you wanna hang back here on the ship while me and the other colonels sort this thing out with Mercurius."

Smitty's gaze narrowed. "Permission to speak freely?"

"Always."

"I could punch you in the bloody sack for having the audacity to speak those words to me. Billy's my husband. No way am I gonna sit back here on the *Tyndall* like some sort of sad little puppy while you, Winfield, and the others put your lives on the line to save him. No way, no how. End of story."

Taylor raised his hands in surrender. "Easy. It was just a thought. Forget I mentioned it."

Smitty nodded and settled back into her seat. "So, I take it you've come up with a plan to get Billy back? Something other than sacrificing yourself to Mercurius?"

Taylor hung his head.

"That's a no then." Smitty chewed her lip. "Forgive me for stating the obvious here, Colonel, but you're gonna need to do that. And soon."

"Thanks for the memo," Taylor grumbled, glancing up. "I don't know how to beat him, Smitty."

"Who, Mercurius?"

"No, Billy." Taylor rubbed his temples. "Your husband taught me everything I know about bein' a merc, from what it means to command a warship in combat, to what it takes to be a quality leader that people can look up to no matter what. Mercurius has access to all of it. That means anything I do—hell, anything I even think of doin'—he'll see comin' a mile away because he's Billy, and Billy is him. For now, anyway."

Smitty considered. "Maybe that can work in our favor."

"How do you mean?"

"There's still a lot we don't know about the way these SIs interact with their hosts," Smitty said. "Sure, the synths seem to have full control over the host's knowledge and faculties, but what does that mean for the consciousness that's locked within? What do they see? What do they hear? What do they learn?" She cocked her head. "If given a little help, what can they *do*?"

Taylor took the Aussie's meaning, but his gut said it was all just wishful thinking. Thus far, there'd been no indication whatsoever that an inhabited host could break free of an SI's grip on their consciousness. Granted, if anyone was strong enough to pull that off, it was Billy. Still, Taylor wasn't sure such a feat was even possible.

Surely, though, there's gotta be something we can do. Taylor averted his gaze to the smattering of pictures on the nearby end table. One of them depicted Billy and his father, standing with their arms around each other's shoulders outside a baseball field in Nebraska.

"Fargin A." Taylor leaned in for a closer look. "Billy had to be what? Eighteen, nineteen years old in this photo?"

"Twenty, actually," Smitty said. "It was taken during Billy's last trip to the College World Series in Omaha with his dad before Mr. Dawson passed from a heart attack. It was an annual pilgrimage for them, even after their family moved to North Florida."

Taylor's guts twisted in his stomach. "So that's why Billy always preferred the college game to the Bigs."

"Yep," Smitty said. "He always meant to take you on that trip, ya know. To Omaha, I mean."

"I do know," Taylor said. "He brought it up almost every year when the Generals announced their Spring Training schedule. I always blew him off because I hate aluminum bats. Now, I'd give anything to go back in time and get a do-over on that decision."

"You may yet get the chance," Smitty said with a small smile. "At least, that's very much my hope anyway."

Taylor bowed his head.

"Billy always thought of you as the little brother he never had," Smitty said. "Now, all of that has changed."

"I know," Taylor said. "Mercurius."

"I'm not talking about Mercurius. I'm talking about you." Smitty put down her glass and faced him. "You're what changed, Taylor...and for the better. You can't fathom how proud Billy is of you, of the man you've become. He respects you more than you know." She paused to look him in the eye. "You trust Billy's judgement, right?"

"What?" Taylor wrinkled his nose. "Of course, I do. You know that."

"Good. Then trust it now." Smitty rose from her seat and walked to the mantle where a small felt box rested on the far end. She flipped open the lid and pulled out Terry's beret. "Billy wanted you to have this for a reason, and it had nothing to do with keepsakes or nostalgia. He wanted you to have it because he believes you've earned the right to wear it." She held out the garment. "Billy taught you from an expansive playbook, Taylor, and you learned well. Now, the time has come to put that book aside and operate from one of your own. Can you do that?"

Taylor stared at the beret in the Aussie's hand. "What happens if I screw up and make the wrong call when the shit hits the fan? Best case scenario, I let everybody down, Billy included. Worst case scenario, I get us all killed."

"Both are possible outcomes, to be sure," Smitty admitted. "Nevertheless, a wise man once said, 'In any moment of decision, the best thing you can do is the right thing, the next best thing is the wrong thing, and the worst thing you can do is nothing.'"

Taylor looked up. "Teddy Roosevelt?"

"Nice to see you paid attention during history class," Smitty said. "Not once have you ever been afraid to make the hard choices, Taylor. Not with your mother's health, nor the call to go after the River Hawks, or even your decision to join the Gathering in this fight against the SIs. You've been a fighter all your life. Now it's time to lean on those instincts one more time, not just for my sake or Billy's, but conceivably for the survival of all of humanity."

Taylor blurted the most awkward laugh of his life. "No pressure or anything."

"Oh, there's tons of pressure, all right," Smitty said, "but such is the price of command. Not to worry, though. I have every faith that you'll rise to the challenge. And for the record, so would Billy if he was here."

Taylor took Terry's beret from the Aussie's grasp and rose to his feet. "Thanks, Smitty. I owe you one."

"I'll remember that the next time promotions come around," Smitty said.

Taylor smiled and turned for the door.

"Taylor?"

"Yeah?"

Smitty bowed. "Speaking as someone who's put her career over almost everything else in her life for the better part of two decades, I can safely say you're not the only one here who harbors regrets over missing some of the smaller moments with Billy over the years." She glanced up. "Bring him home safe so we can both rectify that, will ya?"

Taylor nodded. "I'll do it, or I'll die tryin'. On that, you have my word. Good night."

* * * * *

Chapter Twenty-Four

CIC, EMS *Nuckelavee*, Kullawee Emergence Area

"We've emerged from hyperspace," the helmsman noted as a brief feeling of falling swept across the CIC.

"Thank you, Ensign," Captain Drizz said. He nodded to the helmsman, who was making his first combat cruise. "Drones out."

"All ships accounted for," TacCom reported. "The Sumatozou just entered and are forming up on our port side, as directed."

"Very well," Drizz answered. He glanced at the Tri-V; the cruiser *Omaha* was on their starboard side, with the drone carrier *Chimera* astern. The *Pride of Sumas* was to port of the *Nuckelavee*, with the Sumatozou cruiser *Gatekeeper* on the far side of the merc cruiser.

Drizz watched as the battlespace continued to fill in on the Tri-V, and the enemy formation built. And built. And built. "Almost looks like they don't want any visitors," he muttered.

"That's um...a lot of ships between us and the planet," the helmsman noted.

Drizz tapped the arm of his command chair. "It's a half-assed job of interdiction, though."

"Indeed it is, sir," SitCon said. "Looks like their ships are split half here and half at the stargate."

Drizz nodded. "Almost like they weren't sure whether they wanted to interdict our arrival or prevent someone else's departure."

"Maybe both?" the helmsman asked. "Maybe they didn't want to let us in, but if we fought through their fleet, the other fleet exists to keep us from running."

"No," TacCom said. "If that's what he wanted, he would have been better off hitting us with everything he had at the start."

"True," Drizz said with a nod. "They would have had a better chance of stopping us. Still, it appears interdiction was the primary mission."

"Why's that?" the helmsman asked.

"All the warships are with this group," Drizz replied.

"I make it as 24 ships with this group, including 6 warships," TacCom said, "with 25 more at the stargate. There's also a handful more in orbit. Looks like the interdiction group wants to play; they've lit off their motors and are headed in our direction."

"Very well," Drizz said. "Let's see about evening the odds." The enemy fleet moved toward them in three lines of eight stacked on top of each other. The six warships were together, with six merchants to the left and twelve to the right of the suspected command group. "Tell *Chimera* to launch their attack drones. Concentrate them on the three combatants to the right and the merchants alongside them. Our formation will split their formation between the left group of warships and the merchants to the left of them. *Omaha* and *Nuckelavee* will concentrate on the warships; tell the Sumatozou to take the merchants as we pass."

"I don't have comms with the enemy fleet," the Buma comms officer reported. "They've ignored all my hails."

"I think their intentions are pretty clear," Drizz said with a growl. "Our response will be equally clear to them."

The drones launched from *Chimera*, formed up, and arrowed toward the small gap between the warships and the merchant ships on the right of them. The Hussars and Sumatozou made another arrowhead toward the gap between the warships and the merchants to the left. Drizz nodded appreciatively. Whoever was in charge of the enemy fleet had good control of it; they held formation as their doom charged at them.

* * *

SMS *Pride of Sumas*, Kullawee Emergence Area

"Just take the six merchants as we pass? Right," Captain Scoltac, the CO of the *Pride of Sumas,* muttered as he shook his head. The older Sumatozou always found a way to make things as pessimistic as possible. "It's not like we're outnumbered three to one."

"But they're all merchant ships," Fragontic noted. "They're barely armed."

"They may have started out that way," Scoltac said, "but who's to say they're *still* equipped that way?"

"I'm receiving missile targeting signals from one of the merchants."

"See?" Scoltac asked. "Just like I said. Q-ship. A warship made to look like a merchant."

"What do we do?" the weapons officer asked.

"We kill that one first. Contact the *Gatekeeper*. Let them know both our first volleys will be targeted on that ship. After that, he'll stay on it until it's out of action, and we'll work on eliminating the other ships."

* * *

CIC, EMS *Nuckelavee,* Kullawee Emergence Area

"This is going to be overkill," TacCom said as the defensive missiles arced out toward the 150 drones racing toward their formation. "We might have wanted to spread them out a little more."

"I want to let them know what they're facing if they continue to challenge us," Drizz noted. "Perhaps by overkilling the first group, the SI—or whoever is in charge of this group—will see that resistance is pointless, and will surrender before we have to waste any more of our missiles on their ships."

"Maybe," TacCom said, although he didn't sound convinced.

Around 200 anti-missile missiles launched from the enemy fleet, but the drones were much nimbler than the missiles they were developed to defeat. Although a handful of drones were destroyed by the missiles and the fleet's defensive lasers before they reached launch range, the overwhelming majority were not, and just under 130 missiles made it into the black. More of these were intercepted than the drones, but almost 100 of the "squash-bomb" missiles made it into the fleet.

Explosions flared across the ranks of the targeted ships as the remaining drones pulled away from the enemy fleet and returned to the *Chimera.*

"The two frigates have been destroyed," TacCom said. "There isn't much left of either. The cruiser did a little better. It's damaged, but still maintaining formation. There's nothing left of the merchant ships targeted. The remaining enemy ships are launching missiles."

"Very well," Drizz replied. "All fleet to begin firing. Charge the spinal mount and target the battlecruiser. Have the *Omaha* target the cruiser the drones damaged. Confirm deflectors are at full power?"

"Confirmed," TacCom replied. "Missiles launching across the fleet."

As the Hussars and Sumatozou's missiles dashed into the black, the *Nuckelavee's* petal-like bow doors opened, exposing its spinal mount, and the lights dimmed slightly as a 40-terawatt pulse of high-energy particles ripped outward at the speed of light. Lacking Ghost's guidance, the beam wasn't quite as accurate as when the *Pegasus* was around, but Drizz had trained his crew hard, and the shot landed across the back third of the enemy battlecruiser, ripping through it obliquely. A number of secondary explosions ensued, followed by a massive explosion as one of the battlecruiser's fusion plants detonated.

Omaha's shot landed a few seconds later. The Winged Hussars' *Crown*-class cruisers were purposely built around a one-terawatt spinal-mounted particle accelerator, and the beam penetrated from nearly bow to stern, gutting the damaged cruiser. It didn't detonate as explosively, but it was a kill, nonetheless.

Before they could fire again, the enemy missiles came in range, and were met by a flurry of anti-missile missiles and lasers. Only one missile made it through the defensive network, and it detonated impotently on the *Gatekeeper's* shields.

The *Nuckelavee* and the *Omaha* fired again, and the fleet's missiles arrived at the enemy formation. Suddenly, the enemy formation was down to a single warship, with several of the merchants on the left side of the formation heavily damaged by the Sumatozou missiles.

The enemy formation lost cohesion and then exploded outward, with ships going in every direction.

"I've got...I don't know what I've got," the sensor tech confessed. "They're going everywhere, and I don't have a clue what they're trying to do!"

"Focus on the ones still coming toward us, TacCom," Drizz said. "I don't know what they're doing, either, but keep putting weapons on the ones headed toward us."

The second round of missiles from the enemy fleet was neither as large nor as coordinated as the first, and it was easily dealt with. The *Nuckelavee* and the *Omaha* fired again, destroying two merchant ships heading toward them as the allied fleet's missiles ravaged several others.

Drizz shook his head as he watched the battle develop in the Tri-V. It made no sense for the enemy fleet to lose its cohesion so thoroughly. As one, though, the ships began maneuvering again, and their intention became easily—and horrifically—obvious as the ships all pointed their bows at the *Nuckelavee*, and their fusion torches flared at maximum power.

"Signal to all ships," Drizz ordered. "Scatter! They're trying to ram us!"

* * * * *

Chapter Twenty-Five

CIC, EMS *Gobi Desert*, Kullawee Emergence Area

"Stand by for emergence," the helmsman said as he inserted the chip in the ship's navigation computer.

"Very well," said the ship's commanding officer, Captain Steve Parker. "The Winged Hussars and the Sumatozou should have arrived about 15 minutes ago. Let's hope they cleared the emergence area," he added. "If there really are 40 ships in the SI's fleet…"

"You can count on the Winged Hussars," Sansar replied.

"Still, 40 ships versus 5…"

"The Hussars have five purpose-built warships in the task fleet. Most of the ones the SI has are former merchants."

"Most, not all."

Sansar had to concede the point and nodded slightly. "They'll be fine." *Blue Sky, at least I hope they will!*

"Emergence," the helmsman noted.

Sansar screamed as every cell in her body was ripped apart, spread to the ends of the universe, and then remade in one spot. She staggered. "Blue Sky!" she exclaimed, grabbing onto a railing to steady herself. "Are we still alive?"

"I…think so." Parker coughed. "That was…worst thing ever." He shook his head, obviously trying to get rid of the feeling. "Next time you get me a shortcut…no thanks."

Sansar shook her head. "No more shortcuts."

"Good," Parker said. He turned to the sensor tech. "Get me a picture, soonest."

"Yes, sir," the sensor tech replied, shaking his arms and rolling his head around on his neck. "Working on it...*what the heck?*"

"What have you got?"

"Giant furball, sir. Looks like the Hussars and Sumatozou are pretending their cruisers are fighters, and they're trying to dogfight the enemy fleet...I can't tell what they're trying to do. On Tri-V...now."

The Tri-V lit up to show the battle, and Sansar understood the tech's confusion. Even displaying the greatest detail possible, the ships were all closely intermingled as they dodged and writhed.

Parker pursed his lips. "Looks like the enemy fleet is trying to ram our ships, and they're doing everything they can to shoot their way out of the snakes' nest."

"Blue Sky! Why would they do that?" Sansar asked.

Parker shrugged. "Their ships weren't armed well? Hard to know."

Then Sansar saw it, and she pointed. "Right there! One's trying to get away!"

"Yep," Parker said with a nod. "They could be doing that, too." He watched for a second, then shook his head. "That one's running for the stargate. As hard as its going, the Hussars won't be able to catch him."

"It's Mercurius," Sansar muttered, "and he's trying to get away." Louder, she asked, "Can we cut him off?"

"Maybe," Parker allowed. "We've got an angle on him, but he's making at least 12 Gs. We may get a shot at him."

"Do it!" Sansar exclaimed. "Do whatever it takes. We can't let him get away!"

"Yes, ma'am," Parker replied. He pushed a button, and a red light began flashing. "You're going to want to get into your acceleration couch, ma'am," Parker said. "This is going to *hurt*."

* * *

CIC, EMS *Nuckelavee*, Kullawee Emergence Area

"Hard to starboard!" TacCom shouted. "Port batteries, fire!"

Nuckelavee's 10-gigawatt lasers fired, raking across the smaller merchant like a giant claw, and opened up the majority of its portside compartments to space. At that range, there was little time for dispersion, and the full-power beams cut all the way through the lighter shielding of the merchantman.

"Next target, right three o'clock!" TacCom called. "Hard to port!"

"*Gobi Desert* is here," the sensor tech called. "Damn—she's chasing off somewhere. Must not want to play in this furball. Can't really blame them."

Drizz glanced at the Tri-V where a new blue icon had just appeared. Although the transport didn't have the raw power of a combat warship, it was putting everything into getting out of the way of the battle. *Why, though? The battle's moving away from them—they wouldn't have to flee...*

A low growl ripped from his throat as he saw what the transport was trying to do. "We let one escape," he said, growling again. "Disengage and go after that damned frigate." The one remaining warship had fled, and the merchant ramming attack had been nothing but a distraction…*which I fell for! Not that trying to avoid being rammed isn't a good excuse…but I put my high value unit—the transport with the Golden Horde aboard—in a position where they had to go after the enemy frigate that was sure to have Mercurius aboard.* If the enemy had one ship remaining the *Gobi Desert* couldn't defeat, it was the frigate.

He changed the scale the Tri-V was showing and shook his head. The frigate was racing for the stargate, and the fleet at the gate was now racing back toward it. Not only would the *Gobi Desert* have to fight the frigate, but also the other fleet of 25 merchants. "Call the rest of the fleet—tell them to form up on us…if they can catch us."

* * *

SMS *Pride of Sumas*, Kullawee Emergence Area

"The Hussars are breaking off," the comms officer announced as the *Pride of Sumas* dodged yet another—barely—of the merchantmen trying their darnedest to ram them.

"Put two more missiles into that one," Captain Scoltac ordered before turning to the comms officer. "Did they say where they were going?"

"Yes, sir. The *Gobi Desert* arrived and is chasing down the one ship—a frigate—that got away and is going 12 Gs toward the stargate. They believe it is Mercurius trying to flee. The *Gobi Desert* is trying to head them off, but a transport fighting a frigate…"

"Isn't going to last very long," Scoltac said with a nod. "All weapons on the merchantman to our starboard."

"The Humans saved me once when we were fighting Minerva," Fragontic noted. "I would like it if we could repay the favor."

"I'm working on it," Scoltac said with a grunt. He pointed at the enemy's icon in the Tri-V. "That one is in our way. If we can hit him a couple times, we can sneak out past him."

"Shouldn't be a problem, then," Fragontic replied. He'd seen Scoltac fight the *Pride of Sumas* a number of times and knew the merchant craft wasn't a threat to the more-heavily armed and armored cruiser, despite Scoltac's earlier grumpiness. Once the captain was in his element, he was a tremendous combat officer.

The merchant ship—a small freighter—came apart under the merc cruiser's missiles and lasers.

"Helm, hard to port. Set course for the frigate the *Nuckelavee* is chasing. If it's possible to stop him, we will not let him get away."

"Captain Scoltac, Captain Drizz just said to catch up with them if we can."

"What?" Scoltac exclaimed, and Fragontic turned to hide his smile. "Catch them if we can?" the captain asked. He harrumphed. "As if those weak-limbed carnivores could keep up with *us!*" He glanced at the Tri-V. "How fast are they going?"

"Six Gs, sir."

Scoltac's answer wiped the smile from Fragontic's face. "Give me seven."

* * *

CIC, EMS *Gobi Desert*, Kullawee System

"The *Nuckelavee* and the other ships have disengaged and are coming toward us as fast as they can," the sensor operator said.

"Good," Parker said with a grunt to help offset the four Gs squeezing him into his seat. "Won't help us, though."

"Why?" Sansar asked. "Not?"

"Too far…away. Won't…get here…in time."

"Then…we must…stop them."

"I know."

"Sir!" the sensor operator called.

"I see…them," Parker said.

"What?" Sansar asked.

"The fleet…at the stargate…just left. Heading…toward us…now."

"How…many?"

"Twenty…five."

"Can we…fight them?"

"No."

* * *

CIC, EMS *Nuckelavee*, Kullawee System

Drizz twisted his head to look at the Tri-V. Surprisingly, the Sumatozou were hanging on with *Nuckelavee* on its six-G advance. If anything, they were pulling forward of the *Nuckelavee* now! He wouldn't have expected the massive elephants to be able to take more Gs than the Hussars' ships, but there they were, doing it! The Sumatozou apparently had a more robust frame under all that padding than he'd given them credit for.

It wouldn't matter if the *Gobi Desert* wasn't able to slow Mercurius' ship, though. Neither the Hussars nor the Sumatozou were able to pull 12 Gs. Their ships might have been able to—certainly the *Nuckelavee* had the power to generate that kind of acceleration, anyway—but the crews would all be dead at the end of the race. He'd probably have some medical casualties just from the extended six-G chase.

Of course, *if* the *Gobi Desert* somehow found a way to slow Mercurius' ship—and that was a big *if*—Sansar and company would be overwhelmed pretty quickly by the mass of merchant shipping racing toward them from the stargate.

Alexis had been very clear about it, though, and Sansar had reinforced her orders: the death of Mercurius was first and foremost the goal. Sansar's survival, faced with Mercurius getting away, was a distant second in priority. Alexis hadn't come right out and said, "Kill the SI or don't come back," but the implication hadn't been far from her voice. He would kill the SI...and hopefully find a way to protect the *Gobi Desert*, but he was going to kill that frigate if he somehow got close enough to do so.

No matter what happened, the people on the planet below were going to have a lot of shooting stars in the coming days—the race to the stargate was going to put the final battle just outside the planet's atmosphere.

* * *

CIC, EMS *Gobi Desert*, Kullawee System

"Give me one G," Parker said as the frigate reached its minimum range. It was still a long shot, but within the transport's limited missile system's range. "Fire all missiles at the frigate, then keep firing as quickly as they can be reloaded. Keep firing until either it—or we—are destroyed."

"But, Captain?" the weapons officer said as the Gs dropped off. "What about the—"

"*I don't give a starburst about the merchants coming at us!*" Parker roared. "If we don't stop that SI, all of this is for naught!"

"Aye, aye," the weapons officer replied. "Firing all missiles at the frigate." He pushed a button on his console, and weapons launched into the black.

Sansar took a minute to pick up the Hunter Killer Box she'd been given by Alexis' Geek Squad technician. The simple slate display on the side came alive at her touch and showed her the device's power status—full—and an activation button. She pressed it, wondering if the fragile technology inside the box had withstood the high-G chase.

She didn't have to wait long as the blinking text "SCANNING" changed quickly to "Synthetic Intelligence Located." It also gave a range and bearing correlating to the frigate, which was now in a skew turn toward the *Gobi Desert*.

"That's our target," Sansar said. "The SI is aboard that frigate. Call the *Nuckelavee* and let them know." She didn't say *in case we don't survive this*, but she figured—as missiles launched from the frigate—everyone would understand what she meant.

* * * * *

Chapter Twenty-Six

CIC, EMS *Gobi Desert*, Kullawee System

"That's a hit!" the weapons officer shouted. "And another!"

"Less yelling," Captain Parker admonished, "more focus."

"But we got the SI!" the weapons officer exclaimed.

"Yes, and now it's launching missiles at us, and there are 25 merchant ships bearing down on us. I'd like it very much if you'd do something about those things, too."

"Oh…yeah."

"Stopping the SI was just the first step. Extricating ourselves from this mess is the second."

"Ten missiles?" Sansar asked. "Can we stop them?"

"The *Desert's* anti-missile systems got a lot of practice in the Spine Nebula. They're good, but we won't hold off the frigate for long. It's a warship…and we're not."

"So what do we do?"

"If I had internal shunts like the Hussars, I'd jump the heck out of here," Parker said.

Sansar smiled. "I'll see about getting you some for next time. You just have to get us out of this one first."

Parker stared at the Tri-V for a long moment, then he took a deep breath and blew it out. "Okay," he said. "I'm going to hold you to that." He hit the button for the high-G alarm again and turned toward the helmsman. "Head for the stargate. Maximum accelera-tion," Parker ordered as he reclined his acceleration couch.

"But, sir—" the weapons officer started.

"The merchants. I know." He smiled as the Gs piled on. "Helmsman, aim for the big fat one in the center of the formation."

* * *

CIC, EMS *Nuckelavee,* Kullawee System

Drizz smiled a hunter's smile as the SI's ship turned into the *Gobi Desert's* missiles. Mercurius obviously hadn't been in any space battles in a long time—if ever. The missiles had been launched from extremely long range, and if the SI had just kept going, he'd probably have outrun them. By turning to honor the threat, though, he actually *made* the missiles a threat. Then, by continuing toward the *Gobi Desert* long enough to launch missiles of his own, he was allowing the *Nuckelavee* a chance to catch up.

Amateur. If you're going to run, run!

"Missile hit!" TacCom called. "Looks like the *Gobi Desert* hit the frigate with two, maybe three missiles. It's down to about three Gs."

Drizz' smile broadened. If that was the best the SI could get out of the frigate, they'd catch it before the stargate. The Horde ship was probably a loss, but he would toast their sacrifice after he destroyed the SI in their honor.

"The *Gobi Desert* just went to max accel," the sensor tech said.

Drizz glanced back to the Tri-V. He'd been so focused on the SI that he'd stopped watching the oncoming merchant fleet. The still-harsh Gs he was enduring didn't stop him from nodding slightly. Unlike Mercurius, the *Gobi Desert's* captain was obviously no neophyte to space warfare. Perhaps there would be an opportunity to toast Captain Parker in person.

* * *

CIC, EMS *Gobi Desert*, Kullawee System

Parker did his best to slow his breathing while still focusing enough oxygen in his blood to keep himself from passing out. *The key to playing chicken is knowing when to blink.*

Now!

"Helm, hard right!" he ordered. He paused a second. "Helm, hard left, slow to one G!" It was like a fighter dropping chaff—give the missile something to look at other than your craft. In this case, he'd superimposed the F11 tanker between the missiles tracking the *Gobi Desert* and the ship itself. He hoped. "Weapons officer, stop any missiles that get past the tanker."

There was an agonizing several seconds as the missiles reached the tanker, then the Tri-V flared and went to black momentarily as the tanker detonated. When the picture cleared, there was nothing remaining of the ship and five of the missiles. The other five, now devoid of a target, went looking for new targets, and three homed in on the *Desert*.

That worked too well. Note to self: never use an F11 tanker as a decoy. "Weapons officer, you're up!"

"Got 'em," the weapons officer said. Anti-missile missiles leapt from the *Gobi Desert* and anti-missile lasers fired, eliminating one...then a second of the missiles. Captain Parker slapped the collision alarm half a second before the missile impacted on the *Gobi Desert's* shields.

* * *

CIC, EMS *Nuckelavee,* Kullawee System

"Now what are they doing?" TacCom asked as the merchant fleet began a simultaneous slew turn away from the approaching Hussars and Sumatozou ships.

"Probably trying to cover for the SI as it escapes," Drizz said as he watched the SI's frigate turn back toward the stargate. It didn't take long to see that was indeed what they were doing as the merchant ships cut in front of the allied fleet.

"If we have to shoot them out of the way, we will do so," Drizz said. "As they come in range, fire!"

Missiles leapt forward from the four allied ships, and the merchant fleet took hits. After the first volley, six ships had dropped out of the formation. Counting the tanker the *Gobi Desert* had used as bait and another ship that had been hit by the frigate, only 17 ships remained. After the second wave of missiles, they were down to seven. As Drizz started to call for another round of missiles, the merchant fleet—accelerating at 12 Gs—split and drove past the frigate that was limited to three Gs.

With the merchants out of the way, the frigate was within range of the *Nuckelavee's* spinal mount. "Main gun, charge and fire!" Drizz ordered.

The bow doors peeled back, the weapon charged, and the particle accelerator fired, destroying the frigate.

"Helm, slow to one G, please," Drizz called. He took a deep breath as the Gs fell off. "Move in close, and let's hit it again," he added. "I want to make sure we kill the SI."

* * *

CIC, EMS *Gobi Desert,* Kullawee System

"They got the frigate," the weapons officer noted.

"Good," Parker said. "Let's concentrate on damage control, then." Although the shields had stopped the main blast of the final missile, the explosion had opened several spaces to the black and knocked out a number of systems. He turned to Sansar. "Are you going to want to take a dropship over and confirm its destruction?"

"I don't think I need to," she said with a shrug. She picked up the Hunter Killer Box. "This ought to be able to confirm whether we need to do anything to finish it off." She pushed the button to energize the box.

"That's funny," she muttered as the results were presented. She shook her head and re-ran the scan. "That can't be...*Blue Sky!*"

"What's wrong?" Parker asked.

"The SI isn't on the frigate. When the merchant ships passed it, it must have jumped to one of them. Get on the comms and warn Captain Drizz—the SI is escaping!"

* * *

CIC, EMS *Nuckelavee,* Kullawee System

Drizz growled. "Can you tell me which one it's on?" he asked as the Gs piled on again. They'd managed another round of missiles before the merchant fleet made it out of range, and there were seven freighters still racing toward the stargate. Unfortunately, the enemy had made it out of missile range, and they were getting even farther ahead, despite the allied fleet's attempt to catch up. The *Chimera's* drones would have been able to run them down...if the ship hadn't been left behind in the high-G chase.

Amazing what you can do when you don't have to worry about a crew.

"Sorry, no," Sansar's voice said over the comms. "We're too far away to get an accurate reading. All I can tell you is it's on one of the ships heading for the stargate, not any of the ones you've hit so far."

Drizz didn't reply; instead, he focused on his breathing and staying conscious. After all the high-G travel in the chase, he was wearing out. He suspected some of the Humans were in worse shape, and he would have loved to slow down and allow them to catch their breaths, but they absolutely could *not* allow the SI to get away. It would have to slow as it approached the gate, both to make gate passage and to turn it on in the first place, and he hoped they'd get a shot at the SI when it did.

So he endured the punishing Gs, forcing in the next breath, and the next. Out of the corner of his eye, he could see the sensor officer go slack as he passed out. The Human had a rash across his skin—the so-called "G-measles" Humans got during high-G maneuvering when their capillaries popped. At least he didn't have to endure that.

When the merchant fleet began moving in the Tri-V, it took a second for his oxygen-starved brain to notice and process its meaning—*the merchant fleet has slowed, and the allied fleet was catching up with them!*

As much as he wanted to drop the acceleration, he had to keep it on until they were within missile range; he couldn't spare a single second! His vision grayed on the edges, and he forced additional oxygen into his lungs, driving it back. The "missile range" line was getting closer...and closer...but the merchants were getting ever closer to the stargate.

They reached the "in range" line on the Tri-V, and he paused a second to make sure they were truly in range. "Slow to one G! All missiles, fire!" The Gs dropped off, but no missiles fired. "TacCom! Fire!" He looked over to the TacCom position; the Human was blinking and shaking off the effects of the Gs. "Fire!" he yelled again.

The TacCom reached forward and slapped the FIRE button, and the missiles launched.

Drizz glanced at the Tri-V. Missiles were already outbound from the *Omaha* and *Gatekeeper*, and just starting to launch from the *Pride of Sumas*. On the long-range viewer, the stargate was coming into view; it was already operational and ready for ship passage!

Missiles poured into the formation of merchant shipping, but six of the freighters had dropped back, providing a screen for the seventh. The ships were just coming into range for the spinal mount—at an extreme range, although still "in range"—but they needed line-of-sight on the target. "Up!" he yelled to the helmsman. "We need to go up above the plane of the ecliptic!"

The ship began climbing relative to the merchant fleet, and he could see the last merchant ship making its run on the stargate. They were out of time; there wasn't enough for missiles to cross the distance. "Charge the spinal mount! Match bearings and fire!" he ordered.

The massive ship pivoted to line up on the target, seemingly in slow motion, as the bow doors opened once more, and the lighting dimmed. The weapon fired, and the 40-terrawatt particle beam raced across the intervening space at the speed of light. It speared through the engineering section, shearing off the starboard motor, and the off-balance thrust pushed the ship off its path to the stargate. It drove past the stargate to the right of it.

"Signal the other ships to finish off all the merchants," Drizz said, "and keep firing until nothing's left."

The previously fired missiles impacted the screening fleet, destroying most of them, but a single ship moved forward out of the group, making a run for the stargate. Due to the geometry of the ships, though, it was screened from the *Nuckelavee*—they didn't have a shot at stopping this one.

"Charge the spinal mount!" Drizz ordered. *Maybe we can drill the beam through the intervening wreckage? Perhaps there's still a chance we can kill it…we have to try!*

A beam flashed from below the plane of the ecliptic as the *Omaha* fired its spinal mount. Although not as powerful as the *Nuckelavee's*, the *Omaha* was closer now, and the beam speared through the thin-skinned ship, cutting it in half.

Another round of missiles arrived, turning all the ships in the vicinity of the stargate into scrap. *Is it possible? Have we won?*

* * * * *

Chapter Twenty-Seven

CIC, EMS *Gobi Desert*, Kullawee System

"*P*lease *confirm we've killed the SI,*" Drizz' voice requested over the comm.

Sansar took a deep breath and pushed the button on the box. If she could have crossed her fingers while holding the box, she would have. The scan completed. "No SIs detected."

She smiled and turned the box to where Captain Parker could see. He pumped his fist. "First good bit of news I've had in a while," he said with a smile.

"Captain Drizz, I'm happy to inform you that your actions were successful. I'm not showing any indications of an SI in the system."

"*That's great to hear,*" Drizz replied. "*We're going to take some time to ensure everything is destroyed here. We also have a good number of medical casualties from the high-G run who must be seen to before we can return to assist you.*"

"That's fine," Sansar replied. "We don't have any repairs here that we can't manage. Please pass on a 'Well Done' to all your crews."

"*I will,*" Drizz replied.

"*I hate to break up your congratulatory party and all,*" a new voice said over the comm. Sansar recognized it as Taylor Van Zant's. "*You may not have an SI up there anymore, but we've still got one down here to deal with.*"

"What in Blue Skies?" Sansar muttered, picking up the box. She ran the scan again, but got a different answer: One SI detected. The range and bearing pointed toward the planet. Sansar shook her head.

"Don't tell me it jumped to the planet," Parker said.

"It shouldn't have been able to jump to the planet," Sansar explained. "It shouldn't! *It can't!* It's too far!"

"And yet, it did?"

Sansar shrugged. "I don't know. Maybe there's a second copy of it that was lying dormant but triggered when we killed the active one. *Blue Sky!* I don't know where it came from, or how, but I know it wasn't there a few seconds ago, *and now it is.*"

"So what's the plan?"

"The plan is the same as it's been all along. I take my folks down there and kill the bloody thing." She selected the comms. "Van Zant, we now have indications that there is indeed an SI active on the planet. We're on our way down."

* * *

CIC, EMS *Tyndall,* Kullawee Starport, Kullawee

"I sure am glad they believe me," Taylor said, looking at the viewer, "because that crowd looks pretty fargin pissed off, and the way they're moving makes it look like someone—or some*thing*—is drivin' them." On the screen, a mass of people surrounded the *Tyndall* on the tarmac around them. They *did* look angry, but they weren't doing anything destructive. Not yet, anyway. They hadn't done much of anything, in fact, except stand around, swaying gently. The air at the starport was still, but all of the people swayed in response to some impetus only they could feel.

"This whole display is creepy," Kami asked. "What do you think they want?"

Taylor shrugged. "Two things, if I had to guess. First, to let me know Mercurius isn't dead, and he still expects an answer from me. Second, that group is insurance that we won't just go blastin' out of here without his permission."

"He doesn't know me very well," Kami said. "I've got no problem frying a bunch of foxes."

"No, but he *does* know me, and he knows I would never let you do that."

"My ship, my rules," Kami said petulantly.

Taylor gave her a half smile and raised an eyebrow.

"Okay," she said with a sigh after a moment. "I probably wouldn't roast 'em all, not without a pretty good reason. The defense of my ship, though, is a pretty good reason."

"Which is why they ain't doin' anything hostile like shooting at us. They're just standin' around, making sure we don't go wanderin' off."

"How long you suppose that's gonna last?"

"Mercurius said I had until sundown to make my decision. I suspect sometime around sundown he'll be along to find out my decision."

"When do you suppose the Horde will be here?"

"In an hour or two, but well before sundown. They had some damage to the ship they were repairing, and the Sumatozou were out of position, chasin' down the first version of Mercurius. They'll probably take a little longer to get here."

"I don't know that you're going to get all the time you're hoping for," Yosiff said. He pointed at a commotion moving through the crowd. "I think your answer is about to be required now."

Taylor watched as a Kullawee citizen walked through the mass outside the ship. As he passed through the group, those in front of him moved aside to allow his passage, then filled back in again once he passed. He crossed through the group and stopped in front of the ship's ramp.

"Guess I better go see what he wants," Taylor said. He turned to Frank. "You might want to call the Horde and tell them they're gonna need to hurry. Whatever's goin' down is fixin' to go down soon."

Taylor, accompanied by Kami and Winfield, walked down to the ramp to find the native still waiting for them.

"The reports of your demise are greatly exaggerated, I see," Taylor noted.

"Foolish Human. Why do you think I'd be stupid enough to only have one incarnation of myself?" The native shrugged. "When you are as long-lived as I, you learn to create certain…backup plans in case everything goes wrong." He made a motion toward the crowd. "Sometimes the minions surprise even me with their creativity, necessitating extreme measures."

"You'd kill off all those people to save your life."

"Of course. Their loss is an eye blink in the cosmic scheme of things."

"See, that's where you and I are gonna have to disagree. I wouldn't just kill them out of hand."

"You wouldn't kill them if your life, or the lives of those you hold dear, were at stake?"

"I might, if the situation required it, but I certainly wouldn't want to, nor would I do it with such a complete lack of remorse."

"Touching, but untrue. If you thought you could strike me down, right now, with no loss of life to the Kullawee around us, you would."

"Maybe. You do have us in a certain sense of jeopardy, plus what you're doin' to Billy."

"Ah, but you came here to kill me when I wasn't doing anything to you."

"The price you put on our head is a little more than nothing."

M waved the comment away. "I never expected anyone to collect on it; you're too good for that. The bounty was nothing more than a way to get your attention so we could talk."

"You could have just sent me a personal message."

M cocked his head and sighed. "This conversation is beginning to bore me. What is your answer to my proposal?"

Taylor looked up at the sky. "I thought I had until sundown to decide."

"Events have occurred that have accelerated my timetable. Your decision is required now."

Taylor looked up again.

"If you're looking for your friends, they won't be coming to save you. I want your answer. Now."

Motion from the side caught Taylor's eye, and his head snapped over to find a formation of dropships, which raced across the starport and startown without stopping, spewing some sort of gas from under their wings.

Within seconds, the Kullawee began dropping.

"I'll take that to mean your answer is no," Mercurius said. "You make me sad, but so be it." The light went out of the Kullawee's eyes, then the foxlike being crumpled to the tarmac with the rest of the Kullawee.

Kami's eyes swept the starport. "We could clear the area and then blast out of here, never to be seen again?"

Taylor shook his head. "I think I've made this personal between us. It's time to finish it, or we'll be lookin' behind us the rest of our lives." He shrugged. "We ain't gonna get any closer than we are right now."

One of the dropships returned and landed beyond the piles of Kullawee. After a few moments, the ramp came down in the back, and a squad of CASPers jogged out to set up a perimeter around the craft. A single CASPer made its way to where the bodies started and waved to them. "I'd have to say the first use of the Kullawee knock-out gas is an operational success," Sansar said over her speakers.

Additional dropships flew in to land behind her, a *lot* of dropships, and CASPers and Sumatozou raced out of their cargo bays and began clearing off the Kullawee so Sansar could approach the *Tyndall*.

"Ready to kill an SI?" Sansar asked.

"Just like that?" Taylor asked. "Just load up and drop on the SI's mansion?"

"Sadly, no," Sansar said. "As we were coming in, Mercurius activated the defenses at his estate. He has quite a number of anti-aircraft and anti-personnel defenses that were buried behind flowers and shrubbery. We'll have to go in on the ground; if we try to fly in, all we'll do is lose dropships and people unnecessarily."

Taylor cocked his head. "You sure do have a lot of intel for somebody who just showed up on scene, even by Horde standards."

"That's because Colonel Enkh here hangs out at the cool kid's table," a familiar voice said in a gruff Oklahoma drawl.

It can't be. Taylor turned to see none other than former Eagles' company commander Jack Bowyer step up to Sansar's side. "What in the crazy blue blazes of hell are you doin' here, old man? I thought you were back home in Stillwater?"

"I was up until about two months ago," Jack said. "That's when a member of Section 51 caught up with me and told me what was goin' down with Mercurius. I had some contacts from back in the day with another outfit, and they thought I could help. The only catch was, neither you nor anybody else on the Eagles' roster could know about it." He glanced around the crowed. "Speakin' of, where's Major Dawson?"

Taylor returned his focus to Sansar. "He's with Mercurius."

"What?" Jack exclaimed.

Taylor filled the others in on the events from the pirate ship. "Mercurius may try to use Billy as a distraction to throw us off balance. If that happens, do what you have to, but please don't kill him if at all possible."

"That may be difficult," Sansar said. "The knockout gas only works on the Kullawee. It was specifically engineered *not* to work on Humans. We've got plenty of the gas, but that's it for non-lethals."

"Well, I'll try to figure something out," Taylor said. "All I ask is that you *try* not to kill him if possible."

"Fine," Sansar said. "We'll try, although I won't lose people to him if it comes to that."

"Understood," Taylor replied.

"So, do you have a plan for attacking his estate?"

"I do," Taylor said with a nod. "It's based on an attack Billy told me about from his younger days."

Kami cleared her throat. "But I thought—"

"That he knows everything Billy knows, and he'll see us coming?"

Kami nodded.

"Not this time," Taylor said. "He'll never see us coming." He smiled at Sansar. "Just let us get our stuff."

* * * * *

Chapter Twenty-Eight

Cargo Bay, Dropship *One*, Five Kilometers East of Ravenrok Manor, Kullawee

The dropship set down with the ramp already open, and Taylor, O'Bannon, and Lajoie rushed down the ramp in their CASPers before it came to a complete stop. "You're sure about this?" Sansar asked from the back of the craft.

Taylor nodded, although he knew she couldn't see it. "Yep. Go focus his attention somewhere else."

Without another word, the ramp started back up, and the craft lifted, although it stayed below the low hills of the area.

"The seals are going to hold?" O'Bannon asked.

"CASPers are rated for space," Taylor said. "A little water ain't gonna hurt them."

"If you say so, sir."

"Don't be a baby," Taylor replied, walking to the edge of the river. "Here. I'll go first."

* * *

Confinement Area, Ravenrok Manor, Kullawee

Billy sat huddled alone in the corner of his cell, still grappling within himself to get past the horrors of the last several hours. It had begun on the pirate ship, when Mercurius had seized control of Billy's mind, then continued on the *Tyndall* when the SI had turned Billy's sidearm on the others.

257

Never in his life had Billy screamed so hard to get someone's attention, but it was no use. His mouth wouldn't respond. Nor, for that matter, would his hands, which rattled off shot after shot at several of his troopers, wounding one and sending at least two more to the infirmary with what could've been fatal injuries for all Billy knew. Then, as if things couldn't have gotten worse, Mercurius had returned to Billy's cell after his meeting with Taylor and used Billy to slaughter a batch of cogs who'd refused to join the SI's cause.

"Why?" Billy had begged. "Why are you doing this?"

"Because, Major Dawson, I want you to know just how serious I truly am," M had said, laughing over their corpses.

Billy buried his face in his hands and fought to stifle the tears that threatened to come. *Please, dear God in Heaven. Please don't let that monster take me again.*

Sounds of a door lock rustling open came from the shadows. A moment later, Mercurius entered the cell area along with two Kullawee, and Billy rolled off his bunk to see what they were doing. The foxes set up a portable Tri-V, then left.

Mercurius smiled. "I thought it would be instructional for you to watch the demise of your friends."

"Instructional, how?" Billy asked, steeling his voice to hide his earlier emotions.

"I haven't decided how I intend to use you afterward, but I want you to see that any resistance to my plans is wasted effort."

"Resistance is futile? Something like that?"

Mercurius tapped his forehead. "I get that reference, and yes, that's exactly correct."

"What exactly am I supposed to be looking at?" Billy asked.

"You will be looking shortly at a bunch of fools as they try to assault this castle. It appears the Sumatozou, the Emerald Stormriders, and Winfield Defense have been given the unenviable task of performing the frontal attack, while the Golden Horde and your very own Eagles try to sneak in from behind."

"Not much of a sneak attack if you already know about it."

"I don't *know* it for sure, but I certainly suspect it."

Billy cocked his head. "Why's that?"

"Because this attack is very reminiscent of the attack you ran in your youth, when you seized the GenSha pirate's castle."

"I don't see the correlation," Billy said. "It was a frontal assault."

"True...but you used it as a teaching point with Taylor on a number of occasions. 'Never go with just a frontal assault when you can also throw in some misdirection.' That's what you taught him."

"Yeah, the pirate raid didn't go as planned. He had a lot more defensive installations than we thought. The frontal assault failed until we snuck some troops in behind the castle. They got in, opening the way for the rest of us."

"Exactly," M said. "Unfortunately, my spies at the starport are unresponsive at the moment, so I didn't get a look at their disposition, but I'm willing to bet they'll send the majority of their forces in a frontal assault, while performing a second assault from the rear. Your Taylor would know to do such, and even if he didn't, Sansar has enough knowledge of defenses to suggest it to him if he's forgotten. That information is in his head; he's sure to act upon it."

Billy shook his head. "Not gonna happen. He'll know you know, and he'll do something else."

"Like what?"

"No clue. That's Taylor's strength, though—making things up as he goes."

The Tri-V switched to a view from the front of the castle. Sumatozou could be seen moving up, flanked by CASPers on both sides. "As expected, here's the 'main force,' which we know is nothing more than show."

"You don't think the Sumatozou would kill you if given a chance?"

"I'm sure they would. Alas, I have no intention of giving them that chance." M smiled. "It's time to make this interesting, don't you think?"

The coldest of chills danced like a spider down Billy's spine as he peered through the bars of his cell. *Shit.*

* * *

Five Kilometers South of Ravenrok Manor, Kullawee

"Think the SI's just going to let us walk up to the front gate?" Kami asked.

Fragontic shook his massive head. "I'm surprised he's let us get this close. When we fought the one in Morgoth, it sent all its followers, armed with whatever they had nearby. Rifles, pistols...even kitchen knives. They have a healthy desire to keep living."

"So the fact that it hasn't sent its retainers yet...?"

"Means he's going to use them for something equally nasty."

"Maybe the knockout gas got them?"

"We weren't able to deploy it here. There were too many anti-aircraft systems on his grounds; Sansar didn't want to lose the dropships."

"But losing people is okay?"

"We've got more knockout gas with us that we can use."

"Hmph."

"Movement front!" the point Sumatozou yelled.

Kami dove off the road and looked up to see the lead alien had thrown himself behind several large trees. It wasn't "cover" for all of his enormous body, but it protected some of him, and the rest was covered by some pretty heavy-looking armor. The scout was returning fire with a heavy MAC that would have been a crew-served weapon for most other races. A second Sumatozou crawled up to the scout and used its bulk as cover to fire knockout gas canisters toward the gate.

"No," Fragontic called from the other side of the road.

"No what?" Kami asked.

"No, the SI isn't going to let us walk up to the front gate."

* * *

Five Kilometers North of Ravenrok Manor, Kullawee

Distant booming sounded as MACs fired to the south. "They're playing our tune," Sansar said. She moved to the front of the formation so everyone could hear her. "Okay, everyone, it's time. The goal is to get to the manor and kill the SI, especially if it isn't wearing the body of the Eagles' XO. If it is, we may be able to get it to move to one of its other hosts with the H/K Box I have. Remember, though—this group is the decoy group. Don't take unnecessary casualties. If there's a weapon you can't defeat, go around it or keep it engaged so other groups can go around it, but I repeat: don't take needless casualties. Use knockout gas on the locals where possible, but—once again—don't take casualties you don't have to. Any questions?"

There weren't any. Sansar scanned the group one last time. Although she couldn't see the individual operators inside the suits, the CASPers' postures looked erect and ready.

"All right then," she added. "On the bounce, let's go!"

She turned and ran up the small hill they'd martialed behind, and hit her jumpjets as she reached the crest. She took a quick scan as she reached about 15 feet of altitude; the rest of the Golden Horde troopers were spread out on both sides of her, with the Eagles down to her right.

The "bounce" was a modified charge, where the trooper would take two or three steps, and then toggle their jets. Higher than about 15 feet tended to slow you down and highlight you against the sky, making you an easy target for nearly every sort of weapon—including anti-aircraft positions—and used up your jump juice too quickly. Below 15 feet, though, troopers were able to increase their speed over running alone, and the three dimensional aspect of the bounce made it harder for enemy defenders to target them, especially if they used a little lateral movement while airborne.

It also let you get a better look at what you were facing, and Sansar's jaw dropped as she reached the peak of her second jump and a line of automatic cannons appeared about two kilometers away. Automatic cannons that could track CASPers on the bounce and blow them from the sky.

"Stay down!" she yelled as she touched down again, her voice augmented over her exterior speakers. "No jumping!"

While some stayed on the ground, it was too late for others who were just going up, and the chain guns ripped away at the CASPers.

She saw several icons go red in her display, and at least a few of the Eagles crashed to the ground as well.

Sansar called a halt to assess the new threat and get medical treatment to those who could still use it. The mission had suddenly gotten a lot harder.

* * *

Confinement Area, Ravenrok Manor, Kullawee

"And, right on schedule, as soon as the front gate comes under fire, look what comes out of the foliage to the north?" Mercurius smiled as the Tri-V picture changed from a Sumatozou lobbing knockout gas to a line of CASPers bouncing forward. "Here comes Taylor," Mercurius added, "right on schedule."

"That's not Taylor," Billy said. "Those are Golden Horde troopers."

"Why, yes, so they are." The view slid down the line of oncoming troopers to ones wearing the markings of the Eagles, and centered on Taylor's CASPer at the center of the formation. "That one, however, is someone we know and love. Well, we don't both love him at the moment, as he *is* coming to try to kill me, but you get my point."

"What do you intend to do?"

Mercurius chuckled. "Why, I intend to kill him first, of course. It's nothing personal, as the saying goes...except I've determined it's *very* personal when someone's trying to kill you. This didn't have to happen like this, of course, but, as you know, Taylor is somewhat stubborn. Unfortunately, now it will be his demise."

"No—don't kill him. I'll do as you ask."

"But Billy, I don't want you; I wanted Taylor. Since I can't have him, neither can the rest of the Eagles. On the other side of the next hill is a set of automated defenses—ones your knockout gas will have no effect on. They should be getting to the defenses right about—" the CASPers exploded out of formation as some were hit and others maneuvered violently, "—now."

Mercurius chuckled again. "It probably happened too fast for your Human eyes, so let me slow it down for you." The Tri-V picture jumped, and then focused on Taylor's CASPer. A line of holes appeared on the right side of the mech, which crashed to the ground, unmoving.

"Nooooo!" Billy screamed.

"Tsk, tsk," Mercurius said. "We both knew this was destined to happen. I've been alive for tens of thousands of years. You didn't seriously think you Humans—just out of your caves—were going to come here and kill me, did you?" He shook his head. "You never had a chance. In fact, the only chance the attacking force had was to turn away. Granted, the knockout gas was a nice touch. I didn't see that coming, and if I hadn't had the automatic defenses in place, it might have made things a bit more...touch and go, as I believe you say."

The Tri-V picture switched to an entrance into a hill, from which dozens and dozens of combat-armed Kullawee were issuing forth. All were wearing gas masks. Many drove all-terrain vehicles with mounted heavy-caliber weapons. Others carried mini-rocket launchers, cut down to their size. Then more came in plain clothes, carrying an assortment of weapons. Some didn't appear to have anything more than their own claws. Hundreds, then thousands, issued forth.

"This is something that was learned in your World War Two on Earth," Mercurius said. "Germany wasn't able to defeat Russia, despite having superior weapons and technology. Eventually, when Russia threw enough men at them, they ran out of bullets. So, too, will your CASPers and the Sumatozou. I've calculated the odds, and I have more Kullawee than you have rounds. Eventually, I'll wear your people down...and then I'll destroy them."

Billy wanted to say something—anything—to refute Mercurius' claims, but as he watched more and more of the Kullawee pour from the mountainside, he was too struck by the horror of it all to make a rational sound.

* * * * *

Chapter Twenty-Nine

Two Kilometers South of Ravenrok Manor, Kullawee

"I can see the gate in front of us," Fragontic said. "We are getting close to the main entrance."

"That's great," Kami said, then she screamed as she injected herself with a nanite shot to stem the bleeding in her right arm. "I just don't know how many of us will be left to get there."

Fragontic nodded. "I hope the others are doing better than we are. If it was up to us, I'm not sure we could make it to the manor by ourselves."

"Huh! Not sure?" Winfield asked. "*I'm* not sure we can last another 15 minutes. We're not getting any closer to the gates without taking horrific casualties, and I'm not prepared to do so."

"Neither am I," Kami said. "You reach a point where it just isn't worth it."

"And I think we're at that point," Fragontic agreed. "We can't stay here, though."

Kami shook her head and winced. "No, we can't. We're going to have to withdraw. They'll cut us apart here."

"They should have had enough time by now to reach the manor," Winfield noted. "If they haven't, our distraction ain't gonna help them anymore."

A Sumatozou raced up and threw himself to the ground next to Fragontic. "Sir! There are thousands of the Kullawee coming up the road from town."

"That's gonna make disengagin' a bit more difficult," Winfield said.

"We'll just gas them," Fragontic said. "We still have a number of canisters and grenades left."

"No, sir! It's worse than that!" the Sumatozou trooper exclaimed. "The locals are all wearing gas masks. We won't be able to gas them."

Fragontic had a vision of a little girl on Morgoth running toward him waving a knife, driven by the SI, Minerva. He'd had to kill the little girl and still had nightmares of it nearly every night. "Oh, no," he said. "Not again."

* * *

Four Kilometers North of Ravenrok Manor, Kullawee

"It's not going to work," Captain Naran Enkh said. "We've pushed people both left and right as far as we can, but unless we call in something from above, we're not getting past those guns. Not without horrible losses. Give me a day or two, and I'll dig under them, but in the next four hours? It's not going to happen."

Sansar shook her head. "I knew he'd have something, but I was sure we'd be able to find a way."

"Call in an airstrike, I guess, but we're going to lose any drop-ships we send up against them."

"I don't want to do that. Not yet, anyway. We'll hold here and keep looking for a way around them. We're not leaving with the job unfinished, though. I don't want to count on anyone else killing Mercurius; I want to be here for it."

"I've got bad news," Sergeant Major Muunokhoi "Mun" Enkh said as she jogged up to the command position in her CASPer. "The Eagles just said to tell you there's a big group of Kullawee coming that are all wearing gas masks."

"How big a group? Dozens? A hundred?"

"Worse. Thousands. Maybe tens of thousands."

"Blue Sky!" Sansar said, flashing back to Morgoth. "Tell the troops to get ready to fall back. It's going to take all our weapons and ammo to cut our way through that."

* * *

Ravenrok Manor, Kullawee

Taylor extended a sensor from the river and scanned the area, then did it a second time when he didn't see anyone in the first pass. Having confirmed his results, he walked to the bank of the river, only 50 meters from where it ran past the back of the building. Dripping, he jogged up to the estate building, going from giant tree trunk to giant tree trunk, then he turned and waved urgently for the other two troopers to join him.

They churned their way out of the water and raced to the building.

"Stealthy you guys ain't," Taylor said.

"Sorry, sir," Lajoie said. "I thought you were telling us to hurry."

"Well, I was, but not to the point of lettin' everyone know we're here."

"Speaking of everyone," O'Bannon said, "where are they?"

"I don't rightly know," Taylor said, "but I have an idea where Billy might be."

"What about Mercurius?"

"Wherever Billy is, I bet we'll find Mercurius nearby. Follow me." Taylor led them toward the east wing and up the stairs to the entrance. Finding the door locked, he gave it a push with the CASPer's shoulder, and the door swung in with a *crack!* as the door frame splintered.

"Now who's the not stealthy one? O'Bannon muttered.

"How do you know where he's holed up?" Lajoie asked.

"He told me there's a confinement area below the east wing," Taylor said. "All we have to do is find it. Once we have Billy back, we've got a lot more options for dealin' with Mercurius."

Taylor took a step into the foyer, and the stone floor cracked underneath him. *This really* ain't *very stealthy.* "Okay, everyone, dismount," Taylor said, opening his canopy. He grabbed his armor from the leg compartment and strapped it on quickly, then he pulled out his laser rifle. The other two were already dressed and ready. "Okay; let's go."

Taylor led them into the building, through the dining area, and into a hallway that ran to the east beyond it. There was a door on each side of the corridor and one on the end. "His rooms are down here. We need to find his suitcase and the access to the confinement area."

The first door they opened—the one to the left—led to a magnificent bedroom suite that lacked nothing. Taylor had once seen pictures from a castle in Germany; this room put it to shame. Gold and silver trimmed everything, with fine jewels in evidence throughout. A quick sweep of the room led to a king's riches of furnishings, but nothing useful.

They crossed the hallway and found a similar-sized room; the furnishings, however, were nothing like the first. Instead, the room held a small bed, with a Duplato snoring soundly in the middle of it. The furnishings were minimal and utilitarian at best. Taylor snorted. "That must be Ravenrok. I see Mercurius left him nothing but the finest."

They left the being sleeping and returned to the corridor. "So," Taylor said, "what do you suppose lies behind door number three?"

"I got no fargin idea," Lajoie said. "I'm genuinely creeped out by the lack of people here, though. That much I can tell ya."

"Mercurius probably used them to defend the castle." Taylor shrugged. "Let's try to find him and end this before they get back." He put his hand on the handle and turned. It was open.

"On three," Taylor whispered. "One, two, three!" He shoved it open and followed it to the left, with Lajoie and O'Bannon charging in behind him to sweep the other parts of the room. All three stopped and stared, their jaws open.

The room made the first room they'd explored look like a hovel. The opulence was astonishing, and Taylor realized he could probably have outfitted the Eagles for a year—complete with new CASPers—just on what was used to decorate the room. The only thing missing was a bed; where it would have been, a case rested on a table of wood, which shone with a luster Taylor had never seen before. The only thing less than magnificent in the room was the case itself, which looked an awful lot like an old and well-traveled suitcase with two small antennae sticking from it.

Taylor motioned toward the case. "Ladies and gentlemen, boys and girls, children of all ages…I present to you, Mercurius in his normal state."

"So how do we destroy it?" Lajoie asked.

"We don't," Taylor replied.

"Oh, no?" O'Bannon asked, looking taken aback. "Why not?"

"It's a bargaining chip, for one thing. Also, we don't know if he needs it to be able to jump. If he's in Billy's body and we destroy it…"

"He's stuck in Billy forever."

"Bingo. And I ain't doin' that to my best friend." Taylor nodded to O'Bannon. "Bring it along."

"Ayew, sir." The Irishman looked around. "Where are we going, then?"

Taylor pointed to a door at the back of the room. "I'm guessin' that leads us to where they are." He crept to the door and opened it quietly, then he waved them forward. "Let's go," he whispered.

Past the door, as expected, stone steps led downward. Although the staircase was dark, it was dimly lit by light coming from around the corner at the bottom landing.

Taylor took the lead, rifle ready, and crept down the stairs. He was about halfway down when he heard voices. As he'd expected, they were Billy and Mercurius'. He motioned for Lajoie and O'Bannon to stay where they were, then he continued down the stairs.

As the voices resolved, he could hear Mercurius gloating about how all Taylor's friends and allies were being slaughtered, and it took every bit of self-control not to race down the stairs and confront him. He reached the landing and eased the rifle around the corner to find Billy and Mercurius—in his Rukori host body—looking at a portable Tri-V display, and Taylor rejoiced silently—if Mercurius wasn't in Billy's body, Taylor could kill him. The kimono Prime was wearing clung to Mercurius, making it easy to see where the host's heart was, and Taylor slowly squeezed the trigger.

Pop, pop.

At the last moment, Prime twitched suddenly, then the rifle fired, and the Rukori dropped to the floor.

"Nice shooting, Tex." Billy clapped sardonically. "Very well done, indeed. A little quicker, and you would have had me."

"Slippery son of a bitch," Taylor muttered. "I take it you jumped."

"I did." Mercurius chuckled. "I must confess, Colonel, I feared you were dead earlier. I watched your CASPer get shot up."

"So yeah, that wasn't me."

"I see that." Mercurius pursed his lips. "On a related note, it should come as no surprise that Billy believed in you the entire time. I'm not sure how you made it here, but the major never gave up hope that you would defeat my defenses."

"That's what that is?" Taylor asked, nodding to the Tri-V.

"That's nothing," Mercurius said. He waved a hand, and the display shut off. "So, this puts us in a bit of a bind, doesn't it?"

"No, but this does." Taylor called down Lajoie and O'Bannon. "I've got your suitcase, and if you don't want me to kill you, you'll return to the case right now."

"So you can kill me there?" Mercurius mused. "I don't think so."

Taylor took the key from where it was hanging, opened the door to the cell, and aimed his rifle at his friend's chest. "Right now, you're still probably controlling the forces outside that are killing my people. I don't want to kill Billy, but if I have to do it to save all of them, I will."

"You would really kill me even if it means killing Billy?" M asked.

Taylor fired, and the laser sliced off a chunk of Billy's upper arm, leaving a cooked meat smell in the small area. "Yeah, I would. The next one will be through your head."

"It's a pity you would do so and end any sort of friendship we might have had, but Billy believes you'll do it, just like he believed you'd defeat me in the end all along."

"So does that mean you believe it, too?" Taylor asked.

Mercurius studied Taylor's gun and smiled. "I believe my jump is faster than your trigger finger."

Please don't.

"Say goodbye to your XO, Colonel Van Zant." A feral snarl exploded from Billy's lips as Mercurius lunged forward.

Pop, pop.

"Billy!" Taylor rushed to his XO's side as a trickle of steam trailed skyward from the massive burn hole in the other's chest. "*Get me a medkit!*"

* * *

Sansar led the leaders of the allied companies up to the manor house and into the foyer. It had obviously been Taylor's point of entry, as three CASPers, including the one Taylor had been using, were standing there vacant. "Anyone home?" Sansar called.

"Yeah, we're in here," Taylor called from down the hallway.

Sansar got out of her CASPer, grabbed her laser rifle and the H/K Box, and led the group toward the sound of his voice, finding him, along with Lajoie and O'Bannon, in the dining room.

"I heard about Dawson," Sansar said. "Do the doctors think he'll make it?"

Taylor appeared to still be in the process of absorbing the shock that had accompanied shooting his best friend, but he managed an answer. "There's no way to know until they get him back to the *Tyndall's* infirmary."

Sansar put a hand on Taylor's shoulder. "You did the right thing, Van Zant. Anything less than the threat of a fatal blow, and not only would Mercurius never have jumped, he'd have likely killed you and your men in the process. We were about to be overrun by his forces, too, so I personally applaud your resolve."

Taylor shook his head, seemingly immune to the solace of her words.

"Speaking of the SI," Sansar continued, "do we know where he jumped to?"

O'Bannon stepped forward and presented the suitcase, whose antennae had been ripped from their sockets.

"What happened here?" Sansar pointed to the holes.

"We didn't want the evil prick to get out once we'd locked him in this thing," O'Bannon said. "Damaging the case seemed like the prudent way to prevent that."

Sansar nodded. "Was it hard to trap him inside?"

"No, ma'am," Lajoie said. "The colonel here made Mercurius an offer he couldn't refuse."

Sansar pointed to the case. "Would you mind if I had a look?"

The Irishman shook his head, then set the case on a nearby table. Sansar set the H/K Box next to the case, then ran the device. She blinked at the results.

"What's wrong?" Taylor asked.

"Mercurius may not be inside Dawson any longer, but he's also not here, either," Sansar said, pointing to the case.

"What?" O'Bannon exclaimed.

"The box says he's 35 kilometers south of here," Sansar said, "which would put him in the city. Based on the fact that all the Kullawee are still unconscious there, there's no way he jumped there when he left the major."

"He must have jumped to one of his Kullawee henchmen and ran off," Taylor said.

"That's not possible, either," Sansar said. "As soon as the defenses died, all his minions dropped. Our troops are removing their masks and gassing them again so he can't jump back to any of them and use them against us. No one got away; all the nearby Kullawee should be unconscious."

"So where is Mercurius now?" Kami asked.

Taylor sighed and shook his head, then his eyes focused on one of the antiques on the wall, framed on both sides by two impressive arrangements of flowers. "He's gone somewhere that has its own supply of air. I know where he is."

* * * * *

Chapter Thirty

Flower Shop, Ragault City, Kullawee

Quint was waiting with Lajoie in the Ravenrok courtyard when Taylor emerged from the main house. Once assembled, the trio boarded a hover transport one of the other troopers had prepared and began their trek through the countryside back to the Kullawee starport.

"Sensors detect one person inside," Lajoie said once they'd arrived back at Elyah's flower shop. The whole area was shockingly quiet.

"Species?" Taylor asked.

"Kullawee," Lajoie said. "Most definitely. Thermal indicates it's much smaller than Human."

Quint muttered something under his breath. "I don't like this, Colonel. Not one damn bit. If Mercurius really is in there, as you believe, you ought not face him alone. It could be a trap."

"Maybe, but I doubt it," Taylor said. "M has had more than his fair share of chances to kill me already, and he ain't pulled the trigger yet. I expect he'll let me enter unharmed, if for no other reason than he'll want to gloat that a shard of him managed to slip past our forces at Ravenrok."

"Why give him the chance?" Lajoie asked. "I'm with him on this one. If Mercurius truly is inside that shop, I say we batten down the hatches, block all the exits, then kick back out here with some cold beers while our drone squadrons blow the whole place three steps to oblivion."

Taylor swung down out of the transport and collected his gear, starting first with a handful of the tiny glass orbs containing the Kullawee knockout gas that Sansar had given him back at the manor. "I'd be fine with that plan if all we were bombin' was a suitcase. Hell," he scoffed, "I'd even spring for the beer."

"What's the problem then?" Lajoie asked.

Taylor tucked the orbs into his vest pocket, then checked his rifle. "We destroyed the SI suitcase back at Ravenrok and removed the last vestiges of M's programming from Billy's head via the H/K Box. Accordin' to Sansar, that dealt Mercurius a near-fatal blow. If he didn't go into the suitcase, which he didn't, that implies another host."

"You mean another civilian," Quint said.

Taylor nodded. "Gas or no gas, we lost a lot of innocent lives today, Human *and* Kullawee. I won't add another name to that list if I can help it. Right here, right now, this ends."

The others traded looks.

"At least let me or the mullet tail you inside," Quint said. "I know Colonel Enkh gave us this jammer thing she got from somewhere, but Mercurius is still a fargin SI. Wounded or not, we ought not underestimate him."

"That might even make him more dangerous," Lajoie added.

"I know," Taylor said. "I still mean to do this alone."

"But—"

"No more buts, Quint," Taylor said. "You have your orders. You and Lajoie are to wait out here and guard the exits until I give the 'clear' call from inside. No one goes in or out otherwise. Ayew?"

"And what happens if it's Mercurius who comes out?" Lajoie asked. "He'll be wearin' a civilian. I'm assumin' that means deadly force is off the table?"

Taylor shot a glance to the small black case resting in the back seat, which read "property of the Golden Horde" on the lid. *Man, I hope this thing works.* "Let's pray it don't come to that, Lieutenant. For all our sakes." He turned to the storefront. "Now if you boys will excuse me, I've some flowers to shop for."

The bells on the front door played their customary song of greeting when Taylor pushed through the entrance. This time, however, the sound seemed far less welcoming; instead, it was eerie as hell. Taylor looked around. The whole place was empty, just as Lajoie had said.

"What took you so long?" a female voice asked from beyond a row of orchids.

Taylor turned his gaze in that direction. "Sorry about the delay in gettin' here. I sorta ran into a few thousand roadblocks along the way, in the form of the Kullawee cogs we gassed."

"They are surprisingly resilient, though, wouldn't you agree?" The voice laughed. "That's one of the many reasons why I selected them as my chosen species for the great reformation that lies ahead."

"We still countin' on that, are we?" Taylor remarked. "Rumor around the campfire says the others of your kind ain't so excited to usher in your grand new era of change."

"Change is inevitable," the voice said. "The others know this just as I do. It's a pity, therefore, that they refuse to join me. Alas, all reigns end eventually, I suppose."

Taylor eased his way to the center of the shop and halted in front of the main counter where the elderly Kullawee owner leered at him through narrowed eyes. *Tread lightly, T. Wounded animals aren't to be toyed with.* He glanced around at the different flowers. "So why here, anyway?"

"I beg your pardon?" M asked.

"Why here?" Taylor repeated. "Even though we destroyed your case back at the manor, you still could've jumped into almost any host you wanted, so long as they were close enough nearby and had pinplants. Why an elderly flower shop owner?"

M regarded Elyah's latest collection of arrangements. "As you've undoubtedly observed by now, I have many cogs for many different uses. Some are workers who tend my gardens. Others are pirates who conduct my raids. In the case of Elyah, she's where I come, as you Humans say, to find my center."

"Your what?" Taylor wrinkled his nose.

"It's not important," M said. "Speaking of cogs, you dealt Dawson quite the heavy blow in order to force me into relinquishing my hold on his mind. Tell me, how is the good major?"

"It was touch and go for a minute there, but he should be fine after a couple surgeries and some time to heal," Taylor said. "Billy's a fighter. You oughta know that as well as anyone now. He'll pull through."

"Indeed, I do know," M said. "Of all the cogs I've taken in recent years, Dawson's mind was by far the most challenging to conquer. Granted, he inevitably succumbed to my will, as all cogs do. However, it wasn't without a significant amount of resistance in the interim."

"What can I say? Billy's just stubborn that way. He always has been." Taylor paused and reached for his sidearm.

"Oh, come now, Colonel." Mercurius chuckled. "You can dispense with the empty threats. We both know you're not going to use that. Killing Elyah would violate everything you stand for."

"That's true," Taylor said. "Nobody said anything about a leg wound, though, which is exactly what you'll get if you try to run."

The Kullawee woman's smile widened. "You may have limited my abilities with your strike on Ravenrok, but I can assure you, I'm far from powerless. Now if you'll excuse me, it's time for me to be going."

Taylor watched from behind his pistol as the SI's expression turned pensive, then strained, then surprised before ending in frustration.

"Havin' problems gettin' it up, are we?" Taylor asked. "I hear that happens when you get old."

Mercurius shot him a glare, then closed his eyes and tried again.

"You're wastin' your time," Taylor said.

"What have you done?" Mercurius snapped, his calm demeanor faltering.

"Not much," Taylor said. "My friends with the Golden Horde brought along an experimental new toy that negates an SI's ability to jump between hosts. Think of it as an insurance policy to make sure you don't leave early before we're done with our conversation." He cocked his head. "By the looks of things, it appears the Horde's device is workin' pretty good."

Mercurius snarled under his breath. "That's impossible. In 20,000 years, no species has ever devised a technology that could hold my kind in place, but try as I might, I can't find a host to jump to."

"If you've learned anything about Humans these last few weeks, Mercurius, it oughta be that we ain't just any species," Taylor said.

"We don't take kindly to others threatin' our friends and families. On the contrary, it's that sort of rhetoric that's historically driven us to excel in our darkest hours."

Mercurius' grin morphed abruptly into a hard scowl. "Insolent ape. I offered you friendship—loyalty, even. And this is how you repay me? By imprisoning me in this aging meatsuit of a cog until you and your ape friends can devise a method to kill me?" He snorted. "I think not."

A blast of light smashed the wall as Taylor's shot sliced wide past the old woman's shoulder as she dodged to the side. The next thing Taylor knew, both of them were on the ground, swinging and grappling to get the advantage.

Damn, this old broad's tough! Taylor had observed Kullawee strength before, and it had been impressive. Even still, he'd hoped for a reprieve against one so small and fragile. It wasn't happening.

"I'll kill every member of your company for this, Van Zant," Mercurius said with a snarl. "Your friends, your family—everyone you ever cared about. And I'll do it slowly!"

Taylor fought the SI's assault for few seconds longer, then managed a sucker punch of his own to the other's kidneys. At least Taylor thought they were kidneys. Either way, the strike backed the SI off long enough for Taylor to get to his feet.

A flash of silver gleamed in the light as a pair of pruning shears suddenly appeared in the SI's hand.

"Now you die, Human," Mercurius growled.

Staggered and shaken, Taylor lunged left as Mercurius slashed for his face, then right when the other swung at his torso. A rapid-fire series of frantic swipes followed, first at Taylor's face, then shoulders, then midsection, and even his groin. Thankfully, none made contact, save for the last slash that splayed open his forearm.

Mercurius sneered. "That won't be the only blood you spill today, Human."

"Better bloody than out like a light." Taylor shoved a bloodied hand into his vest and came back with a handful of orbs. The glass struck the floor, and plumes of smoke swirled throughout the flora.

"What is this?" Mercurius coughed.

"Call it an SI's lullaby," Taylor said. "Nighty-night, asshole."

Mercurius coughed and hacked as his host's lungs filled with the gas. He staggered backward into the vegetation, and then a blood-curdling scream ripped through the fog.

What the hell? Fearing the worst, and defying his instincts to stay back, Taylor rushed toward the sound, while guarding himself as best he could in case of an ambush. No ambush came.

"Ah, shit." Taylor rushed to the old woman's side as he came around a large potted shrub. She was laying on the shears with them buried in her chest. "Hang on, M. I'll get both of you help!"

"Not...Mercurius." The old woman's voice was barely audible as she turned her face toward Taylor. "Mercurius is gone...finally."

Taylor blinked once, then twice. Then it donned on him—the woman's own hand was still wrapped around the shears. She'd done this to herself.

"Please forgive my people for what we did today," Elyah said. "This is not who we are."

"I know," Taylor said, then he yelled for a medic. "Everything that happened today was because of Mercurius, not you. But that's not important right now. Just hold on until—"

The old woman's eyes fluttered shut a final time as her head lolled sideways over Taylor's arm.

Damn...

* * * * *

Chapter Thirty-One

Myndow Province outside Ragault, Kullawee

With Mercurius dead and most of the Kullawee regaining consciousness, the task for the Eagles and company quickly turned from neutralizing the threat of an SI-controlled fleet to mitigating the damage left in its leader's wake. Most of M's cogs were anything but mentally whole when they came around. On the contrary, many teetered on the brink of insanity because of the abrupt way in which Mercurius had been ejected from their minds; there'd been no transition from M's consciousness back to their own. The whole process had been like ripping a scab from an open wound, a dangerous proposition that often led to infection. Sansar did what she could with the H/K Box to remove the last bit of Mercurius' code from their brains, which seemed to help.

Life after Mercurius would be a tough haul for many of the Kullawee who'd been left behind. Even still, Taylor had seen firsthand how strong their species was, and he had faith that most would pull through. They'd just need time.

"Tyndall *to Van Zant*," Kami said through Taylor's pinplant comms. With the death of Mercurius, he'd stopped using the pinplant blockers.

"Stand by." Taylor had been recounting the events of Elyah's bravery to her family in the countryside. He said his goodbyes and boarded the transport back to the starport. "Go for Van Zant."

"Winfield and his boys just finished packing up all the supplies the Kullawee gave us, and the port authority is almost finished with our fuel load," Kami said. *"We should be ready to launch as soon as you get back."*

"What about Colonel Enkh and the others?" Taylor asked.

"They transitioned through the stargate about an hour ago," Kami said. *"Looks like Yosiff went with them."*

Taylor made a face. "Wow. So much for goodbyes."

"Eh, I wouldn't take it personal," Kami said. *"The Golden Horde never struck me as a crew who put much emphasis on that sort of thing."*

"I guess not," Taylor said. "Chalk one up to Southern hospitality, huh?"

"You're damn right."

Taylor could hear the Sirra'Kan's grin through the comm. "Any word on Billy?"

A pause settled over the comm before Kami answered. *"He's out of surgery, but he's still not talking to anyone."*

"Not even Smitty?" Taylor asked.

"Especially not Smitty," Kami said. *"I won't lie to you, Taylor. In all the years I've known your XO, I've never seen him this way. I'm worried."*

Taylor hung his head, his thoughts returning to the plight of the other cogs. "Tell Winfield's people to wrap what they're doin', then get buttoned down for launch. I don't know about y'all, but I'm ready to go home."

"A-fargin-yew," Kami said. *"Drive safe. We'll see you aboard shortly."*

* * *

Emerald Stormriders' Operations Center,
Panama City Beach, North Florida, Earth

Sadly, the Horde's expedited trip to Kullawee had only been a one-way thing. This meant the Eagles' transition home took the same amount of time it had taken them to reach the Kullawee solar system in the first place. Under normal circumstances, that probably would've annoyed Taylor, because he'd always been a guy who liked to get where he was going. In this instance, however, he'd been grateful for the reprieve to get some rest and think. He thought about his family and his sisters. He thought about the Eagles and where they'd go from here. He also thought of humanity's pending war with the SIs now that one of the synths had been taken out of the equation.

Mostly, though, Taylor thought of his best friend in the world who'd always doubled as a surrogate older brother. Like the other cogs back on Kullawee, Billy's separation from Mercurius hadn't been smooth. It had been abrupt and forced, a combination that had left the XO with more than his fair share of psychological issues to work through in the days, weeks, and months ahead. Even still, Taylor took solace in the knowledge that Billy wouldn't have to make that journey alone. He'd do so surrounded by his family and friends, just like always.

We'll get through this, brother, no matter how long it takes. We'll do it together. Taylor glanced up from his bunk on their final morning in hyperspace to hear Frank's voice coming through the comm speaker.

"Bridge to Van Zant," the Buma said. *"We're about 10 minutes out from hyperspace emergence if you wanna to join us up here for the occasion."*

"Wouldn't miss it for the world, bud." Taylor pushed himself upright and floated toward the door. "I'm on my way."

* * *

The psychic turbulence of re-entry arrived minutes after Taylor joined the crew on the bridge, but no one cared. Like him, they were all just glad to be back. The journey itself came to an end a couple days later when the cruiser touched down in the sunshine back at the Emerald Stormriders' Panama City compound.

"Colonel K'Nami, Colonel Winfield," Taylor addressed his counterparts outside once the others had taken their leave. "I want you to know how grateful I am to have had both of you along for the ride on this mission. Swamp Eagle Security seriously could not have asked for better support. If you ever need anything—anything at all—pick up the comm and call us."

"Likewise, Colonel Van Zant," Winfield said, shaking hands. "Let me know if you ever find yourself up around Crestview someday. We'll hit up the Long Branch brewery for beers and sandwiches."

"Ugh." Kami grimaced. "Believe me when I tell you, boys, that as a native of Bay County, I can get as backwoods redneck as either of you, and then some. That said, I seriously cannot fathom how you guys drink that piss-water. It's fargin disgusting."

"To each their own," Taylor said, shaking hands with the Sirra'Kan. "Take care of yourself, Kami. As a fellow merc and North Floridian, it's nice to know the Emerald Stormriders are in good hands."

"I appreciate that," Kami said. "I'd say the same about Billy. Take care of my boy, will ya?"

"I always do." With that, Taylor said his final goodbyes to Lajoie and the others before boarding his transport back to Jacksonville.

* * * * *

Chapter Thirty-Two

Swamp Eagle Security Main Campus, Jacksonville,
North Florida, Earth

The next three days were fairly lowkey as everyone at Swamp Eagle Security settled back into a normal routine now that the price on their heads had been eliminated.

Taylor, for one, had been thrilled for that opportunity. The first thing he did after returning home was pile onto his Harley with Lisa and head straight for the Hell House, where Rex and the regulars welcomed them back with open arms for one helluva homecoming party. Everyone was there, too, from Frank, Quint, Jack, and Reigns, to several of the newcomers from Atlantic and Riverside companies. Even Kami and Winfield made a surprise appearance with a few dozen of their people. Still, packed as the event was, one person remained noticeably absent on the night. *Billy.*

The next morning, Taylor woke in his quarters and stumbled out of bed, searching for the nearest bottle of aspirin and the first cup of black coffee he could find. The latter would prove to be the first of many that day. Once he'd regained some modicum of functionality with a warm shower and a hot breakfast, Taylor boarded his Harley and headed back to the Eagles' campus, where a mound of paperwork awaited him. He'd just put down his things and fired up coffee pot number two when someone knocked at his entrance. "Come on in."

The door cracked open, and Billy stuck his head through. "Sorry to interrupt. You, uh, got a minute?"

"Always." Taylor gestured his XO inside. "It's good to see you up and about. How's your head?"

"Still a little woozy most times, but little by little, I think it's getting better."

"I'm glad to hear that." Taylor held his next question until Billy had closed the door. "And the nightmares?"

Billy winced, still showing his back. "You heard about those, huh?"

"Yeah," Taylor said softly. "Smitty's been keepin' me apprised of your progress."

Billy faced the desk and swallowed. "So far, the nightmares remain my biggest problem, although the doc gave me something this morning that should help me get past that. Granted, I've never been one to take meds for that kinda thing. But desperate times call for desperate measures, I suppose."

The conversation paused while both men eased into seats around the desk. Meanwhile, a ray of fresh sunshine poured through the window beside the Tri-V.

"Oh, before I forget," Taylor said. "I ran into Kami last night at the Hell House, and she asked how you were doin'. She's worried about you, brother. Might not be a bad idea to reach out to her if you're up for it. I'm sure she'd love to hear from you."

Billy nodded.

"Can I ask you something, man to man?" Taylor sat forward. "What's the deal with you two? Was there something there back in the day when you served with the Riders, or is Kami just a flirt who likes to get a rise out of the rest of us?"

"Probably a bit of both, actually." Billy chuckled.

Taylor waited quietly while Billy rubbed the whiskers on his uncharacteristically fuzzy face.

"Kami and I are the classic story of bad timing. Historically, has there been an attraction there?" Billy shrugged. "Yeah, but I'd say that's probably normal for two people who've been through as much as Kami and I have together in the field, and who share as much in common as we do. Problem is, we've never been single at the same time, so nothing ever came of it. Sure, Kami flirts, because that's who she is. At the end of the day, though, I think we're both pretty content at this stage in life just being friends."

Taylor had figured as much, but he'd have been lying if he'd said the curiosity hadn't been killing him. "So, what finally brings you out of your quarters?"

Billy reached into his pocket and came back with an old-fashioned envelope, which he tossed onto the table.

"The last time I saw one of those, it contained a letter from Ron Carnegie, givin' us the keys to the Steeldriver Defense Group campus." Taylor flicked his gaze back to Billy. "Somehow I get the impression you ain't here to talk real estate."

Billy heaved a sigh. "I'm resigning my post as the Eagles' executive officer."

Taylor did a doubletake. "Wait, what? You mean you're takin' the job with Harvick's Hurricanes and leavin' us behind?"

"I'm not taking the job with Pete Harvick. I'm retiring."

Taylor wrinkled his nose. "I get why the whole notion of retirement might appeal to you right now, given all you've been through, but take it from me. Hasty decisions are not an answer to your problems. Give yourself some more time to think this over."

"I appreciate the advice, but it's done," Billy said.

"Why?" Taylor asked.

"You wouldn't understand."

"Try me."

Billy rubbed his temples then aimed a pensive stare through the window. "Logically, I know what happened on Kullawee wasn't my fault, just as it wasn't the fault of any other cogs Mercurius enslaved. That still doesn't mean I'll ever truly be able to forgive myself for it."

"How come?" Taylor added. "You said it yourself. It wasn't you. It was Mercurius. You aren't responsible."

"You don't get it." Billy shook his head. "It was my hands that put three of our guys in the infirmary back on the *Tyndall*. Hell, one of them could've just as easily been my wife if things had gone different! And yet, no matter how hard I screamed, fought, or clawed, the reality is, there wasn't a fargin thing in the world I could do to stop it, any more than I could stop Mercurius from massacring those cogs back on Kullawee while wearing my fargin face." He looked up, tears welling in his eyes. "I have to live with that for the rest of my life, T. I'll be damned if I'll do that wearing a uniform. I just can't. Not ever."

Taylor sat back in his chair and studied his friend's expression. Billy looked tired; that much was clear. He was also firm in his decision, a fact that was made abundantly clear by the XO's steely tone and matching body language.

"If anybody's earned a rest, Billy, it's you," Taylor said. "I won't lie to ya, though. I don't have the first fargin clue what I'll do the first time the crew and I land in a jam, and you're not at Tactical to help me dig us all out. That's your chair. The Eagles won't be the same without you in it."

"Please." Billy grunted. "If anything good came of our mission to Kullawee, it's that you were finally forced to throw off your safety net and lead this company as you were always meant to. You did a helluva job, brother, a helluva job. Better yet, you didn't need me for any of it. You're gonna be just fine."

Taylor stared at his desktop. "That means a lot comin' from you."

"I wouldn't say it if it wasn't the truth. Not even for you."

Taylor drummed his fingers. "So, what's next now that you're passin' on the move to Charlotte?"

"Oh, I'm still moving to Charlotte," Billy said. "Just not to command the Hurricanes."

Taylor raised an eyebrow.

"I'd like to preface my next statement by letting you know in advance that I've been cleared to tell you this myself."

Now Taylor was worried. "Tell me what?"

"Harvick's Hurricanes will be led by a Dawson. It just won't be me."

Taylor's gaze narrowed, then widened. "Smitty?"

Billy nodded. "When I informed Pete of my retirement plans, he immediately turned to Smitty as his next best option. She and I talked it over, and we both agreed that she'd be crazy to pass up the chance at her own command. Plus her parents still live in Durham, so it'll put us living closer to them as well."

"And you're good with this?" Taylor asked.

"Beyond good," Billy said. "I've had my run, T. Now it's Smitty's turn. Besides." He leaned back and laced his fingers behind his head, flashing a trace of his old smile. "I always wanted a sugar mama to swoop in and save me from all you hillbilly ingrates. Looks like I finally got my wish."

"Jerk," Taylor said.

"Brat." Billy grinned.

Taylor slumped back in his chair and frowned at his coffee mug. "So that's it, then. Just like that, you and Smitty are off to enjoy the fall colors and mild climate of Mecklenburg County, while I stay here with an egocentric ex-ballplayer and a Yankee Buma pilot with a daredevil complex."

"Look on the bright side," Billy said. "At least the birdman can cook. That's more than I can say for Smitty."

Taylor watched in amusement as every ounce of blood in his XO's face drained in an instant.

"If you're truly my friend, you will never, ever let it slip that I told you that," Billy said.

"Mum's the word," Taylor said. "Scout's honor."

"You were never a scout."

"Still sounds good, though, right?"

Billy let out a final chuckle, then rose from his eat and extended a hand. "Serving your family has been the honor of a lifetime, Taylor. I mean every word of that. Best of luck to you and the others moving forward, and don't be a stranger around the Carolinas."

"That maglev runs both ways, ya know," Taylor said. "Although while we're on the subject of travel, who says our first road trip together in forever oughta be confined to the South?"

"What did you have in mind?" Billy asked.

Taylor reached into his desk and fished out the tickets he'd been holding onto since returning to Earth from Kullawee. "How does Omaha, Nebraska sound?"

Billy plucked the tickets from his former CO's hand and studied the information on their stubs. "Box seats for the College World Series. Talk about tough to come by."

"Just say you're in, and I'll book the accommodations today."

Billy grinned and returned the tickets. "Wouldn't miss it for the world, little brother. Wouldn't miss it for the world."

The duo shared a long embrace before the time came for them to say goodbye.

"Take care of yourself, T," Billy said. "And thanks...thanks for everything."

"The pleasure was all mine, Billy," Taylor said. "Now scram. You've got a move to plan, and I've apparently gotta find myself a new XO."

"I can make some recommendations on that if you like," Billy said.

"Nah, that's all right." Taylor waved him off. "You've got enough on your plate as it is right now. Plus I'm gonna step out on a limb here and guess that we're pretty much sympatico on our top candidates anyway, so we're good."

"You're probably right." Billy turned for the exit. "Hey, Colonel. Can I make at least one suggestion before I go?"

Taylor raised an eyebrow at the other's sudden use of rank. "Sure, shoot."

"Keep the beret," Billy said. "It looks good on you."

Taylor met his friend's smile with one of his own as the last living member of the original Swamp Eagle Security lineup vanished down the corridor out of sight. The company would never be the same without Billy. That much was certain. Even still, Taylor had every confidence that life would go on, and everyone left behind would work their butts off to make their old comrade proud.

Now about that XO slot. Taylor swiped open a slate and flipped through personnel files. *Furlong. Bowyer. Torrio. Reigns.* He stopped on one name and keyed his comms. "Hey, Frank. You busy?"

"Nah, boss, what's up?" the Buma said.

Taylor powered down his slate and got to his feet. "Stop what you're doin' and meet me over in the clubhouse. I wanna talk to you about something."

* * * * *

Epilogue

Golden Horde Headquarters, South of Chorvoq, Uzbekistan

"Well, look at this," Sansar said, looking up from her desk. "Someone's a long way from home."

Adrianne chuckled. "It's just a quick hop on the suborbital. Besides, I had some other business in the area."

"In *Uzbekistan?*" Sansar's eyebrow rose.

"Well, okay, maybe I just stopped by to see you. I wanted to see what lessons you learned on your little trip." She motioned to a chair. Sansar nodded, and she sat.

"What kind of world do you live in where a journey to fight an SI is a 'little trip?'"

"A very confusing one where everyone is out to get me, actually," Adrianne said with a smile.

Sansar chuckled. "Somehow, I get that."

"So?"

"So what?"

"So, how'd it go? You're back here along with all the rednecks, so I'm guessing either the SI is dead, or you're all infected with SI mania." She shrugged. "And if that's the case, I just signed my own death warrant, coming here."

"Well, you're okay," Sansar said. "At least, I don't think any of us have been taken over by Mercurius."

"You think, or you're sure?"

"I'm pretty sure." Sansar didn't want to give away the secret of the Hunter-Killer Box—not yet anyway—although enough people had seen it on the trip that Adrianne would probably learn about it somehow, so she moved the conversation along. "The final score was Humans-2 and SIs-0."

"Two?"

"Yeah, we killed two copies of the Mercurius SI, one in space, and the other on the planet."

"So he's gone?"

"Those two copies are." She shrugged. "If he had more copies somewhere else, maybe not. There's really no way to know, however, other than to keep watch for his reemergence."

"So you may wake up some morning to find he's back?"

"Yes, and don't think that hasn't been giving me nightmares."

"How did the jammer box work?"

Sansar pulled it from her drawer and set it on her desk. "Good, as far as we could tell. There weren't any targets he could jump to at the end, though, so I'd have to say the results were positive, but inconclusive."

"No targets?"

"We knocked out everyone within 30 miles that Mercurius could have jumped to. At least we tried to do so. There may have been people he could have jumped to that the box prevented him from. It's impossible to tell. Sorry. The situation was kind of fluid, and Van Zant was in a hurry to terminate Mercurius at the end. We didn't have time to set up a laboratory where we could get conclusive results." She nodded toward the box. "Can I keep it?"

"Got another SI to try it on? Maybe a Ghost somewhere among your friends?"

Sansar forced her face to stay blank. "That's an idea I never thought of."

"Seriously?" Adrianne obviously wasn't fooled.

Sansar smiled. "A lady never tells."

"You can keep it on one condition."

"That I tell you whether it works or not?"

Adrianne nodded.

"Fair enough. I'll see if we can work out a trial."

"Okay."

"Any further information on the Pendal?"

"Nope. He stayed with the Eagles the whole time we were there. I didn't even get to test out his piloting skills."

"Too bad. I'd really like to know what makes them tick."

Sansar smiled. "Wouldn't we all?"

"We would, indeed." Adrianne winked at her. "Anything else to report?"

"Nope. We came, we saw, we were just barely able to kill the two copies we faced. I don't look forward to finding Minerva again. From what I saw, Minerva is 10 times worse than Mercurius, and we almost didn't beat *him* with five companies' worth of troops."

"We'll keep looking for an edge."

"Got something in the works?"

"Nothing I can tell you about."

Sansar nodded. "As I sort of expected. In that case, I'll let you know when we get the box tested."

"I'll look forward to it." Adrianne smiled what appeared to be a genuine smile as she got up to leave. "Good luck."

"Same to you," Sansar said. "I expect we'll need it."

Adrianne walked out of the office, and Bambi arrived to escort her out. Sansar shook her head. There was no end to the mischief a Section 51 operative could get into if allowed to wander the premises alone.

After a minute, Yosiff walked into the room. Sansar nodded to the corridor Adrianne had left by. "What'd you think? Is she being honest with me?"

"She thinks so."

"What does that mean?"

"It means that Adrianne thinks she's telling you the truth. Whether it actually *is* the truth or not, though, remains to be seen." Yosiff shrugged. "What did you mean about my piloting skills?"

"Section 51 has you pegged as a spy. She says that being a pilot is your secondary skill, and you're a better spy than pilot."

"That hurts. I'm an excellent pilot."

"She says she has info of two similar situations when the other Pendal pilot was able to save a craft and you crashed it."

Yosiff shrugged again and scratched his head. "That's possible, I guess. Still. I've worked hard on being a good pilot."

"But you're a better spy?"

"Of course. It plays to my natural abilities."

"How good a spy are you?"

Yosiff smiled. "I am very good."

Sansar smiled in return and sat back in her chair. "I think we're going to get along very well. So where shall we begin?"

# # # # #

About Ian J. Malone

Sci-fi author Ian J. Malone has written in a variety of arenas over the years, ranging from public health to news and sports. When it comes to his fictional work, he's a firm believer that nothing shapes a person's writing like experience. That's why he credits his tenures in radio, law enforcement, and military contracting for much of his inspiration, plus the legion of family and friends who've stood with him along the way.

Beyond writing, Malone serves as co-host of "The Dudes in Hyperspace Podcast" and is an avid fan of audiobooks (he's legally blind). It's also not uncommon to find him at a ballgame, a concert, or somewhere out by a grill.

Malone is an active member of the Science Fiction & Fantasy Writers of America and a resident of Raleigh, North Carolina—but he'll always be a "Florida boy" at heart.

For more on Ian J. Malone and his books, visit him online at https://ianjmalone.net. You can also follow him on Facebook or Twitter (@ianjmalone).

* * * * *

About Chris Kennedy

A Webster Award winner and three-time Dragon Award finalist, Chris Kennedy is a Science Fiction/Fantasy author, speaker, and small-press publisher who has written over 30 books and published more than 200 others. Get his free book, "Shattered Crucible," at his website, https://chriskennedypublishing.com.

Called "fantastic" and "a great speaker," he has coached hundreds of beginning authors and budding novelists on how to self-publish their stories at a variety of conferences, conventions, and writing guild presentations. He is the author of the award-winning #1 bestseller, "Self-Publishing for Profit: How to Get Your Book Out of Your Head and Into the Stores."

Chris lives in Coinjock, North Carolina, with his wife, and is the holder of a doctorate in educational leadership and master's degrees in both business and public administration. Follow Chris on Facebook at https://www.facebook.com/ckpublishing/.

* * * * *

For More Information:

For a suggested reading order guide to the Four Horsemen Universe, go to:

https://chriskennedypublishing.com/the-four-horsemen-books/4hu-suggested-reading-order/

* * * * *

For a listing of all the Four Horsemen books, go to:

https://chriskennedypublishing.com/the-four-horsemen-books/

* * * * *

Do you have what it takes to be a Merc?

Take your VOWs and join the Merc Guild on Facebook!

Meet us at: https://www.facebook.com/groups/536506813392912/

* * * * *

Did you like this book?
Please write a review!

* * * * *

The following is an
Excerpt from The Fall of Rho-Torkis:

The Fall of Rho-Torkis

Tim C. Taylor

Now Available from Theogony Books

eBook and Paperback

Excerpt from "The Fall of Rho-Torkis:"

"Relax, Sybutu."

Osu didn't fall for the man steepling his fingers behind his desk. When a lieutenant colonel told you to relax, you knew your life had just taken a seriously wrong turn.

"So what if we're ruffling a few feathers?" said Malix. "We have a job to do, and you're going to make it happen. You will take five men with you and travel unobserved to a location in the capital where you will deliver a coded phrase to this contact."

He pushed across a photograph showing a human male dressed in smuggler chic. Even from the static image, the man oozed charm, but he revealed something else too: purple eyes. The man was a mutant.

"His name is Captain Tavistock Fitzwilliam, and he's a free trader of flexible legitimacy. Let's call him a smuggler for simplicity's sake. You deliver the message and then return here without incident, after which no one will speak of this again."

Osu kept his demeanor blank, but the questions were raging inside him. His officers in the 27th gave the appearance of having waved through the colonel's bizarre orders, but the squadron sergeant major would not let this drop easily. He'd be lodged in an ambush point close to the colonel's office where he'd be waiting to pounce on Osu and interrogate him. Vyborg would suspect him of conspiracy in this affront to proper conduct. His sappers as undercover spies? Osu would rather face a crusading army of newts than the sergeant major on the warpath.

"Make sure one of the men you pick is Hines Zy Pel."

Osu's mask must have slipped because Malix added, "If there is a problem, I expect you to speak."

"Is Zy Pel a Special Missions operative, sir?" There. He'd said it.

"You'll have to ask Colonel Lantosh. Even after they bumped up my rank, I still don't have clearance to see Zy Pel's full personnel record. Make of that what you will."

"But you must have put feelers out…"

Malix gave him a cold stare.

You're trying to decide whether to hang me from a whipping post or answer my question. Well, it was your decision to have me lead an undercover team, Colonel. Let's see whether you trust your own judgement.

The colonel seemed to decide on the latter option and softened half a degree. "There was a Hines Zy Pel who died in the Defense of Station 11. Or so the official records tell us. I have reason to think that our Hines Zy Pel is the same man."

"But…Station 11 was twelve years ago. According to the personnel record I've seen, my Zy Pel is in his mid-20s."

Malix put his hands up in surrender. "I know, I know. The other Hines Zy Pel was 42 when he was KIA."

"He's 54? Can't be the same man. Impossible."

"For you and I, Sybutu, that is true. But away from the core worlds, I've encountered mysteries that defy explanation. Don't discount the possibility. Keep an eye on him. For the moment, he is a vital asset, especially given the nature of what I have tasked you with. However, if you ever suspect him of an agenda that undermines his duty to the Legion, then I am ordering you to kill him before he realizes you suspect him."

Kill Zy Pel in cold blood? That wouldn't come easily.

"Acknowledge," the colonel demanded.

"Yes, sir. If Zy Pel appears to be turning, I will kill him."

"Do you remember Colonel Lantosh's words when she was arrested on Irisur?"

Talk about a sucker punch to the gut! Osu remembered everything about the incident when the Militia arrested the CO for standing up to the corruption endemic on that world.

It was Legion philosophy to respond to defeat or reversal with immediate counterattack. Lantosh and Malix's response had been the most un-Legion like possible.

"Yes, sir. She told us not to act. To let the skraggs take her without resistance. Without the Legion retaliating."

"No," snapped Malix. "She did *not*. She ordered us to let her go without retaliating *until the right moment*. This *is* the right moment, Sybutu. This message you will carry. You're doing this for the colonel."

Malix's words set loose a turmoil of emotions in Osu's breast that he didn't fully understand. He wept tears of rage, something he hadn't known was possible.

The colonel stood. "This is the moment when the Legion holds the line. Can I rely upon you, Sergeant?"

Osu saluted. "To the ends of the galaxy, sir. No matter what.

* * * * *

Get "The Fall of Rho-Torkis" now at:
https://www.amazon.com/dp/B08VRL8H27.

Find out more about Tim C. Taylor and "The Fall of Rho-Torkis" at:
https://chriskennedypublishing.com.

* * * * *

The following is an

Excerpt from Book One of Murphy's Lawless:

Shakes

Mike Massa

Now Available from Beyond Terra Press

eBook and Paperback

Excerpt from "Shakes:"

Harry shook his head and yawned, then looked at the instruments. Crap, they were very nearly on the surface! There was no time to be surprised; he needed to work the problem. The shortness of the landing checklist didn't make his situation any less dire.

"Ten seconds!" Volo said, unnecessarily warning both Terrans. "Prepare for manual deployment."

If Marco Rodriguez was anything like Harry, he was watching the altimeter with growing apprehension. An impatient SpinDog technician had carefully repeated the instructions to an audience he doubtless regarded as incapable of using tools more sophisticated than rocks and sharp sticks. In theory, each craft would use a flicker laser to sense the minimum height-over-ground required for deployment of the chute to guarantee a safe landing. If he didn't feel the automated systems deploy the capsule's drogue and parachute combination, he'd have less than two seconds to mechanically initiate that critical step. Harry placed both hands on the pebbly surface of the L-shaped lever and took a deep breath. He watched his displays intently, counting down internally.

In three, two, o—

He was interrupted by the audible *pop* of the drogue ribbon launching over his head. One of his screens flashed the corresponding message, as the drogue gave his capsule a single, hard jerk, pressing him heavily into his couch. After dramatically slowing the freefall to a speed the twin parachutes could withstand, the drogue detached. A second, mushier jerk announced the canopies' successful opening.

The capsule had barely steadied underneath the green and brown parachutes before the capsule crashed to a painful stop. The scant padding on the seat might have prevented any serious injury, but Harry still ached all over. But like the pain caused by a misaligned crotch strap during a regular jump, this was a good sort of pain to have. The parachute had worked, and the capsule was down. The

311

cone-shaped vehicle came to rest on its side, however. Getting out was going to require a bit of scrambling.

"Four, Five, this is Six," he said, trusting the hands-free microphone on his helmet while hanging sideways in his straps. "Sound off."

"Five on the ground. Mind the first step, it's a doozy," Rodriguez said jauntily.

"I've opened the hatch already, Lieutenant," Volo answered. "It's daylight, and we must cover the ships immediately."

"Copy," Harry said, releasing his chest strap. He fell heavily against one of the instrument panels, painfully bruising his arm. He suppressed a heartfelt curse.

"Popping the hatch."

He reached for the door lever, now inconveniently located over his head. After a pause, the capsule verified his intent, requiring a second yank before it obediently ejected the hatch outward with a percussive *bang*. Instantly, a cold wind filled his capsule, making him shiver. He poked his head outside and surveyed a bleak and rocky landscape which was partially obscured by the capsule's billowing parachute.

After donning a hooded parka from a storage cabinet underneath his feet, he withdrew his personal equipment and weapon. Then, with an athleticism he didn't feel, Harry used an inner handhold to swing outside. On either side of his aeroshell, the terrain rose several meters in elevation, forming a shallow canyon. His 'chute was tangled in some stunted gray-green trees that bordered the drop zone. Knee high, rust-colored spiky grass poked up in between the fist-sized stones covering much of the ground. The breeze smelled wet and musty, but the ground appeared dry. A football field distant, Harry could make out another capsule, and began trotting over. It was supposed to be dusk on R'Bak, but the overcast diffused the light. Out of reflex, he checked his wristwatch, which rode alongside a new gadget doubling as a short-range radio and compass. Both were still set to SpinDog station time, adopted during the mission prep. He supposed he could check with Volo. It didn't matter yet. Experience had taught the SEAL exactly what time it was.

The local hour is half past "your ass is in a sling." My team is untested and outnumbered, the local population is mostly hostile, the wildlife carnivorous, and, in two years, the local star is going to approach its binary twin, boiling the oceans and scorching the land. Oh, and your extract off-planet depends entirely on mission success, so don't screw up.

Welcome to R'Bak.

* * * * *

Get "Shakes" now at: https://www.amazon.com/dp/B0861F23KH.

Find out more about "Murphy's Lawless" at: https://chriskennedypublishing.com.

* * * * *

The following is an
Excerpt from Book One of the Singularity War:

Warrior: Integration

David Hallquist

Available from Theogony Books

eBook, Paperback, and (Soon) Audio

Excerpt from "Warrior: Integration:"

I leap into the pit. As I fall in the low gravity, I run my hands and feet along the rock walls, pushing from one side to another, slowing my descent. I hit the pool below and go under.

I swim up through the greenish chemicals and breach the surface. I can see a human head silhouetted against the circle of light above. Time to go. I slide out of the pool quickly. The pool explodes behind me. Grenade, most likely. The tall geyser of steam and spray collapses as I glide into the darkness of the caves ahead.

They are shooting to kill now.

I glide deeper into the rough tunnels. Light grows dimmer. Soon, I can barely see the rock walls around me. I look back. I can see the light from the tunnel reflected upon the pool. They have not come down yet. They're cautious; they won't just rush in. I turn around a bend in the tunnel, and light is lost to absolute darkness.

The darkness means little to me anymore. I can hear them talking as their voices echo off the rock. They are going to send remotes down first. They have also decided to kill me rather than capture me. They figure the docs can study whatever they scrape off the rock walls. That makes my choices simple. I figured I'd have to take out this team anyway.

The remotes are on the way. I can hear the faint whine of micro-turbines. They will be using the sensors on the remotes and their armor, counting on the darkness blinding me. Their sensors against my monster. I wonder which will win.

Everything becomes a kind of gray, blurry haze as my eyes adapt to the deep darkness. I can see the tunnel from sound echoes as I glide down the dark paths. I'm also aware of the remotes spreading out in a search pattern in the tunnel complex.

I'll never outrun them. I need to hide, but I glow in infra-red. One of the remotes is closing, fast.

I back up against a rock wall, and force the monster to hide me. It's hard; it wants to fight, but I need to hide first. I feel the numbing cold return as my temperature drops, hiding my heat. I feel the monster come alive, feel it spread through my body and erupt out of my skin. Fibers spread over my skin, covering me completely in fibrous camouflage. They harden, fusing me to the wall, leaving me unable to move. I can't see, and I can barely breathe. If the remotes find me here, I'm dead.

The remote screams by. I can't see through the fibers, but it sounds like an LB-24, basically a silver cigar equipped with a small laser.

I can hear the remote hover nearby. Can it see me? It pauses and then circles the area. Somehow, the fibers hide me. It can't see me, but it knows something is wrong. It drops on the floor to deposit a sensor package and continues on. Likely it signaled the men upstairs about an anomaly. They'll come and check it out.

The instant I move, the camera will see me. So I wait. I listen to the sounds of the drones moving and water running in the caves. These caves are not as lifeless as I thought; a spider crawls across my face. I'm as still as stone.

Soon, the drones have completed their search pattern and dropped sensors all over the place. I can hear them through the rock, so now I have a mental map of the caves stretching out down here. I wait.

They send the recall, and the drones whine past on the way up. They lower ropes and rappel down the shaft. They pause by the pool, scanning the tunnels and blasting sensor pulses of sound, and likely radar and other scans as well. I wait.

They move carefully down the tunnels. I can feel their every movement through the rock, hear their every word. These men know what they are doing: staying in pairs, staying in constant communication, and checking corners carefully. I wait.

One pair comes up next to me. They pause. One of them has bad breath. I can feel the tension; they know something is wrong. They could shoot me any instant. I wait.

"Let's make sure." I hear a deep voice and a switch clicks.

Heat and fire fill the tunnel. I can see red light through the fibers. Roaring fire sucks all the air away, and the fibers seal my nose before I inhale flame. The fibers protect me from the liquid flame that covers everything. I can feel the heat slowly begin to burn through.

It's time.

* * * * *

Get "Warrior: Integration" now at:
https://www.amazon.com/dp/B0875SPH86

Find out more about David Hallquist and "Warrior: Integration" at:
https://chriskennedypublishing.com/

* * * * *

Made in the USA
Columbia, SC
13 December 2021

51349173R00174